Nelson & MacIlwraith
Moon Murder Mysteries III

K. Sterling

Copyright © 2024 by K. Sterling

ISBN: 9798884521537

All rights reserved.

No part of this book may be reproduced in any form or by any electronic or mechanical means, including information storage and retrieval systems, without written permission from the author, except for the use of brief quotations in a book review.

*For Jared "light of my life" Rosenberg.
Thank you for being the sweetest, brightest muse. Your kindness,
amazing heart, and humor inspire me every day and I am so
grateful for your support.
You are pure magick. Never stop shining.*

*Once again, I am so blessed to have the World's Greatest PA,
Lindsey Middlemiss.
It's been amazing, sharing the same weird wavelength with you and
it's made this trilogy a joy to write. Thank you for your patience and
for truly **getting** me.*

*And for my Melissa. She is truly the bee's knees and adds a little bit
of her magick every time she helps me prepare another manuscript. I
am so blessed by her kindness and friendship.*

*My love and eternal gratitude to my sister witches.
Roshni and Lesley.
Thank you for inspiring me every day and helping me shine.*

A Note About Magickal Appropriation

Much of the magick described in this book is made-up and should not resemble magickal practices outside of the characters' or the author's cultural identities. A great deal of research went into creating a practice that was both unique and authentic to ancient druidic healing and rituals in 2nd century BCE Gaul, Ireland, and Britain, before the Roman conquest.

There is so little known about the culture and practice of the ancient Celtic druids because they existed in a time between prehistory and the rise of the Roman empire. And so much of what we do know is translated through Roman accounts of the Celts. Thanks to the American witch trials, it's difficult to find much magickal lore or a strong tradition of witchcraft being practiced in the US Appalachian region before the more modern Wiccan practices of the 1950s. For the author, this presented a blank page to create new lore and a unique magick system for our characters.

That being said, the Tuatha Dé Danann and the Dagda belong to ancient Ireland and my interpretation of these legends includes a few variations to traditional beliefs to fit this story.

Also, the nature and practice of this book's modern Tuath Dé are not intended to resemble or accurately portray those of their ancient predecessors.

Content Warnings and an Apology

Assault: one character is assaulted in the line of duty.

Bigotry/Hate: Nelson and Nox interview a character in prison who is racist and antisemitic. A swastika and other racist symbols are mentioned.

Brain trauma: a secondary character experiences brain trauma.

Breath play: characters engage in risk-aware breath play as part of sex.

Cancer and loss of a parent/loved one: the past diagnosis and loss of a parent to cancer is discussed, along with the loss of another parent.

Criticism of Christianity: includes anthropologist characters deconstructing Christianity in the context of cults.

Dementia: a character is stated to be in a long-term care facility and suffering from dementia.

Kink: characters engage in aspects of kink, including chastity cages.

Poisoning: mention of fatal poisonings.

Recreational drug use: a character uses opium for Magickal purposes.

Secret life: romantic partner with a secret life.

Sexual assault and violence: the investigation into the Moon Murders and abductions includes details and discussions of graphic violence and sexual assault that may be difficult for some readers.

.

Finally, to the town and people of New Castle, my apologies. So small and out in the middle of Virginia's Western Highlands with a name I could easily remember *and* remember how to spell... This author has never visited New Castle and bears no ill will toward its 125 residents or its law enforcement. All representations are purely fictional and not intended to offend or malign the people or the town of New Castle.

Pronunciation & Translation Guide

*As requested, the author has done her best to include pronunciations for non-English words, but some of the Gaelic words and phrases used are archaic and haven't been used in centuries. And pronunciations may vary based on regions and dialects.

Sorcha (Surka): Nox's mother, died when Nox was 12.

The Dagda (Dag-duh or Day-duh): An important god in Irish mythology likened to the Germanic god Odin. One of the Tuatha Dé Danann, the Dagda is portrayed as a father-figure, king, and a high druid. He is associated with fertility, agriculture, manliness and strength, as well as magic, druidry, and wisdom. He can control life and death, the weather and crops, as well as time and the seasons. His name means "the good god" or "the great god."

Badb (Bive or Beev): A crow, and associated with the battle goddess **Badb Catha** (Bive Caha) the battle crow and one of the trio of war goddesses known as the **Morrígan/Mór-Ríoghain** (Mo Ree-an).

Darach (Da-rock): an old Gaelic name meaning "oak tree" or "oak grove."

Tuatha Dé Danann (Too-Wah day dan-ann) Acknowledged as the early gods of Ireland (an earlier form of their name, **Tuath Dé** (Too-Ah day) means "tribe of gods").

Samhain (Sau-win) a Celtic festival celebrated on 1 November marking the end of the harvest season and beginning of winter or "darker half" of the year. It is also the Gaelic name for November. Celebrations begin on the evening of 31 October, since the Celtic day began and ended at sunset. It is about halfway between the autumnal equinox and winter solstice.

The Cath Maige Tuired (Caw-Mwee-Turra) from before the ninth Century A.D., is two saga texts of the Mythological Cycle of Irish Mythology detailing the epic battle between the mythical Tuatha De Danann and Fomoire for Ireland.

Fomorians (Faw-mah-reean) mythological beasts often depicted as giants.

Uaithne (Oof-na): The Dagda's magic harp that could change seasons, turn the tides of battle, and see into the hearts of men.

Du thabairt dorais du glé, for mu muid céin am messe (NA): I am the knowledge and the door, turning the darkness into light.

Cunomaglus (Koo-no Mag-lus) artifacts found in the Cotswolds, in southwest England, suggest the worship of an early Celtic deity whose name translates to "Hound Lord" and is identified with the god Apollo.

Coire Ansic (Kwee-ra On-sik): The Dagda's magick cauldron of plenty, said to never run empty and please all who sat with the Dagda.

Log Mór (Lo-rich Moor): The Dagda's magick club or staff, said to have the power to kill with one end or restore life with the other.

Cunús (Coo-Nyoos) Dirty, foul thing.

Go ndéana an diabhal dréimire de chnámh do dhroma ag piocadh úll i ngairdín Ifrinn! (NA) May the devil make a ladder of your backbone while picking apples in the garden of Hell!

Nocht (NhocT) Reveal

Cathal (Co-Hull) Irish name meaning vigilant.

Nách mór an diabhal thú. (NA) You're the devil.

Ó Murchadha (O-Murra-khoo): Old Irish surname and origin of the surname Murphy.

Eithne (Eeth-nah) meaning "kernel" or "grain."

Aodh (AY) name meaning fire and traced back to the worship of the druids.

Glaisne (Glash-ne) name meaning calm or serene.

Ríonach (Ree-Uh-na) name meaning royal or queen.

Alban Eiler - (AHL-bahn eye-ear) Druid name for the festival of the spring equinox, which means "The Light of the Earth."

Bullán (Bul-AWN) A stone with a natural or manmade depression found at many pagan sites. They hold water and occasionally pebbles and other offerings and were believed to have been used by the druids for rituals and divination.

Fuirich air falbh on grian! (Fwirr-ick err voliv on gree-an) Stay away from the sun!

Mo anam cara (muh ann-imm carrah) my soulmate, my soul friend.

A chuisle mo chroí (A quish-leh muh kree) my treasure, my beloved.

Stad! (Stadd) Stop!

Más (mahs) Spanish for "more."

Iroquois (Ir-ah-Koy/Ir-oh-Kwa) Native Americans of northeast North America and Upstate New York. They were known during the colonial years to the French as the "Iroquois League," and later as the "Iroquois Confederacy." The English called them the "Five Nations," including the **Mohawk** (Mo-Hawk), **Oneida** (Oh-ny-dah), **Onondaga** (On-on-dah-gah), **Cayuga** (Kay-yu-gah), and **Seneca** (Sen-uh-kuh). After 1722, the Iroquoian-speaking **Tuscarora** (Tus-cah-ro-rah) from the southeast were accepted into the confederacy, which became known as the Six Nations. The Confederacy likely came about between the years 1450 CE and 1660 CE as a result of the Great Law of Peace, said to have been composed by **Deganawidah** (Day-Gon-Na-We-Dah) the Great Peacemaker, **Hiawatha** (Hi-Ah-Wah-Thah), and **Jigonsaseh** (Gee-Gon-Saw-Say) the Mother of Nations.

Glooskap (Klue-skopp or Kuh-loo-skopp) a sun god of the **Algonquian** (Al-gon-kew-an) peoples, one of the most populous and widespread North American native language groups. Glooskap was described as kind, benevolent, a warrior against evil, and the possessor of magickal powers.

Malsum (Mawl-som) a malevolent trickster god and twin brother of Glooskap.

Quah-beet (NA) translates to "Great Beaver," a river deity.

Odin (Oh-din) a prominent god in Norse mythology worshiped by the Germanic peoples of Northern Europe. Odin[1] is associated with wisdom, healing, death, knowledge, war, battle, victory, sorcery, poetry, and frenzy, and is depicted as the husband of the goddess Frigg. Odin is also associated with the divine battlefield maidens, the valkyries, and he oversees Valhalla, where he receives half of those who die in battle. Odin fathered many children, including Thor, Baldr, Hoor, Vioarr and Vali.

Loki (Loh-kee) a god in Norse mythology. Loki is the son of the **jötunn** (Yo-tun) Fárbauti and the goddess Laufey, he sometimes assists the gods and sometimes behaves maliciously towards them. Loki is a shapeshifter and in separate incidents appears in the form of a salmon, a mare, a fly, and possibly an elderly woman.

Apollo (Uh-pol-oh) one of the Olympian deities in classical Greek and Roman mythology. Apollo has been recognized as a god of archery, music and dance, truth and prophecy, healing and diseases, the sun and light, poetry, and more. One of the most important and complex of the Greek gods, he is the son of Zeus and Leto, and the twin brother of Artemis, goddess of the hunt. He is considered to be the most beautiful god and is represented as the ideal of the **kouros**—a sculpture of a beardless, athletic youth.

Thor (Thorr) a prominent god in Germanic paganism. In Norse mythology, he is a hammer-wielding god associated with lightning, thunder, storms, sacred groves and trees, strength, the protection of humankind, hallowing, and fertility.

Huginn and Muninn (Hoo-gin and Moo-nin) are a pair of ravens that fly all over the world, Midgard, and bring information to the god Odin.

Valkyrie (Val-kuh-ree) name meaning "chooser of the slain," a host of Norse female deities who guide souls of the dead to Valhalla. Valkyries also appear as lovers of heroes and other mortals, where they are sometimes described as the daughters of royalty, sometimes accompanied by ravens and sometimes connected to swans or horses.

Poetic Edda (Ed-Duh) the modern name for an untitled collection of Old Norse anonymous narrative poems in alliterative verse. It is distinct from the closely related Prose Edda, although both works are seminal to the study of Old Norse poetry. Several versions of the Poetic Edda exist. Especially notable is the medieval Icelandic Manuscript, Codex Regius, which contains 31 poems.

Valhalla (Val-hal-luh) "hall of the slain." It is described as a majestic hall located in Asgard and presided over by the god Odin. Half of those who die in combat enter Valhalla, while the other half are chosen by the goddess **Freyja** (Fray-yuh) to reside in **Fólkvangr** (Volk-fan-gir). The masses of those killed in combat, along with various legendary Germanic heroes and kings, live in Valhalla until Ragnarök when they will march out of its many doors to fight in aid of Odin.

Ragnarök (Rahg-nuh-rok) in Norse mythology, a foretold series of impending events, including a great battle in which numerous great Norse mythological figures will perish, including the gods Odin, Thor, Týr, Freyr, Heimdall, and Loki. It will entail a catastrophic series of natural disasters, including the burning of the world, and culminate in the submersion of the world underwater. After these events, the world will rise again, cleansed and fertile, the surviving and returning gods will meet, and the world will be repopulated by two human survivors, **Líf and Lífþrasir** (Leef and Leef-thrahss-eer) Life, and the Love of Life.

Hamartia (Huh-mar-dee-ah) a fatal flaw in a character of a tragedy that leads to their downfall.

Do chara (Duh ca-Ha-rah) Your beloved

Mo stór (Muh stohr) My most beloved, my treasure.

Ghrian (Gyree-un) Sun

Eochaid Ollathair (YOKH-adh oll-UH-hurh): The Dagda, the allfather. He is known as the good or great god and the lord of the heavens.

Saol fada chugat, mo rí. (Sail faddah coogit, muh ree) Long life to you, my king.

1.

Prologue

Tuatha Dé Danann of the glorious light.
Who rose from the mists in the time before kings.
These Druids complete in their wisdom and gifts.
They came in ships like smoke, full of magick and valor in service of the One.
The Dagda. He is the light and the truth. He is the mist from which the Tuatha sprang.
The Father of the Druids and on Him the crown of all kings.
Out of the mist, the Dagda raised His strong and noble people.
His blood from the womb of every mother and on the field with the slain.
Then, His time came and He was laid in the earth under a mound to rest.
His treasure entrusted to the glory of the kings of Ireland
Until His people arise and mighty Uaithne calls Him forth with the sun.
A new age of glorious light.
Tuatha.
It begins.

. . .

Tuatha Dé Danann of the glorious light.

Who were the keepers of the sacred sun and protectors of His treasure.

These Druids, most trusted and loyal, guardians of the heir.

They hold the memory of the fallen and call Him forth with the spring.

The Dagda. He is the light and the truth. He is the mist from which the Tuatha sprang.

The Father of the Druids and on Him the crown of all kings.

Under the mound he rests, awaiting the rise of His most beloved and worthy of sons.

His hearth kept warm with the Coire Ansic and His line defended by a ruthless Log Mór.

Then, His faithful will pray and join with Him under a youthful, growing moon.

Until His people arise and mighty Uaithne calls Him forth with the sun.

A new age of glorious light.

Tuatha.

It begins.

Tuatha Dé Danann of the glorious light.

Who remained, loyal and vigilant to the One and His heir.

These Druids with timeless, ageless wisdom and faith.

They gather His faithful to await His return with the coming of the spring.

The Dagda. He is the light and the truth. He is the mist from which the Tuatha sprang.

The Father of the Druids and given to Him, the crown of all kings.

With the new Sun He rises, brighter than the dawn, He the Lord of all Wild Things.

At His side, His noble Three: the Coire Ansic, the Log Mór, and His mighty, fearless Uaithne.

For He is master of all life, consort of the dead and Lord of sacred night.

His glory eternal and His reign of love and Sun everlasting.

A new age of glorious light.

Tuatha.

It begins.

—Translated by P. Columb from *Leabhar Fintan mac Bóchra* (c. 1106)

One

Nox was asleep on the kitchen floor, wrapped around the teapot and snuggled under his favorite quilt. An easy, peaceful smile rested on his face and Nelson was calling it a win as he quietly backed away and stepped out onto the terrace, closing the door silently and dialing Merlin's number.

"How is he?" Merlin asked, answering immediately.

"He looks okay. He isn't sleeping on the work table anymore."

Nelson put a stop to that after Nox rolled off in the middle of the night and landed in his dinner. Because one slept on a table and ate on the floor when they were in an opium stupor, apparently. Nelson had been asleep in the study on the sofa and had aged decades when he awoke to a loud crash and Nox's terrified squawk.

"I'm alright," Nox had slurred as he flicked a noodle off his cheek. Soup dripped from his chin and the end of his nose but Nox swiped it away with a drowsy shrug. "Back to sleep."

"Don't even think about it!" Nelson had said when Nox attempted to push himself up and return to the work table. "Not until you figure out how to defy gravity or bounce."

"Fine," Nox had grumbled. He slid the tray away and curled

around his knees, soft snores huffing from his lips a few moments later.

Nelson had brought a pillow and covered him with the quilt, but it had been days since Nox had eaten or consumed anything more than a few spoons of soup or pot of Merlin's tea. "What if he becomes addicted?"

"To that tea?" Merlin chuckled dubiously. "It's very gentle and Nox has drunk stronger potions, I can assure you," he added suggestively.

"You know, Clancy had a point before about Nox needing more supervision."

"Hush. We cannot understand what we're afraid to see and Nox has never shied away from learning first-hand and expanding his mind. That's why he is such a gifted witch, because he has far more than a theoretical understanding of that which he practices."

"You taught him that it was okay to use himself as a guinea pig," Nelson accused, then waited for Merlin to deny it or apologize. "Hello?"

"Do you know how young knights were trained for battle in the Middle Ages?"

"How?" Nelson asked, preparing for another one of Merlin's little lessons.

"In the melee, and later, the joust. So many knights were killed in 'recreational,' practice combat that there were papal edicts and monarchs made laws banning those activities. It was a brutal and wasteful way to train a young man of noble birth. But, knowing how to wield a sword or block a curse *in theory* doesn't do you much good when you're in the thick of it, in the heat of battle, does it, Nelson? *Knowing* how a plant or dark magick works can only get you so far. It's practice and experience that save your life during a fight."

"Speaking of fighting..." Nelson would never approve of Merlin's methods and the ambiguously older man would never

Chapter One

repent because the ends justified the means in his batty little mind. "Have you and Clancy settled your differences?"

There was a heavy, shaking sigh. "He says he no longer blames me for Sorcha's[1] and Lucas's deaths and I believe him," Merlin began slowly.

"But?" Nelson prodded threateningly. "I hid the tea because I need Nox to wake up soon and I need you two here so we can figure out what happens next. You're not getting anywhere near him if you're still holding a grudge against Clancy. That's nonnegotiable."

"I know," Merlin said with another sigh, this one even more pained. It had been two days since Nox had banished Merlin and Clancy and banished himself to the kitchen in hopes of finding answers in a pot of opium-laced tea. Thankfully, Clancy was more of a text person and checked in every few hours, whereas Merlin called almost hourly, groveling and fretting. "I have forgiven Clancy for the things he's said and done *to me*. I can put that part of the past behind us because it has always been in Clancy's nature to be ruthlessly pragmatic and a touch...controlling. He has the heart of a general and he will always be ready for war."

"But?" This time, Nelson was gentle because he had seen what Clancy had been willing to risk and hadn't quite forgiven him yet himself. His feelings toward Clancy weren't the problem, though, and hadn't created a web of awful complications for Nox and the investigation.

"I'm not sure I can ever forgive him for what happened to those girls. Not completely." Merlin's voice quivered until it crumbled and his hoarse, exhausted cries hurt Nelson. "Because that would mean that I'd forgiven myself for my part in that and I can't, Nelson."

"What do you mean?"

Merlin pulled in a watery, reinforcing breath. "Of course, I knew about that wild clan of witches down in New Castle. They're not the only ones hiding in those mountains, but I knew they were Tuath Dé and that they were up to something. And I knew Clancy had a hand in it when I heard about students finding them and whispers of a new Dagda[2]. Just as I suspected that Clancy would foment any cult that rose around them. That was always the point and why he teaches about cults and works for the FBI. But I was scared of how far Clancy had gone when those girls went missing. I didn't send Nox to New Castle and to the rave just because of the prophecy. I sent him to put a stop to the horror *I* helped unleash by looking the other way."

"I don't believe Clancy knew about the league or the plan to sacrifice those girls," Nelson interrupted, making Merlin gasp.

"No! Neither do I. *Now*," he qualified. "I couldn't put it past him because there isn't much else that Clancy *wouldn't* sacrifice for Nox. I didn't think he'd hesitate to give his own life or even his girls' to protect *and save* Nox."

"Because he couldn't save Lucas," Nelson realized, earning a sad hum of agreement from Merlin.

"He's never been attached to an heir like he was to Lucas and his love for Lucas brought out the human in Clancy. He never married or had a life before. He always behaved like a monk!" Merlin sounded incredulous as he laughed but it faded, the mood turning solemn. "He *was* a monk for a few centuries and Lucas was the first to crack Clancy's shield and awaken the human in him. I'd never known Clancy to follow or listen to his heart before and it broke when we lost Sorcha and Lucas. Clancy doesn't just love Nox because it's his duty, he loves Nox because Lucas gave him the capacity to love like a father. And I had feared that his ruthless nature and his fatherly love for Nox had twisted Clancy."

It had, but not as far or in the way Merlin had imagined. "He gave Nox a cult and they were building him an army to fulfill the prophecy. They just didn't know *who* they were building all of it for and someone else saw the potential and took advantage," Nelson guessed.

"That does seem to be the case..." Merlin replied hesitantly. "Clancy and I have discussed this Badb[3] and we have an idea as to who it could be."

"Really?" Nelson asked, not ready to get his hopes up. "You two had a discussion and something productive occurred?"

"We see how much trouble we've caused and we both agreed to set the past and our differences aside. All that matters now is helping you find the Badb and freeing Nox. He's all that's ever mattered, we just let our hearts and our pride get in the way."

A loud breath whooshed from Nelson and he was lightheaded at the thought. "That's a miracle. I was afraid we'd have to figure this out without any backup."

"*No,*" Merlin said firmly. "We are in complete agreement now. We're sorry for *everything* we've done and all we want is to come back and help."

"Good." Nelson turned, feeling the sun warming his back as he headed inside, and nodded. "That's really good. I'll wake Nox up and tell him it's time to get back to work."

---

1. **Sorcha** (Surka): Nox's mother, died when Nox was 12.
2. **The Dagda** (Dag-duh or Day-duh): An important god in Irish mythology likened to the Germanic god Odin. One of the Tuatha Dé Danann, the Dagda is portrayed as a father-figure, king, and a high druid. He is associated with fertility, agriculture, manliness and strength, as well as magic, druidry, and wisdom. He can control life and death, the weather and crops, as well as time and the seasons. His name means "the good god" or "the great god."
3. **Badb** (Bive or Beev): A crow, and associated with the battle goddess **Badb Catha** (Bive Caha) the battle crow and one of the trio of war goddesses known as the **Morrígan/Mór-Ríoghain** (Mo Ree-an).

Two

"It's time to wake up."

Nelson's tender reverence made the return to consciousness and reality less dreadful. Nox had missed him but...

"Elsa's still dead and Clancy and Merlin are still backstabbing assholes, aren't they?"

"Elsa's still dead," Nelson confirmed sadly, making consciousness and reality dreadful again. She was dead and six girls had their lives shattered because of Nox, and the two people he loved and trusted most had betrayed him.

"I think I could use more tea," Nox said, looking around the kitchen from the floor. He couldn't see his teapot or the tin of Nelson's *extra special* bedtime blend.

"I hid it," Nelson said as he scooped Nox up by his armpits, then held him at arm's length. "You need a shower."

"Probably." Nox opened his robe and gave himself a sniff, gagging at the pungent fumes as he was guided out of the kitchen and down the hall. "Why do I smell like body odor and chicken soup?"

"You've had an eventful two days."

Chapter Two

"And did I miss anything important while I was away?" he asked as they climbed the stairs.

"Merlin and Clancy would like to come back," Nelson said, then gave an apologetic wince when Nox snarled. "They have settled their differences and are working together—in a non-dysfunctional way, I've been promised—and they know who the Badb is," he added.

"Oh! Well, then!" Nox clapped his hands together, feigning delight. "Is that all it took? All that running around and questioning witnesses to find him when we could have tried devastation and opium and saved ourselves all those weeks." He rolled his eyes as he strode into the bedroom and headed for the bathroom and his toothbrush.

"I'm not going to make excuses for them," Nelson began as he went into the closet and appeared a moment later with a pile of clothes while Nox brushed his teeth. "You weren't in a listening frame of mind, before, and they were trying to save you in their twisted, dysfunctional way."

Nox flashed Nelson a hard, warning look. "None of that was done out of love," he said around the head of the brush. He gave his head a shake, then quickly finished at the sink.

"Nox..."

"No!" He slashed at the air as he went to start the shower. "I don't care what was at stake. No one who loves me would have allowed that nightmare of a cult to exist and I would have died before I sacrificed my father." He laughed as he imagined what would have happened if he had died instead of Lucas. "*That* would have stopped the prophecy in its tracks and Dad and everyone else might have lived happily ever after as long as he didn't have another son."

Nelson shrugged as he leaned against the counter. "I could have recorded a country album."

"What?" Nox laughed as he dropped his robe, turning to Nelson.

He shrugged again, gesturing for Nox to get on with it and get in the shower. "I got roped into singing in a Christmas thing in college because someone in my roommate's a cappella group got sick. His dad was a producer with some record label and he wanted me to come into the studio and give it a shot but I passed."

"You passed?" Nox asked loudly as he stepped under the water. "With your looks and that deep range. You could have been a star!"

"I guess you could say I opted out because I didn't want to be a star. I wanted to be an FBI agent. And I never would have met you."

That stopped Nox. He stared at the tile for several moments, contemplating whether it would have been better if Nelson had accepted that offer and if they'd never met and gone to New Castle together. "Would the world be better or safer now if I had died and you became a country star?"

Nelson snorted, shaking Nox from his thoughts. "The world would *not* be better. And I don't care, I'd never give you up or change the past just because it would be easier. The cult and those girls weren't your fault, but they're *our* mess—you, me, Clancy, and Merlin. We're the only ones who can make this right now and end it."

"I can *almost* forgive Merlin," Nox said while lathering his hair. "He was always more transparent and it was me who refused to listen when he urged me to act. He faced me here, directly, and he didn't play with other people's lives like they were meaningless or beneath him."

"I don't think Clancy—" Nelson started but Nox pointed a bubble-covered finger at him.

"Clancy knew—he *knows*—how combustible zealotry and fanaticism can be, especially when combined with religion and the possibility of immortality. There is *nothing* more irresistible to humans, it draws them like bees to nectar."

"Them?" Nelson asked, waiting with a towel.

Nox pushed out a weary breath as he scrubbed his chest and

neck with salty, eucalyptus and juniper shower gel. "You know what I mean."

"I honestly don't. Are you still one of us?"

"I must be. My stomach feels like an empty, acid-burned hull and my back is killing me," he said with a rueful smirk. "I don't think humans would be as excited about immortality if they knew eternal back pain was a possibility."

"I think you're still feeling the effects of that tea," Nelson replied, making Nox chuckle as he turned off the water.

He thanked Nelson for the towel and surveyed his senses as he dried himself. "I am experiencing some mild euphoria that's helping me stay relaxed and I'm still seeing a slight technicolor haze, but my reflexes and the rest of my brain seem to be alert and functioning relatively normally."

"Thank goodness," Nelson replied, sounding utterly sincere.

Nox stopped and captured his lips for a slow, clinging kiss. "I did miss you while I was away," he whispered as he pecked. The starchy crispness of Nelson's shirt against Nox's bare skin and the firm hand sliding down his back to cup his ass felt like a balm as they kissed. Soft sunlight filled the bathroom and it was quiet. Nox sank into the peace and was reassured by how good and right it felt when he was in Nelson's arms.

"I missed you too." He angled his head, taking the kiss deeper for just a moment. "No more tea. We'll figure this out together. Just stay with me and let me help you."

Nox hummed in agreement as he stroked Nelson's jaw and traced his lip. "I've gone as deep as I can go into my psyche and found all the secrets that were hidden in there. And I think that *we* are the key to solving the rest of this puzzle."

"Good." Nelson nodded. "In that case, Merlin and Clancy are downstairs and your oatmeal should be ready. It's time to get back to work."

They were waiting for Nox in the study when he strolled in with a bowl, their heads bowed and staring at their feet in shame. Nox took a seat on top of his desk, crossing his legs as he ate and studied them anew. Gone were the loving uncles who had protected him and filled his head with sweet, Dagda-free dreams of a short, but somewhat normal life.

Now, Nox saw them and regarded Nelson as he was meant to, without their disguises. They were meant to be his counsel: Clancy the general, Merlin the oracle and healer, and Nelson the bodyguard and the bridge to the Dagda and Nox's ultimate destiny. He also considered himself and the role of the leader of their little clan. Of the four of them, only Nelson was free of guilt and had no reason to feel any shame.

"Before I will even *begin* to forgive or trust either of you, I have to know that there is no more bad blood or ill will," Nox began and Clancy's head snapped up as Merlin nodded quickly.

"It's all behind us," Merlin promised, clasping his hands together. "All we want is to help now."

Nox cast Clancy a cynical look. "You've forgiven 'the boggart'?"

"I have," Clancy said firmly. "I blamed him because I couldn't forgive myself."

"And have you forgiven yourself?" Nox challenged, earning an immediate head shake.

"I'll never forgive myself, but we only made things worse when we let our shame grow into grudges."

"Good." Nox nodded, then shoveled a spoonful of oatmeal into his mouth. His eyes narrowed as he chewed and decided the best path forward. "Hug," he said as he waved the spoon at them.

"Excuse me?" Clancy asked, grunting when Merlin's arms lashed around his middle. He chuckled softly and rolled his eyes as he put an arm around Merlin and patted his shoulder. "There. We're fine now," he said but Nox shook his head.

"I want to see a real hug and I'll tell you when you're done." He smiled expectantly at Clancy while Merlin obediently rested a cheek on his chest.

"I don't see why—" Clancy started but Nox hushed him.

"Remember how you made your girls hug it out when they

were little? I want you and Merlin to hug it out now," he said, earning another chuckle and eye roll from Clancy as he wrapped his arms around Merlin and accepted his punishment.

"Very well," he said wearily.

"I forgot how nice you smell, Darach[1]," Merlin murmured, making Nelson's brow hitch and he mouthed a surprised "Darach?" at Nox.

Nox waved it off, more curious and excited at the possibility of Merlin and Clancy coexisting peacefully again. He was a child the last time the two of them had gotten this close to each other without at least one of them swinging or spitting. "Keep hugging," Nox whispered as he ate, allowing the sight to soothe and heal years of drama-induced trauma.

Merlin was the first to crack. He began to sniffle as he rubbed his cheek against Clancy's sweater vest. Then, there was a shuddering gasp as Clancy's arms tightened around Merlin. "I'm sorry for all the times I called you a boggart," he said, crying in earnest and Merlin nodded jerkily as he wept.

"I understand and I'm sorry for most of the times I called you a cunt."

There was a strangled choking sound from Nelson. He looked like he was going to bite through his knuckle or explode, his face was so red as he watched them sob and comfort each other. Nox waited until their crying had settled into regretful, wistful sighs to finally release them.

"Now, I believe it," he said as he hopped off the desk, his bowl empty and his belly full of oats, honey, and fresh berries. "And who is the Badb?"

Clancy's head hung and there was a muttered curse. "It's Walter Forsythe, my assistant."

"Walt?" Nox was only surprised because he was expecting someone more...surprising. "Are you certain?"

"Yes," Clancy said, grimacing at Nox. "As soon as you mentioned that you were looking for the Badb, I knew. Walt's mother was—or still is, I suppose—Wiccan. I can't recall him telling me much about her practice or beliefs except that she was devoted to the Badb before she began to decline. She's in a home now, I think. He wrote his thesis on the Morrígan and their sister deities throughout various cultures and literature. He doesn't show it very often, but he has a crow tattooed on his forearm."

"So it's star pupil versus the golden child," Nox murmured thoughtfully and nodded as he glanced at Nelson. "He might see more in his favorite professor than just a mentor if he was raised by a single mother," he speculated, earning a knowing hum from Nelson.

"He wears the exact same frames," he said, pointing at Clancy's glasses. "I used to go to my father's tailor until Giovanni passed away. It was the easiest box to check for his approval. Dad couldn't complain about my hair or the way I dressed because I looked just like him."

The three of them blinked at Nelson for a moment before Nox cleared his throat. "I don't think it worked in this case either," he guessed, raising a brow at Clancy. "That would explain why he hates me. But how did he *know me* well enough to run straight up to my bedroom and how did he know there was a locket with my hair in it?"

Clancy scrubbed his face with shaking hands and muttered a string of curses. "I never saw that he was fixated on you, I swear. I thought he was just enough of a believer that he would encourage students to seek out the Tuath Dé when they came to us with papers about witches or druids or modern pagans. I had no idea that *he* had gotten involved with that group down in New Castle."

Nox chuckled wryly at Clancy. "He was more than a casual believer, though, wasn't he? You knew his interest was far more than academic or you wouldn't have trusted him to run with this unsupervised. You taught me yourself: your teaching assistant is your voice and your representative. They speak for us and we trust them with our message. You wouldn't have left something this important to a dilettante."

"No..." Clancy agreed hesitantly. "I never thought of it that way. I was too assured in his desire to please me and advance his career that it never occurred to me that Walt would have any other motivations. But he—" His face twisted into a disgusted grimace. "But he practically told me! I was just too arrogant and short-sighted to take him seriously."

"He told you?" Nox asked as he prowled closer and Clancy nodded.

"I only remember it because it was the closest I've ever seen Walt come to being angry. It was the only time he ever raised his voice. At the time, I chalked it up to embarrassment because I had laughed at him."

Nox's head tilted as he watched Clancy closely. "This is it, team. This is his origin story," he whispered. "Why did you laugh at Walt?"

"He said he'd found...things in old books and he wanted to know if I thought the prophecy could be fulfilled and if the Dagda would stir if a new Tuatha Dé Danann[2] were to rise. I said that anything was possible, but that there were other parts of that prophecy—*key figures*—necessary for the waking of the Dagda."

"What did he say to that?" Nox asked, his anticipation rising with Clancy's regret.

"He mentioned the Badb. He said the Dagda might awaken if the Badb returned and rejoined the Tuatha Dé Danann. Walt suggested that the Badb could bind with the Dagda to create a new god."

There was a shocked laugh from Merlin. "Preposterous! He makes a sick stew of only what he wants to believe and defiles the rest," he said and let out a loud gasp as he turned to the rolling boards with all their photos and facts. "That's why he wanted those girls for a Samhain[3] ritual. The Battle of the Plain of Pillars!" he declared, earning a louder gasp from Nox.

"The Cath Maige Tuired!"[4] he said excitedly, nodding as he joined Merlin. "It's bonkers but I get it now!"

"I don't," Nelson called from behind them and Nox smiled as he turned.

"Followers of the Badb or the Morrígan offer sacrifices to the warrior goddess because the lore holds that on the eve of the Battle of the Plain of Pillars—Samhain Eve—she met with and married the Dagda and the two mated. After, she advised him to gather his greatest warriors and that she would wield chaos and destruction when it was time to face the Fomorians[5] in battle the next day. On Samhain, they faced the enemy for the soul of Ireland and it was her ruthlessness that drove the Fomorians into defeat."

A hard humph wafted from Nelson as he nodded. "That is bonkers, but I get it."

"That's why you laughed at him," Nox said to Clancy. "Is that when you told him about me?"

Clancy had never looked more pathetic as he nodded. "I told him that everyone knew the old stories about the Badb and the Fomorians. But I'd found old books and records, too, that hinted at a surviving line that had been unbroken since the time of the last druids. I said that in that family there was an heir that *could* be the new king if the legends were true and if the stars aligned. That even if the Badb were to return, the Dagda would not settle for a crow when *He* could have the sun."

"Hmm..." Nox steepled his hands and tapped his fingertips together, attempting to calculate how much of a spiritual, emotional, and professional slap in the face that would have been for Walt. "Wow! He gets shot down by his father figure who not only craps on his theory but all over his favorite deity as well... The burn would have been severe once he realized you were talking about me."

There was a soft cough from Nelson as he waved his notepad at Clancy. "When did he figure out that you were one of the three and that you had used him to build a cult for your golden boy?"

"I don't know," Clancy replied, shaking his head. "My hope was that Walt would do the math and maybe brag that *he'd* found the heir. I thought the cult would come to Nox once the rumors spread. Those six missing girls and Elsa Hansen were the first signs I saw that something had gone terribly wrong. But I never would have imagined it was Walt, that he was capable of this."

"Now we know the why," Nox summarized, looking around. There were sad, serious murmurs and grunts. He laughed at Clancy, shaking his head. "One would think that an *anthropology* professor would know better. When has it ended in anything but disaster when gods and demigods play with the hearts and aspirations of mortals?" he asked and Merlin clicked his teeth at Nox.

"That job has always been a means to an end. Clancy's primary objective and his *first* duty has always been to build you a cult and to be ready to defend you in battle," he scolded Nox gently, then offered Clancy a gracious nod. "He was smart enough to infiltrate the FBI and recruit from within. How do you think that case found its way to Nelson—the one agent in the bureau who *would* follow you to the ends of the earth? Or New Castle."

Nelson shook his head. "Felton said that Clancy reassured him there was no case."

"Of course, I did," Clancy replied. "I didn't want Felton to hand it off to one of his favorites. And for what it's worth, I did think it was a nuisance case when I first heard about two missing witches. I thought they had *joined* the cult. It never occurred to me that they had been taken and that there might be more. The girls were supposed to lead Nox to the Tuath Dé so it *had to* go to someone he could walk all over. An agent with an ounce of self-preservation wouldn't have taken him seriously. Sorry, Nelson," he added with a wince.

"It's fine," Nelson replied woodenly and there was a sympathetic groan from Merlin.

"But now we see that the two of you were always meant to find each other. Clancy couldn't hand the case directly to Nox so he made sure the case went to Felton with orders for you to shut it down immediately. Just as Clancy relegated the dirty work to Walt, letting him rub elbows with the students and the hillbillies.

It was rather clever and classically Clancy until Walt went rogue and turned against him and Nox."

"I'm so sorry," Clancy said heavily, but Nox waved it off. "You can tell that to Heidi Hansen after we've dealt with Walt." He went to the boards and reached for Elsa's picture, plucking it off. "You were never a nuisance to me." He turned back to his counsel. "We're focusing on Walt now. I want to know him as well as he knows us. Where did he learn dark magick? *Who* taught him? That will tell us as much as the traps he's set. I already know most of his tricks. I just need to know *who* Walt is. Once I do—once I've learned his secrets—he won't stand a chance."

Merlin went straight to work, turning one of the boards to its blank side. "That's an excellent place to start. I've been examining the curses he's left so far and I have some thoughts," he began, mumbling mostly to himself so Nox swung back to Clancy.

"Get me everything you have from him when he was a student and your assistant—papers, tests, emails, texts... Everything."

"Hold on," Nelson interrupted again with another wave of his notepad. "We need better proof connecting Walt to this than Julian's statements about the Badb. None of that was on the record and he can't testify to Walt's involvement. We have to connect Walt to the poisonings in New Castle and the prisons. It would be even better if we could prove *he* was behind the abductions, not Julian. *Without* tipping him off if we can help it," he added with a pointed look at Clancy and Nox.

Clancy's eyes widened. "Walt had access to several federal facilities over the last few months. I recommended him for lead on a research project for the school and I sent him to do a few interviews—some light surveys—for the bureau's behavioral science department."

"He would have needed access to work as your assistant," Nox concurred with a shrug. "That just makes Nelson's life easier. We'll have to be careful when we question Aubrey, but I have a feeling she'll be able to connect Walt to the yew," he said and Nelson snorted in approval.

"That would be a great start. Especially if he's on the visitors' logs and the security videos. It'll take me a while to get them but we'd have enough to connect Walt to the method of poisoning and prove he had access."

"There you go," Nox said to Clancy. "We need everything connected to any tasks you assigned Walt on behalf of the FBI as well. And gods help you if it gets out that *your* assistant used you and the FBI to murder our witnesses," he added and gestured for Clancy to get out of his sight.

"I'll tell them myself as soon as it's safe to," he said, as he took himself off.

Merlin sighed at his back, then cast a cautious look at Nox. "You know, he's more human than demigod these days. We all are and we've all made terrible mistakes," he said gently, but Nox shook his head, still too bitter and shellshocked.

"You're here because you've forgiven each other and because I need you to finish this task that's been forced upon me. But I haven't forgiven the two of you yet," Nox explained. "I can't until this is over and I've seen how much damage has been done and how much we're able to fix."

"I understand," Merlin said with a bow. "I'll find everything I can about his mother, her practice, and their past. I'll tell you everything I can about this Badb," he vowed as he went back to work on the boards.

Nelson raised a brow at Nox. "What do you want me to work on?"

A beatific smile spread across Nox's face. Nelson said it was time to get back to work and work they would. Nox's destiny, reality, the consequences of Clancy's schemes... All of that sucked *hard*, but this was going to be fun.

"I want you upstairs, Uaithne[6]. We're going to master sex magick."

"Oh!" Merlin hooted and clapped excitedly as he spun back to them. "If you'd like I can prepare a—"

"No!" Nelson shouted and shook his head as he backed from the room. "I'm not sure if this is a good idea, but we can talk about it upstairs," he mumbled, then fled.

"I think you must," Merlin whispered out of the side of his mouth and Nox hummed in agreement.

"I won't allow *Him* to manipulate us like that. And if that's how *He* means to control me, then I'll make the most of it."

"That's my boy!" Merlin said proudly as he wiped an eye. "Godspeed, lad."

---

1. **Darach** (Da-rock): an old Gaelic name meaning "oak tree" or "oak grove."
2. **Tuatha Dé Danann** (Too-Wah day dan-ann) Acknowledged as the early gods of Ireland (an earlier form of their name, **Tuath Dé** (Too-Ah day) means "tribe of gods").
3. **Samhain** (Sau-win) a Celtic festival celebrated on 1 November marking the end of the harvest season and beginning of winter or "darker half" of the year. It is also the Gaelic name for November. Celebrations begin on the evening of 31 October, since the Celtic day began and ended at sunset. It is about halfway between the autumnal equinox and winter solstice.
4. **The Cath Maige Tuired** (Caw-Mwee-Turra) from before the ninth Century A.D., is two saga texts of the Mythological Cycle of Irish Mythology detailing the epic battle between the mythical Tuatha De Danann and Fomoire for Ireland.
5. **Fomorians** (Faw-mah-reean) mythological beasts often depicted as giants.
6. **Uaithne** (Oof-na): The Dagda's magic harp that could change seasons, turn the tides of battle, and see into the hearts of men.

Three

Nelson had his notes out and was pacing, gathering reasons for why they *shouldn't* when Nox arrived, whistling cheerfully as he shut the bedroom doors behind him.

"I've put you through a lot, the last few days," Nox began as he sauntered toward Nelson, a teasing grin tilting his lips and his eyes sparking with lust and hunger. "And you've been patient —*incredibly* patient—with me for months. I promise, Nelson, I will find a way to show you how grateful I am without you-know-who sticking *His* infinite nose in the middle of it."

"No." Nelson shook his head and tapped the page when he found the right spot. "You shouldn't thank me. I put you in danger last—"

"Not on purpose," Nox argued, but Nelson snorted dismissively.

"I figured it out after the rave, though, and I thought I could control it myself if I just didn't...*you know* with you." He felt so stupid in hindsight and wondered if the Dagda had counted on Nelson's hubris and ignorance in the bedroom.

Nox made a happy, dreamy sound as he helped Nelson out of his coat, easing it over his shoulders. "Because you see the man—

the human—in me and you loved *him*, not an heir or a pawn in a prophecy you could manipulate."

"We can't keep pretending, though. You aren't just a man and we're playing with fire."

"What would you suggest?" Nox asked warily, earning a cautious wince from Nelson.

"Maybe we shouldn't...for a while. Until we're sure it's safe," he suggested and Nox laughed.

"Could you live like that?" he asked in disbelief, then rolled his eyes. "Of course, *you* could. But absolutely not, Nelson. I'm not going to waste what might be my last few weeks on this *good* earth deprived of true joy and happiness because of *Him*. I don't care who or what we are outside of this bedroom. I belong to you and you belong to me," he said simply as he tossed Nelson's coat at a chair. "And the only way it's ever going to be safe is if we figure out how this works and beat *Him* at *His* own game."

Nelson shook his head, still nervous as he remembered how close he came to losing Nox to the Dagda's trances. "I don't like using you as bait or as a guinea pig. Not if I can't follow you and keep you safe. I took notes after last time because I had a feeling you wouldn't remember everything," he said with a wave of his notepad. "I knew you'd want to learn as much as you could while you were in that trap. I'm just not sure if I got anything useful."

Nox's brows jumped. "You observed and took notes?" he asked and Nelson nodded, averting his eyes as he blushed.

"I didn't know what else to do. Merlin said it was the only kind of magick I was capable of and he told me to stay with you. So, I let you get close enough to see *Him* and tell me what was happening," he explained, causing Nox to splutter.

"You...let me get close? How?"

Nelson's face was so hot and his brow was damp as he scrubbed it with the back of his hand. "I just...tried my best to keep you close to..." he mumbled. "But I kept pulling you back before you could...*you know*." He cleared his throat suggestively, making Nox's eyes widen. "Before *He* could take you."

"Nelson, that's...*brilliant.*"

"What is?" Nelson frowned, shaking his head in confusion. "You seemed pretty frustrated and it was nerve-racking, not knowing if I was doing what you'd want me to do or if I was making things worse."

"You brilliant, brilliant man." Nox groaned as he twisted his hand in Nelson's tie and pulled him close. "Kiss me," he whispered as he offered his lips.

"Okay." Nelson complied, lowering his head and receiving a slow, sultry kiss that left them both winded. "Why am I brilliant?"

"Mystical edging," Nox panted as he backed Nelson toward the bed.

"I don't know what that means, but my notes, Nox."

"I am *very* interested in those notes."

"Are you?" Nelson raised a brow skeptically.

Nox nodded, pausing to pull his T-shirt over his head. "That might be the hottest thing anyone's ever done to me and I can't wait to try it agai—"

"What? *No.*" Nelson stared at Nox in dismay. "I didn't know what I was doing and we're lucky it didn't backfire on us. I took notes so we don't have to do it again," he argued.

"That's the thing!" Nox squealed as he pressed another kiss to Nelson's lips. "Your instincts are spectacular, Nelson! And I think it's because you aren't weakened and distracted by your desires the way most men are. Even when I'm testing every bit of your willpower and your patience, you never miss an opportunity to learn."

"We don't have time for me to learn," he warned. "I don't know what I'm doing most of the time and what I do know, *He* taught me in dreams so I'd be able to please you."

"Maybe." Nox shrugged. "*He* can't override your instinct to love and protect *me*, though."

"How can you be so sure?" Nelson raised his notepad to check something. "You said you saw me and I was a wolf and a warrior priest."

A long, loud gasp rushed from Nox. "Really?! I *have* to see that," he insisted, but Nelson frowned at him over the pad.

"I don't want to be a wolf and a warrior priest. But what if I have those instincts, too? What if there's something in me we don't want to tap into or let loose?"

Nox's eyes glittered and grew so big they could have fallen out. "My gods, if I could pick one way to go…"

"That's not funny," Nelson scolded and Nox's lips split into a wide, mischievous grin.

"That's making the best of it," he countered. "The Dagda gave me a mighty Uaithne and thought *He* could ensnare me with a holy dick. Some kings died in battle, but most of the heirs before me died in the prime of their lives doing silly, mundane things like walking to work or some casual rockhounding," Nox explained, his smile hardening and his eyes gleaming with wild defiance. "Meeting my maker while getting my back well and truly blown out is a far more glorious end."

"Hmm…" Nelson wrinkled his nose and shook his head. "That doesn't sound like something I want to be a part of either."

"That's the worst-case scenario, though!" Nox said quickly. "I think that if we're both compos mentis and we stay together *we* can beat *Him* at his own game. Did we get off at all? Tell me exactly how you did it," he urged while unzipping and shimmying out of his jeans.

"Um…" Nelson didn't need his notes for that, but he blinked at the page until he found the nerve. "I uh…got you off first, to get the first round out of the chamber. You were already so wound up and I wanted to draw it out as long as I could."

"That's so hot," Nox said, looking dizzy and clearly aroused as he reached for Nelson. His cock was hard and straining and Nox groaned as he yanked Nelson's tie loose. "This is why I trust you, Nelson. Implicitly. You stay so clear-headed while I'm practically out of my mind."

"I try," he said with a shrug.

"That's what makes all of this so hot. Let's practice edging

Chapter Three

until we're both able to feel when *He* enters the chat, if you will," Nox suggested, earning a frown from Nelson.

"I think I can tell..." He went back to his notes for the list. "Golden glowing, beautiful harp music, bees buzzing, increased euphoria," he read and Nox chuckled as his head tilted and he licked Nelson's knuckles around the notepad, making his hand shake.

"Increased euphoria? Are you feeling euphoric now, Nelson?" he purred, his eyes taking on a warm glow.

"You're doing it," Nelson warned gently and gave Nox's nose a soft, affectionate swat before kissing him. "*He's* already here," he whispered.

"Okay. Give me a minute." Nox closed his eyes and drew in a slow, steady breath. Nelson had observed Nox while he practiced yoga and meditated, centering himself in the same way so he could focus. "There," Nox said, opening his eyes and smiling. They were cool blue when they met Nelson's and Nox was his again, a laughing idiot in love. "Where were we?"

"I have a list of things I've noticed whenever we're about to... lose each other," Nelson said as he watched Nox closely. "Golden glowing, beautiful harp music, bees buzzing—"

"Oh! That's a *big one* for me!" Nox interrupted, as he turned Nelson's hand so he could see the list. "I certainly notice the increased euphoria and can never tell if that's just me being super horny, but the bees are definitely a giveaway," he said with unfeigned fascination.

Nelson was relieved to have Nox back but it was short-lived. "How do we keep *Him* from spying on us? It's getting more obvious when you're not in control, but what if *He* figures out what we're trying to do and hijacks you before we're ready?"

"I'm working on that!" Nox's cheeks puffed out as he widened his eyes at Nelson. "Dad showed me where to hide in my mind and I spent a lot of time in there when I was in my tea dream. I can find my way back to that part of myself when I'm awake, but it's tricky," he admitted. "That's why I want us to give your mystical edging another shot. It's like learning how to meditate. It's hard to focus and clear your mind in the beginning but with practice, your brain and your subconscious get used to tapping into those quiet parts and tuning out the rest."

Nelson squinted over Nox's shoulder, unsure if that was brilliant or if he was bullshitting. "If we learn *how* to trigger *Him*..."

"Then we can learn how to avoid *Him*," Nox replied and made a giddy sound as he threw his arms around Nelson's neck and jumped, sending the notepad flying. His legs wound around Nelson's waist and he was radiant as they kissed. "And we can choose when we're ready and face *Him* on our terms, not *His*."

"Okay..." Nelson smiled, happy to finally have a purpose and a course of action he understood. "*That* part I like and I think I'm getting the hang of the intimate parts," he added hesitantly but Nox shushed him.

"You've definitely gotten the hang of it, Nelson. The dick is literally out of this world and the rimming, god-tier."

"Thank you?"

"*Thank you.*" Nox swung his chin toward the bed. "We'd better get that first bullet out of the chamber because it's been *days*. I don't know how long I can keep *Him* at bay. I feel almost feral, I want you so badly, Nelson."

"I see." Nelson could feel it rising in Nox as well, the primal urge to be touched, licked, and filled until they were lost in the frenzy.

That enthralled and aroused Nelson, the untamed, burning need Nox held and defended only for them—for him.

"Let me take care of that."

Because that was his duty, and his alone. This was *his* Nox to cherish and protect and Merlin and Clancy—and even the Dagda —would never know the privilege of loving him the way Nelson did.

His heart sang and Nelson gave into the joy as he lowered Nox onto the bed and set about satisfying him. Nelson started with Nox's ears and neck, nibbling and sucking until there were goosebumps and shivers. He burrowed into Nox's armpit, seeking out the hints of natural musk and catching a whiff of sweat as their bodies grew warmer. Nelson licked lazily, enjoying Nox's keening whimper.

"Please!" Nox rolled over, arching his back and presenting his ass to Nelson.

"Come here," Nelson growled, pulling Nox's hips back and parting his cheeks with both hands. "This is mine." He dragged his tongue over Nox's hole, glorying in his delirious moan.

For this was Nelson's purview, his temple, and he didn't need a god to tell him how to serve Nox there. He sucked on the flinching, tender flesh and strummed the delicate wrinkles with the tip of his tongue, drilling when Nox's legs began to shake.

"Yes! Gods, that's so good, Nelson!"

Nelson rumbled in approval, pleased to hear *his* name on his lover's lips as he rolled Nox onto his back. He would have to push Nox to the edge, until he was truly delirious and confused, but for the moment Nelson treasured their bond and how pleased *his* Nox was with him. Soon, they would be caught up in the golden rapture and unbridled lust but it was the way Nox yearned for him that aroused Nelson when they had sex. And it was Nox's pleasure, not the inevitable orgasm, that brought Nelson the most satisfaction.

"Come for *me*, Nox," he begged before working a long string of spit from his lips and sliding two fingers into tight, gripping heat. He took his time, slowly winding Nox up and lapping at the pre-cum dripping from the end of his cock.

"Hah... Hah...." Nox's jaw stretched and his eyes rolled. "Bees, Nelson!"

"Alright." Nelson shushed and squeezed the base of Nox's shaft tight. "Breathe and keep *Him* out. Stay with me and let me have you first. Let me taste you before you go."

Nox nodded jerkily, panting as his fingers twisted in the duvet and Nelson's hair. "Fuck! This is so hot, though!"

"Mmmm..." Nelson wrapped his lips around Nox, sucking

hard as he reached deep with his fingers. They curled around Nox's prostate, stroking firmly in time with the rise and fall of his head.

"Nelson!" Nox screamed as his back came off the bed, a thick burst of cum flooding Nelson's mouth.

He took it, claiming every tart drop until Nox was spent and breathless. "Now, we work," Nelson told Nox, grinning ruthlessly as he snatched a wrist and yanked him upright. "You want to practice, let's practice." Nelson pulled Nox onto his knees, facing him, and cupped the back of his head. "Open for me," he commanded as he guided Nox's lips to his cock.

Nox's eyes glowed and he had taken on a golden haze. "I can get used to you like this. You're really hot when you're bossy." His tongue stretched and he hummed in delight as he covered Nelson's length in long, indulgent licks, making loud, greedy sounds as he sucked. "I've never been much of a sub, but I could pretend," he said before taking Nelson deep into his throat, swallowing the entire shaft, and gagging softly. There was a loud slurp as Nox raised his head. "I could submit and worship this." He panted the words against Nelson's throbbing flesh, his gaze burning with desire.

"I don't want you to submit to me," Nelson countered, taking Nox by the hair and pulling him up for a brutal kiss. "But I'll hang onto you and keep *Him* out any way I can." He turned Nox, locking him against Nelson's chest and holding him close. "I'll dangle you in front of *Him* and use you for bait if that's what it takes but I'd always rather see you wild and free," he breathed in Nox's ear, reaching for the lube. Nelson teased Nox's nipples, pinching and flicking and making him tremble and whimper. "Tell me what you see," he ordered as he gripped Nox's cock, his strokes firm but not fast enough to give him relief.

"Light!" Nox gasped, back bowing and bucking into Nelson's hand. "I can hear the bees and a harp."

"Slow down." Nelson whispered Nox's name and dotted his neck and shoulder with soothing kisses. He waited until Nox's breathing had settled to resume, taking him to the brink again and again. They were both slick and sweating when Nelson bent Nox over and mounted him, filling him with a smooth, driving thrust.

"Nope!" Nox shook his head, the glossy wet strands sticking to his forehead. "We've got bees. And gods, it's hot and bright."

A wry smile yanked at Nelson's lips as his pelvis slapped swift and hard against Nox's ass, the sound carrying through the room as they were bathed in warmth and soft, shimmering light. He could hear the tender strumming of a harp and buzzing as the urge to pin Nox down and breed him swelled. Nelson let the compulsion grow with the heavy pounding in his core, stopping at the first bright pulse and the first lifting of his control.

"No!" Nox's shocked cry shook the chandelier and the frames on the mantle.

Nelson fell forward, bracing a hand on the bed and nuzzling the back of Nox's neck. "Shhhhh!" He stayed with Nox, their bodies interlocked as their hearts thrashed, waiting for them to come down. "Don't go to *Him* yet. Stay with me and see what else you can learn."

"Okay. I'm good." Nox held onto Nelson's wrist and nodded. "I hear *Him* calling. It's not *His* time yet but *He* wants this."

"*He* wants this?" Nelson rolled his hips, grinding hard and forcing little squeaks from Nox.

"Yeah. *He* wants to watch us and *He* wants us to love *Him*," Nox explained in weak huffs, bringing Nelson's thrusts to a halt again.

"Like, love *Him*? Or, *love Him*?" He shook his head. "Don't answer that right now," he decided and continued pumping his hips. Nelson closed his eyes and sank into the slick bliss and the feel of Nox, wild and restless—alive—in his arms. He licked the sweat off of Nox's back, between his shoulder blades, then tucked his face in the corner of his neck and drove harder.

"There! Don't stop!" Nox cried desperately, his nails digging into Nelson's wrist. Nelson hurled him right up to the heavens, reaching around and gripping Nox's shaft. He stroked tight and fast, riding Nox's prostate with every merciless roll of his hips. Nox's cheek dragged on the mattress and his eyes were molten gold as they crossed "Oh, fuuu-! *No!*" Nox punched a pillow, swearing when Nelson pulled out. He used another pillow to muffle his screams.

"Sorry." Nelson rolled Nox onto his back and lowered, stretching his tongue and collecting the sweat from the hairs beneath Nox's navel and nuzzling the patch at the base of his cock.

"Yes!" Nox lolled, enraptured as he reached for Nelson. "Please! I need you!" His voice was hoarse with desire and his body luminous as he pouted and undulated beneath Nelson. "Take me now, Uaithne. Take me to *Him.*"

Nelson clicked his teeth, dragging his lips over the skull and horns tattooed on Nox's abdomen. "Not today." He traced the triskelion on the skull, taunting the god before sweeping lower. "You're still mine."

Nelson took him deep into his throat, sucking hard but fingering Nox slowly and firmly massaging his prostate. "Yes! Yours, Nelson!"

This time, Nelson couldn't swallow fast enough, cum spilled down his chin and Nox's twitching cock. He took his time, listening to Nox babble while licking him clean and giving him time to cool down.

Literally.

Nelson sang some bits of a song Nox liked, crooning and kissing his cheeks and nose and eyelashes until he was drowsy but still playful and turned on.

"May I...please?" Nelson hid his burning face, whispering his love and his undying loyalty to Nox's sternum and his collarbone.

"I need you to," Nox babbled dreamily. "I am utterly spent but I need you to destroy my body now, Nelson. And not for *Him* or any magickal strategic reasons. You slammed that gate closed and now I want you to ride me home."

"Yes." Nelson ached as he reached for the lube. He'd tortured

Nox with 'mystical edging' for a sunny afternoon, but the Dagda had kept them apart and tortured Nelson for weeks. "I want that," he said clumsily, coating his cock and falling into Nox's mouth and his body.

He still didn't crave sex unless he felt Nox craving him first. And Nelson could lose himself in a kiss and feel the same heady rush as an orgasm without Nox touching anything but his face. It was miraculous, though, when Nelson could let go and he yearned to feel his soul spilling into Nox's without the Dagda interfering.

Nelson tangled his fingers in Nox's hair pinning him for a savage kiss. He was rough, reclaiming everything the Dagda had seen and touched. And Nox reveled in it, setting Nelson loose and ordering him to be ruthless.

"Take me, Nelson. Claim me."

Nelson nodded, hooking Nox's leg around his waist. A different fire burned between them as Nelson put his head down, biting into Nox's shoulder and digging in with his knees. Nelson ran right into the inferno, filling Nox with relentless, pounding thrusts. Pleasure licked at his nerves, bright and brutal and cindering the last of Nelson's control. He leaped into the heart of the flames, smothering his howl as he came.

"My gods, Nelson. You truly are an animal." Nox's arms were limp as he cradled Nelson, their bodies slick and their legs tangled. He kissed a trail across Nelson's brow, whispering reverently in Gaelic.

"What did you say?" Nelson checked Nox's eyes but they were blue and he was clear and calm.

"I said I saw you, my fearless, fearsome wolf. My warrior priest."

Nelson snorted and flapped a hand, dismissing the idea that he could be competent at anything in that magickal realm.

"How does that make sense? I can kind of get being a harp now because what does a harp know? I'm hardly a warrior and I'll never know enough magick to be a druid priest."

"You're always selling yourself short," Nox said with a disappointed sigh. "And right after you rocked my world. Deities often took several different forms, remember, and wolves were as ubiquitous as crows."

"Was the Uaithne associated with a wolf?"

"No... Not traditionally. But the Morrígan was also said to take the form of a wolf and many of the Tuath Dé were said to keep a wolf at their side for protection." Nox held up a finger, making Nelson's heart skip a beat. "Again, if you bear in mind that many deities shifted forms, it is possible that those wolf protectors could have been warriors as well. The wolf represents *the moon*, transformation, intuition, and fierce loyalty."

"Huh."

"Not so silly anymore, is it?" Nox challenged. "There is another possibility that comes to mind," he said, growing more excited. "There are Roman accounts of a mysterious Celtic god named Cunomaglus[1] whose name translates to 'Wolf Lord.' He was said to be the guide of a specific god and his intermediary with the dead. They wrote of secret cults dedicated to Cunomaglus."

"Which god did he guide?" Nelson asked and was suddenly suspicious by the wild glimmer in Nox's eyes. They were still the good shade of blue and too focused but Nox often got that look when he was up to something or knew a secret.

"He was the familiar and guide of the horned god, Cernunnos, in some very obscure accounts."

"Cernunnos was the son of the Dagda," Nelson recalled.

"In some early texts," Nox cautioned, his finger rising again. "He's what is called a Proto-Celtic god, from the periods *before* the early Celtic period. Most of those gods we know very little about but we see variations of them or common themes with later gods throughout Celtic and Norse mythology."

"And he's the son of the Dagda?"

Nox smiled, his lips curling in. "That gets a little murky. Sometimes, he's the son. Sometimes, he *is* the Dagda. He's the

Lord of Wild Things. But he was almost always depicted with a wolf companion and serpents."

Nelson gave him a hard look. "No more serpents," he said and Nox hummed seriously.

"I'll let them know, no more serpents."

"Do that," Nelson said, nodding. "I'd be fine if I never laid eyes on another snake before I died."

"Don't talk like that." Nox covered Nelson's lips with a hand. "I won't let go if you don't let go. And we don't know if death will be the end, do we?"

"Can a god die?" Nelson could accept that his body and his consciousness could end but he could go easier knowing that some form of Nox would still exist.

"I don't know!" Nox said, laughing as he rose and straddled Nelson. "I barely know *what* a god is. I've always held that we have never gotten the gods right as academics by trying to describe them with our modern language and concepts. What if they are like everything else in nature and the heavens and are capable of metamorphosis as well? Why assume they hold to the same rules and limitations as humans? It makes perfect sense to me that an Uaithne would be a harp and a priest and a wolf because almost all deities were known by symbols before there were common tongues and alphabets and most of them took animal forms."

"True..." Nelson conceded, his mind spinning with the possibilities as Nox grew more excited and his eyes sparked again.

"What if the gods are like the elements and they have seasons and storms for feelings? What if their souls are like air and they can change like water?" He lowered and licked the sweat that had collected in the hairs between Nelson's pecs. "Water can change and be as light as steam or freeze until it's as hard as a rock. And you can drink water and turn it into blood and sweat and tears. It becomes life until it leaves us as water, a cycle as old as the gods and time. Why in the world would the gods be boring and basic like us when they could change shape and fly like a butterfly or be as infinite as the sea?" Nox opened his palm and tipped it sideways, spilling water onto Nelson's chest.

"How did you—?" Nelson snatched his wrist to get a look at Nox's hand but there was nothing up his sleeve because he was naked.

"I don't know, I had a thought the other day about metamorphosis and transfiguration and pulled some of the water from inside my hand. But I could feel a tide there, if I wanted it," Nox boasted in a whisper.

"Good." Nelson cupped Nox's cheek and drew him closer for a kiss. "I don't want to lose you like we lost the others. Be as infinite as the sea for me."

"Only if I get to keep you," Nox whispered shakily, his lips clinging to Nelson's. "I won't have any use for eternity if you're not by my side."

Nelson made a thoughtful sound, pretending to consider. "Can you promise I won't have to put up with bad breath and back pain?"

"Nope."

"Hmmm... Can I get back to you on eternity?" He sighed heavily, knocking his forehead against Nox's. "Enough practice. We still have a Badb to hunt. Where do *you* want to start?" he asked and watched as Nox's focus shifted and his eyes took on a different, more determined glow.

"Send for Tony. He thinks I'm still unwell after my visit to Julian's. I have to see what he knows and if I've been betrayed by my favorite assistant."

---

1. **Cunomaglus** (Koo-no Mag-lus) artifacts found in the Cotswolds, in southwest England, suggest the worship of an early Celtic deity whose name translates to "Hound Lord" and is identified with the god Apollo.

Four

Nox felt like a fraud and an old movie villain in his disguise. Or an elderly widow on her deathbed as he huddled under a quilt in his pajamas and a robe. "Is this necessary?" He wondered out loud and raised his sunglasses so he could see Nelson better.

"We want Walt to believe you're recovering from your visit to Julian's place and this is best until we know whose side Tony's on. And Walt will just get cockier if he hears and thinks he's responsible for all of this," Nelson said, checking his watch from his spot by the door. Tony was due at any moment and Merlin would show him up.

Nox had to know if he could still trust Tony, but he felt like the Big Bad Wolf waiting for Little Red Riding Hood. It was unbelievable to Nox that Anthony Costa could play the part of the loyal, laid-back, and clueless himbo assistant so well. And for so long. Nox saw Walt a handful of times a month and usually only in passing. But Tony was Nox's right hand and his gatekeeper. He would have had to have been a hell of an actor or an extremely powerful witch. Walt may have created a web of confusion around Nox, but he wasn't capable of enchanting or brainwashing Tony that deeply.

"Not in Walt's wildest dreams could he do this much damage," Nox said to himself and sighed at his feet under the quilt. Nox had never felt more isolated and wounded, but having another lesser monster to chase was a welcome distraction from the fate of all mankind potentially resting on his shoulders. "I'd appreciate the challenge if he hadn't brought those poor girls into it. The rest of it was rather remarkable. Breathtaking, at times," he conceded as he pictured the altar in New Castle. It would have been art and the moment transcendent for Nox if it hadn't been desecrated by death and violence. "Even the puzzle with the MacCrorys and the yew... I'm fascinated by how well Walt played me and I'm keen to settle the score," he admitted, earning a humph from Nelson.

"Keen is fine but be *careful*," he stated, his eyes pinning Nox to the pillows. "We knew *He* was playing games with your memories and now you tell me Walt was using dark magick to tamper with them too."

"I'm learning a lot from the way they hide from me, though," Nox said.

They both dropped the subject and turned towards the doorway when they heard the doorbell ring, followed by Merlin greeting Tony as they came up the stairs.

"Be careful," Nelson rumbled softly, then stepped into the hall and waved. "He's awake and he's glad you could stop by."

"Of course!" Tony said as he leaned around the door and looked for Nox. "Hey, professor." He brightened when he spotted Nox on the bed and hurried in. "I came over as soon as I heard you were hurt. What happened?"

"I'm fine!" Nox insisted and pushed himself up a little straighter. "A little under the weather, maybe," he added when Nelson and Merlin gave him threatening looks.

"The professor doesn't want to worry you," Nelson said as he drifted around the bed for a better view. "But he was attacked a few days ago so we've been keeping a close eye on him."

"Attacked? How?" Tony came around and lowered onto the

foot of the bed, his eyes wide and seeking. The strongest emotions Nox sensed were concern and shock.

"That's...hard to explain," Nox began, wishing he could take off the glasses but his eyes were bloodshot and had a tendency to glow more when he was upset. He gestured for Tony to come closer and take his hands.

"You don't have to explain anything to me, but I'd be the last one to judge you. And you were pretty understanding about my accidental acid trip last week," Tony said as he scooted forward and put his hands in Nox's.

"I know." Nox's smile faded and he was sad as he cradled Tony's hands. "But there's no doubt that your acid trip wasn't an accident, T."

"It was connected to your nemesis and the investigation?" Tony asked, earning a nod from Nox.

"It is and we're afraid that the person who poisoned you also murdered our witnesses and was behind the abductions and the murder we've been investigating."

"God... That's... Oh, God." Tony grew steadily paler until he was as white as the duvet under the quilt. "Wait. I was the target? I thought someone was trying to stop you and I was...collateral damage or something."

"I'm certain he meant to poison you so he could get closer to the professor," Nelson said slowly, his eyes narrowing as he gauged Tony's reaction. "Someone...broke in here last Monday and stole something that had very little monetary value but was priceless to him."

"That doesn't make any sense." Tony swept a hand through his thick black waves and frowned at Nox. "How does getting rid of me get someone closer to y—" His eyes widened until they were like saucers. "You said someone broke in here on Monday and took something?"

"Yes," Nelson confirmed and Tony's lip trembled as his eyes swung to Nox's and they were filled with tears.

"The thing that was stolen, was it a necklace? With a locket?" he asked shakily and Nox nodded.

"It was my mother's locket."

"Oh, shit!" Tony's hand clapped over his mouth and he was visibly shaking as he jumped to his feet. "I think it was Walt!"

"Do you?" Nelson asked, watching Tony closely. "Why?"

"I was going to duck out of school before lunch to drop off the professor's mail last Monday, but Walt said he could do it. We usually go to lunch together. But he was going home early because he—"

"He had a migraine," Nox said and Tony nodded quickly.

"That's right! I stopped by his and Aubrey's place to check on him after work because she was out of town and Walt was *so weird*."

"Weird?" Nelson prodded and had his notepad and pencil ready when Tony nodded, swallowing hard.

"I let myself in because they gave me a key and I usually do," he started, pausing as he revisited the moment.

"He didn't like that?" Nox asked gently and softened the lights and made the room warmer, lulling Tony's nerves.

"No." Tony frowned and shook his head, staring past Nox. "He was in the kitchen and said he was headed out soon. Which was strange because where would he go that late on a Monday evening? And he didn't want me to see whatever he was working on. There was a pile of dirt and odds and ends and I mentioned that the locket looked like the one Professor Mac wears sometimes. But Walt said he found it on one of his walks and was cleaning it up for Aubrey as a surprise. I thought that made sense so I let it go and I told myself he was being weird because he wasn't feeling well. I thought it was the migraine making him extra cranky."

"Do you have any idea why he'd do it? Why he'd have this deep of a grudge against the professor," Nelson asked.

"No." Tony shook his head but looked uncertain. "Actually..." His nose wrinkled and he mouthed an apology at Nox. "It never seemed that serious, but I could tell that Walt was a little jealous of you. A few times, he said that you were kind of...overrated. Or that you weren't as smart as everyone thought you were."

"I'm definitely overrated," Nox replied with a shrug. "But I am incredibly smart. That's not worth as much as Walt thinks it is, fortunately."

"Fortunately?" Tony countered and Nox smiled.

"*Intention.* That's what matters most, most of the time," he said, his heart aching as he thought about Merlin and Clancy and their misguided intentions. "Spite has its own power and it can be a wonderful motivator when we're proving naysayers wrong. But spite can also be incredibly corrosive and it can weigh you down and trip you up. Spite, hate, jealousy, fear... They create monsters in men that devour their hearts and minds and can taint everything they touch. Whatever Walt has planned will fail because of his flawed intentions. His intention will be his downfall," he predicted.

Nelson coughed discreetly. "He has had some success," he said with a loaded look at Nox.

"Right," he said and winced at Tony. "I don't want to put you in any more danger so I asked Clancy about finding something for Walt to do. I want to keep him busy so you don't have to worry about covering for us," he added, glancing at Nelson. He was feeling more reassured but keeping them separated so Tony couldn't give them away—intentionally or accidentally—seemed like a good idea. "Can you pretend to be super busy covering for me while I recover and we 'muddle' our way through this investigation?"

His brow furrowed and Tony looked stricken as he nodded. "Whatever you think is best," he insisted. "I don't want to mess up anything more than I already have."

"What do you mean? You didn't mess anything up," Nox replied, but Tony shook his head.

"I don't know why Walt stole that locket. But I get the feeling he did something really bad with it and that I could have prevented a lot of bad things from happening if I had stopped by with your mail like I had planned."

"I think..." Nox said with a weary, sympathetic sigh. "Walt's been playing the both of us for a very long time and I'm really sorry he used you, T. I know you were a good friend to Walt and you trusted him."

"I did and I..." His hand clapped over his mouth. "I told him so much about you! I didn't think anything of it, but I talk about you all the time!"

There was a soft snort from Nelson. "That's probably why he befriended you. You're an open book and you clearly idolize the professor," he said, causing Tony to blush.

"Well... Professor Mac's the coolest and it's always been an honor," he mumbled at the quilt.

"You're the coolest," Nox said, giving his shoulder a playful punch.

Tony's lips pulled into a hard line as he shook his head. "I missed that my best friend was a psychopath and..." His voice cracked and he gulped loudly. "Those girls you rescued!" Tears puddled in his eyes as they swung between Nox and Nelson as Tony finally grasped the magnitude of Walt's crimes, that the consequences extended so much further than him and Nox and even the university. "You really think he murdered those people and took those girls?"

"He's used a lot of people," Nox said soothingly, absorbing as much of Tony's horror and shame as he could.

"Oh, God. I've helped him, haven't I?" He looked at Nelson, panicked and flushed. "I'm gonna be sick."

"What did I say about intent?" Nox asked, his voice rising as he caught Tony's cheek and gave it a gentle pat. "*I* helped him, Nelson helped him, Clancy helped him, the FBI helped him..."

"Aubrey," Tony groaned, sniffing hard and shaking his head in dismay. "She's going to be devastated. And if Walt used her to poison people—!" He choked back a cry, earning a grimace from Nelson.

"It's probably a good idea if you avoid talking to Walt for a few days."

"I can get it together," Tony said as he mopped at his face with his sleeve. "I have to if he used me to hurt the professor and all those other people. I have to help."

"Then, forgive yourself and be the exact same Tony he's counting on," Nox suggested tenderly. "Have my back while I recuperate and we investigate so he thinks it's business as usual."

"Okay. I can do that." Tony nodded and straightened. "What else?" he asked bravely.

"Spend a few hours with Merlin," Nelson suggested. "Tell him anything and everything you can think of about Walt and his past and tell him *everything* you've told Walt about Nox that could be relevant."

"Brilliant idea!" Nox said and beamed at Nelson. "We're gathering intelligence because he has the advantage at the moment. Help us catch up."

"Alright." Tony had his phone out and was tapping. "We usually have lunch on Mondays because you don't have any classes, but I'll tell him I'm going to hang out here and help with the week's lesson plans."

"That's good," Nox said. "Hint that I'm in bed and have been out of commission all weekend."

"On it," Tony said as he typed, earning a humph of approval from Nelson.

"That's exactly what we need," he told Tony as he helped him up and guided him to the door. "Walt wants the professor to be in disarray and is counting on you to be his source on the inside so keep feeding him disinformation for us. Report to Merlin in the study and tell him everything you can about Walt and his past."

"Okay," Tony said, grimacing at Nox over his shoulder. "I swear, I had no idea, professor."

"It's alright, T. I know," Nox said sincerely as he waved him off, trading a bemused grin with Nelson as they waited for him to leave.

"We'll need to be careful about what we say around Tony, but I believe him," Nelson said quietly, closing the door.

"So do I and I can't tell you how relieved I am," Nox said as he threw back the covers and got up. "I can accept that I was wrong about Walt because I barely know him, but I've known Tony since he was a freshman. I feel like I helped raise him, in a way..."

"He's two years older than you."

"I said 'in a way,'" Nox replied with a dismissive wave of the sunglasses. "Most people are older than me in academia, but Tony isn't stuffy and he doesn't take himself too seriously. He has the potential to be a brilliant lecturer because he loves learning as much as he loves teaching. Students admire *that*, not erudite, elitist professors who are more enamored with the sounds of their own voices."

"I guess Walt would fall with the latter," Nelson mused as he followed Nox into the closet so he could change. "He favors Clancy," he added, making Nox flinch at the stab of disappointment.

"They were both using teaching as a cover it seems," he said sadly. "I knew that Clancy was...like me and Dad. That he was from an ancient Celtic line and was keeping the vow. Merlin, too. I didn't begin to suspect that they were part of the three from the prophecy until you—the Uaithne—appeared. I thought they were..." He frowned at the shelves of shirts and jeans at the back of the closet, feebly attempting to make sense of a lifetime of secrets and self-gaslighting. "Merlin called Clancy an old monk once and I thought they were descended from the families that came from the Old World with my parents' ancestors," he explained. "For a long time, I thought they were there to make sure we *kept* the vow."

"Merlin said Clancy was like a monk but your father changed him." Nelson's hands closed around Nox's shoulders and kneaded tenderly. "His love for you and your father opened his heart."

Nox nodded, unable to speak.

Chapter Four

Nothing mattered more to Lucas MacIlwraith than love and he loved his family and his friends ardently and unabashedly.

"Love as much as you can, Nox. Time will take us, but the love you leave can last for generations and change the world."

"He had that effect on a lot of people and I try my best to make him proud."

"I know he is," Nelson said, kissing Nox's hair.

"He is," Nox replied with a watery laugh, turning in Nelson's arms. "I don't know if I actually saw my dad or if Merlin's tea helped me tap into my subconscious and find some things I'd lost in there, but I know he's proud of me and that he's proud of us."

A soft smile tugged at Nelson's lips. "Good. I'm taking that as a sign that we're on the right track."

"Me too," Nox said, craning his neck and stealing a quick kiss for strength. "He also told me that I'd need Merlin and Clancy and I'm doing my best to remember that when I feel like I don't know them anymore."

Nelson rumbled in agreement as his arms tightened around Nox, comforting him and giving him a moment of shelter. "I don't care if that was your dad or your subconscious, I'm glad you're listening because we do need them."

"They did come through with the Badb," Nox said, sighing as he swiped any shirt off the shelf behind him. "And I have a feeling he's going to regret underestimating Tony and that we've just found a valuable trove of information."

"You might be right," Nelson said and squinted in the direction of the study. "Walt was probably counting on Tony's blind loyalty and for him to be too oblivious to put the pieces together."

"That just shows you how little Walt really gets or cares about Tony. It only took Tony a moment to see it and he didn't hesitate when he had to pick a side. He took responsibility and won't rest until he's made up for his mistakes because that's *my Tony*. That's why he's my assistant."

"I'm glad he's on our side," Nelson said as he reached around

Nox for a pair of jeans. "Let's see what Merlin can get out of him."

Nox laughed, a lewd joke about Merlin's talents forming on his lips, then stopped. "Uh oh..." Nox widened his eyes at Nelson. "We probably shouldn't leave Tony alone with Merlin."

Nelson let out a hard groan and headed for the door. "I'd better go."

"Hurry!"

Five

In the study, Tony was shaken and blaming himself, but he had hit the ground running with Merlin.

"Walt doesn't have any other family. Only his mother, Sheila, but she has dementia," he told Merlin as he chewed on his nails and paced. "His father is a really sore subject so Walt *never* talks about him," he added and Nox hummed thoughtfully as he strolled in a few minutes after Nelson.

He wasn't wearing his sunglasses and waved Nelson off when he raised a brow in concern. "I'm feeling much better now that Tony's here to help," he explained, then pointed at the board and the question mark where Walt's father belonged. "He's sore about his father," he continued. "Is it because he doesn't know and never will, or because Walt *does* know who his father is and is disappointed, or was he rejected by him as well?" he wondered out loud, glancing at Tony in case he had any ideas.

There was a hesitant hiss as he shook his head. "Would it make sense if I said it might be all of the above?"

"Yes," Nox, Nelson, and Merlin stated in unison, surprising Tony.

"Well..." He chuckled and swept a hand through his dark waves. "He used to say that I was so happy and easy-going all the time because I had a dad when I was a kid. He said he never had the luxury of being innocent and irresponsible because he and his mother were on their own, he didn't have a dad to protect and provide for them. But then, he'd hint that he could have had more and been more if their family hadn't been cheated."

"That's interesting!" Merlin said as he wrote the word "family" on the board and circled it. "That would imply that Walt knows something about the rest of his family," he mused, but Tony shook his head.

"That's why I got the feeling he was disappointed or ashamed. He *never* liked talking about anyone but his mom and even then, all he'd say was that she was all he had. She's in a facility somewhere now. He visits her almost every weekend. I can't remember the name, though."

Nelson hummed thoughtfully as he wrote in his notepad. "I'll see if I can track that down."

"Good," Nox said, nodding at them. "Let's find out all we can about Sheila, too. If she was all Walt had, she's either his confidant or she's another thing he's ashamed of."

Tony chuckled again. "That might be another situation where it's a little bit of both. I've offered to go with Walt for emotional support and to help him take care of the house, but he always shot me down. He said it would be too hard and make him uncomfortable."

"The house?" Nelson asked and Tony winced.

"It's in Pennsville, I think. Walt usually visits his mom on the weekends and then stops by her place to keep things from falling apart."

Nox cringed at Sheila's name. "I almost feel bad for him. No father and caring for his sick mother..."

"Unless he's lying," Nelson countered. "What if he is using his mom as an excuse so he can disappear whenever he wants?" he said, making Nox gasp.

"He could be Bunburying!" he said excitedly, earning confused looks from Nelson, Tony, and Merlin. Nox rolled his eyes at them. "Try reading about something other than witchcraft, anthropology, and forensics, please! In *The Importance of Being Earnest*, Algernon makes up a sick friend, Bunbury, so that he can escape the city. Walt could be leading a little double life right under everyone's noses. He might be Bunburying!" he explained and Nelson frowned and nodded slowly.

"I have read that," he replied hesitantly. "And I would say that Walt would have to be...Bunburying to get away with this for as long as he has. I'll track down the house and the mom and see what state both of them are in. Let's find out if he's as attentive as he's let on."

There was a soft *ping!* from Tony's phone. He pulled it from his jeans pocket and smirked at the screen as he read. "It's from Walt. He hopes you're feeling better soon and apologizes for not being able to help more. Clancy's asked him to take over the research on a new project so Walt has to run up to Boston."

"Did he?" Nox asked, pretending to be surprised. "Is the FBI taking another run at the Irish mob?" he mused and winked at Nelson.

He snorted at his notes. "They'll always be a thorn in the bureau's side so it's a safe play. It wouldn't be hard for Walt to find an active investigation into some facet of the Irish mob if he checks."

"Perfect," Nox said, smiling at Tony. "That should give you a few days to come to terms with this before you have to face him and it'll give us some time to catch up."

"I'll be fine," Tony insisted but there was a catch in his voice and he swiped a tear from his cheek.

"No, you won't be," Nox said sadly and offered him a sympathetic smile. "You're a kind and caring person and you've been betrayed by someone you love and trust. You were used by a monster but you have to pretend he's still your friend. It'll be like your best friend died and you have to face the man who killed him. *That* hurts, T."

Tony scrubbed his face with his hands, nodding. "I know. But

I can feel sorry for myself later. I don't know exactly what Walt's been doing or how much I helped. I just know that I have to help you stop him."

Nelson huffed dismissively and shook his head. "We have a source on the inside now and Walt doesn't know that we're on to him yet. Keep working with Merlin so he can build us a good profile and keep feeding Walt disinformation so he doesn't see us coming," he said, giving Tony's arm an encouraging swat with the notepad.

"I can do that," Tony said and sounded relieved as he regarded the board and Merlin's many question marks. "Oh!" He pointed at the one under prior address. "He used to live over in Jersey by the bridge before he moved in with Aubrey."

That earned a curious look from Nox. "Did you ever visit Walt's bachelor's pad?"

"No." Tony shook his head firmly. "He said his roommates were pigs and he was glad to get out of there. Which wouldn't surprise me. Walt's super fastidious. Aubrey's always teasing Walt about how picky he is about his clothes and his half of the closet and the way he can't handle clutter. He's the neatest witch she's ever met and the best roommate she's ever had," he recalled with a chuckle, then it morphed into a hard grimace. "Fuck, what are we going to do about Aubrey?" he worried again and Nox slid Nelson a loaded look.

"How sure are we that she didn't know?" Nelson replied, causing Tony to rear back.

"No way!" He shook his head firmly. "There's *no way* Aubrey would be involved in anything dark like that. She's Wiccan and practices witchcraft, but she's all about healing with plants and crystals, not this evil shit with the kidnapping and sacrifices."

Nox made a soft, thoughtful sound. "That tracks with what I've always sensed from her. She is rather...pure," he explained with a pained look at Nelson. "We'll go with Clancy and pay her a visit. She's about to be another one of Walt's victims. I want to get a sense of how much damage he's already done there and how we can help her recover when the time comes," he said, then turned when Nelson cleared his throat.

"Once we're sure he hasn't brainwashed her like Julian. Has she ever mentioned the Badb?" he asked Tony.

He laughed and pointed at the board again. "No, but Walt got drunk once and rambled about how he could trace his family back to the Badb. I asked him about it the next day and he told me I must have misunderstood because I was drunk too. He doesn't like to drink. Says it makes him ramble and tell tall tales," he added, making Nox jump.

"He told me he doesn't drink very often. That must be why! He can't trust himself when he's tipsy," he said and Tony frowned.

"When did he tell you that?" he asked but Nox waved it off.

"Not important," he replied with a hard look at Nelson. The faint golden glow in his eyes told Nelson that Nox had recalled something else from Walt's shadowy visit to the townhouse. Nelson rubbed the corner of his eye until Nox noticed and nodded. "I'm fine," he said with a wink and his eyes were soft blue again.

Nelson snorted dubiously at his notes and flipped back to their last visit to Julian's. "Did he ever mention the Dagda, the heir, or the three?" He kept his expression neutral.

"Not really..." Tony's brow furrowed and he shook his head at Nelson. "He might have mentioned the Dagda when we were talking about a paper or a lecture, but nothing stands out. He wrote his thesis on the Morrígan and their sister deities so it was probably something to do with that," he mused with a shrug.

"Probably," Nox agreed and smiled airily at Tony. "Did he ever mention meeting any followers of the Dagda or members of a cult? Maybe as part of his research?" he offered, but Tony shook his head.

"No. And that would stand out, considering how many people we know with Irish ancestry," he said with a suggestive glance at Nox.

He chuckled and winked at Tony. "That would be noteworthy," he said and Nelson cleared his throat loudly, shutting the conversation down before Tony had a chance to connect the dots again.

"Back to the topic at hand," he scolded them with a hard look at Nox. "What about after we found those girls?" he asked Tony. "Did Walt mention that cult we uncovered or what happened down in New Castle?"

"Of course! We all talked about it!" Tony said and shuddered. "He seemed just as upset as we were and I think he said something about being glad they sent the professor to help or else those girls wouldn't have been found." He paused, suddenly catching the irony. "That fucking bastard!" he spat as he looked around the room. "He really played us and was lying in our faces the whole time!"

"It does seem that way," Nox agreed with a heavy sigh. "It's going to be important for all of us to remember that in the coming weeks. We need to look out for each other—especially you and Aubrey. The two of you were closest to Walt and you're both going to feel the most betrayed," he predicted.

A faint blush tinted Tony's cheeks as he nodded. "I'll look out for her," he vowed and Nox smiled as he gave Tony's arm a reassuring punch.

"I knew I could count on you. How do you feel about occult shops? I have a friend who owns a really cool one and he could use a hand if you need a distraction. Or if you want to talk to someone who understands exactly what you're about to go through," Nox added gently.

"Yeah..." Tony pushed out a hard breath. "That sounds like it might be a godsend."

Nelson smiled as he made a note to kiss Nox later. "It might be."

There was a loud buzz from Tony's phone and he groaned. "That's my mom. Can I take this out there?" He pointed at the terrace and Nox shooed him off.

Chapter Five

"Give Celia my love," he said sincerely. "Speaking of godsends..." Nox said, wincing hard at Merlin. "You wouldn't happen to remember an old stone circle that my dad would have taken me to for one of our birthday camping trips. It was my eighth birthday," he said hesitantly but Merlin spun, his eyes sparkling.

"Of course, I remember, lad! I took you back every year after we lost your poor mother. Unless you were in the mood for something more rustic and then I'd leave Lucas and Clancy to it," he said with a wrinkle of his nose. "You know how upset I get if my hands are soiled." He held them up and shuddered. "That cabin up in Coudersport is as close as I'm willing to get to roughing it. Unless we're talking about sex. In that case, I like it very ro—"

"No!" everyone but Merlin shouted.

Nox's brow furrowed as his head cocked. "The cabin at Coudersport?" he asked, then gasped as he clutched his forehead, finally recalling where he'd seen the tree in his tea dream. "I think I know where we were!"

"Where? Who?" Nelson asked but Nox smacked his forehead hard.

"I knew it looked familiar because I've been there a dozen times!" He made an incredulous sound. "We were camping in the woods on the opposite side of the meadow. I remember sleeping next to a great, ancient stone and I think I know where it is. Merlin had a cabin built after we lost Mom. I never realized it was the same place," he admitted and Merlin nodded quickly.

"Lucas took you there a few times because we had taken him there as a child. But I abhor discomfort and bugs so I bought that bit of land in nowhere Pennsylvania and built a cabin for us when we realized you'd need to go on yearly retreats."

"We were at Coudersport," Nox murmured to himself in disbelief, then shook his head. "Dad and I camped all over the Appalachians. He always set up camp close to an old altar, stone circle, or a bullán[1] if there was one nearby. But I wonder if that was on purpose, if he was taking me to old druid sites to see what would happen," he mused out loud.

"Are there that many?" Nelson asked, earning a knowing hum from Merlin.

"More than you'd imagine," he replied in a hushed whisper, his eyes taking on a familiar, mischievous shimmer as he prepared to deliver another one of his little lessons. "The first Irishmen to step foot in the New World arrived with the Spanish in 1560 and there are accounts of Irish and Scottish settlers in Virginia as far back as the early 1600's. They used to say that Boston was the next parish to Galway because of the bond New Englanders shared with Ireland. And it wasn't just the Ulster Presbyterians and the Catholics who came over from the old country," he said, his voice trembling with awe. "There were druids and Tuath Dé among them."

Nox nodded jerkily, his gaze glassy and distant. "They must have thought they were home when they found the Appalachians, those intrepid Irish and Scottish druids."

"Yes!" Merlin replied. "They went deep into the woods, away from the bustling ports and growing cities on the eastern coast. There, they could erect stone circles like the ones they had at home and were safe to carry on their practice, away from watchful Puritan eyes."

"Why build the cabin by the circle at Coudersport, though?" Nox asked Merlin. "What's so special about that one?"

A wicked smile curled Merlin's lips and his eyes glittered. "Because it's *ours*."

"It's ours?" Nox parroted. "Why didn't I know about it, then?" he asked and Merlin let out the loudest, bitterest cackle.

"Do you think I didn't want to tell him?" He looked at Nelson, appalled. "I would have loved nothing more than to tell him about how our predecessors—past Coire Ansics[2] and Log Mór[3]—had taken heirs to Coudersport to partake of various rituals through the ages. But how could I when Nox would stick his fingers in his ears and shout me down?"

"You were right," Nox conceded with a bow of his head at Merlin. "I was being stubborn before."

"You're still being stubborn," Nelson observed and Nox held up his hands.

"Probably always will be, but I recognize the pattern and see that there have been consequences," he said, his shoulder bouncing dismissively.

Nelson turned to Merlin, rubbing his brow in frustrated disbelief. "I've been meaning to ask, were all the demigods horny idiots or is this one broken?" he said, waving at Nox.

"Yes," Merlin and Nox replied, nodding in unison.

But Merlin wagged a finger at Nox, sighing heavily. "Across all of mythology it is always a hero's fatal, tragic flaw—be it stubbornness, hubris, curiosity, misplaced trust—that is his undoing. Your stubborn refusal to accept your destiny and embrace the past may be your downfall."

Nox's face fell, his lips tightening into a telling scowl. "You weren't exactly transparent about your actions and your motives. And I made a vow. We all made a vow," he said and raised his brows, daring Merlin to deny it.

"I don't deny that I did dark, terrible things to protect you, lad. There are things I pray you'll never discover," he whispered, large tears forming on his lashes. One dropped, the soft splat carrying through the silent study like a thunderclap. "But I'd do it all again and much worse if I could see you spared. What are you willing to risk, Nox?" he challenged hoarsely, stepping up to him.

"Me?" He shook his head. "I don't want to risk anything but I don't have a choice now, do I?"

"Yes, you do!" Merlin gave him a hard jab in the chest, making Nox flinch. "You know the answer to defeating the lying Badb is to learn all there is to know about Walt and his origin story. But how long will you ignore yours? The answers are there, but you are too stubborn to look and to learn."

"I'm learning now, aren't I?" Nox said loudly, flailing around him, then promptly stormed out of the study.

1. **Bullán** (Bul-AWN) A stone with a natural or manmade depression found at many pagan sites. They hold water and occasionally pebbles and other offerings and were believed to have been used by the druids for rituals and divination.
2. **Coire Ansic** (Kwee-ra On-sik): The Dagda's magick cauldron of plenty, said to never run empty and please all who sat with the Dagda.
3. **Log Mór** (Lo-rich Moor): The Dagda's magick club or staff, said to have the power to kill with one end or restore life with the other.

Six

What was Nox willing to risk?

The question plagued him as they drove to the school to meet Clancy on Wednesday. He was taking them to see Aubrey under the guise of planning Walt's bachelor party.

"This feels a little...like we're the bad guys," Nox complained as they walked across campus. "She's planning the happiest day of her life and we're using it as a cover to bust her fiancé."

Clancy stopped him, looking around before his face twisted into a hard sneer. "Do you think he cares about her? If he's even planning to go through with this wedding," he added and swore under his breath. "I thought Walt had landed himself a dream girl because Aubrey is a lovely, brilliant young woman with a pure, gentle heart. But he never loved her. He used her and lied to her while he kidnapped those girls."

"You're assuming she didn't know," Nelson argued carefully.

"No." Nox shook his head. "I know her a touch better than I knew Walt and there's no way she's involved. Clancy's right. Walt couldn't love someone good like her and do the things he's done. But we're about to use her and lie to her too. It feels gross," he said and Clancy shrugged.

"It seemed like the easiest way to question Aubrey without upsetting her or showing our hand. She isn't a very good liar and we're already pushing our luck with Tony."

"She's going to find out," Nelson interrupted with a grimace. "But we can't risk upsetting her now or she might give us away, so using the bachelor party as an excuse is smart. Her guard will be down and we'll have a reason to ask questions about Walt and his past without raising her suspicions. And she'll keep it a secret from Walt without feeling conflicted because she thinks we're working on a fun surprise," he explained but Nox grumbled about how uncool it was as they continued their journey to the botany department.

Once again, Clancy was being pragmatic—the general. He'd accepted that lying to Aubrey and playing with her emotions was an acceptable risk because Walt had already made her a casualty. It was too late to stop the deep and crushing injury she was about to sustain, but Nox didn't feel right exploiting her. Even if she was another good window into who Walt was and what he had been up to.

Would Nox ever be able to accept the risks that Clancy had taken?

Had Clancy, being old and wise like the trees, lost sight of how fragile humans could be and how easy it was to fall in love with them? For that would be Clancy's fatal flaw. He'd allowed himself to love Lucas, thus opening his heart to real, pure mortal love for his wife, daughters, and Nox.

That, Nox could forgive. For Clancy to selfishly put his own loved ones—including Nox—above the lives of all others was unforgivable. But Nox's certainty wavered when he glanced at Nelson.

There had been many men before Nelson but Nox couldn't remember a single face or any of their names. He'd been too busy, or perhaps, he'd kept too busy to date anyone he could fall in love with, because Nox had feared that aspect of his destiny the most.

How could he give someone a heart that was meant for

another? Not to love another, but to beat with the soul of another with different ideals and an entirely different destiny. How could he promise forever when Nox didn't know if *he'd* see another birthday?

His heart raced and Nox felt frantic when Nelson glanced up from his notepad. His brow hitched in concern but Nox smiled and waved it off, ignoring the itch of desperation. He couldn't think about his upcoming birthday without wanting to scream and beg for a way out, a way to ditch the awful, impossible thing Nox was supposed to prevent.

It was times like these when Nox could fathom doing terrible, unspeakable things to avoid it and stay with Nelson. The ease with which he could do them was terrifying and put Clancy's decisions and actions into a different and haunting perspective for Nox.

"We will help her too," Nox stated when Clancy got the door for him. "We have to be better than the monster we're hunting."

"You're right, of course," Clancy replied, ducking his head. "I had planned to look after her if I was still here and in a position to," he said under his breath, then pointed at the proper hallway. "She's supposed to be in her office."

They found her at her desk, squinting at what looked like GC-MS results. "Come on in!" She hopped to her feet, a petite ginger-haired firecracker and one of Nox's favorites from both his and Clancy's former assistants. "It's so good to see you!" she said, opening her arms to Nox as she hurried to greet them.

"How can we work on the same campus and never see each other?" he asked as he pulled her into a tight hug, using the moment to stifle the rush of guilt and search her aura. She was tickled and buzzed with delight, her spirit as warm and welcoming as it always was.

"I've been spending more time over in the anthropology department lately, but I keep missing you," she said as he released her. "And shame on you, sir!" she said as she went to hug Clancy. "Sending Walt all the way to Boston to search those archives. You know the wedding's in a month." She gave his chest a playful smack. "At least, you better. You're giving him away," she teased and Nox noticed the shimmer in Clancy's eyes and heard a pained grunt.

"I haven't forgotten," he said as he set her away from him. He pretended to give the younger woman a once over and nodded. "You're looking a lot less stressed now that you're no longer working for me."

"Stop! You were strict but kind and always treated us with respect." She winked at Nox and Nelson. "Which is a damn sight better than some of the other professors I TAed for and work with, let me tell you."

"Have you two met?" Nox asked and she shook her head, eyeing Nelson with open curiosity.

"I've heard lots of gossip and I am not disappointed!" she whispered out of the side of her mouth at Nox and held up her hand for him to slap it. "Way to go, professor!"

"Thanks!" He slapped her hand and they bumped fists. "No way I was letting *that* get away from me," he said, wiggling his brows and making her giggle.

"I do not blame you."

Nelson coughed and cleared his throat at them impatiently as he offered his hand to Aubrey, glaring at Nox. "Agent Grady Nelson, but just call me Nelson. It's nice to meet you," he said with a curt nod.

"Aubrey Bright, botany babe extraordinaire at your service," she told him, making Nox chuckle.

"Not a single lie detected," Nox said with a sheepish, apologetic smile. "But I'm afraid it's my fault Clancy had to send Walt away. I've been under the weather lately and I'm in way over my head with this investigation. I'm not as experienced as Clancy when it comes to working with the FBI," he explained, earning a sympathetic groan from Aubrey.

"Of course! And Walt is all too happy to help. He knows how

Chapter Six

important this is. Me too!" she said, nodding emphatically. "If there's anything I can do, please ask!"

Clancy shook his head and waved dismissively. "We're not here for the investigation. This is a secret mission," he said, causing her brows to jump.

"Oh?"

He went to the door and made a show of checking the hall before he closed it. "Bachelor party business," he whispered.

"Oh!" She clapped and pretended to zip her lips. "Your secret is safe with me!"

"Perfect," Clancy said as he fell back against the door and crossed his ankles. "You can tell him we stopped by to ask about Pacific yew if he finds out we were here," he suggested, which was absolutely brilliant in Nox's opinion. She'd either say they were asking perfectly reasonable questions about the case or she'd hint that they were there to discuss the bachelor party.

"Did you have more questions about it?" she asked as she went to her desk. "Were those samples what you were looking for?"

"The samples?" Clancy asked and she stopped, frowning over her shoulder.

"The ones I sent over with Walt. He said you needed some Pacific yew to compare against some samples from one of your crime scenes."

"Right!" Clancy said quickly, nodding and pointing. "I've had Walt running all over lately. When was that?"

"Um..." She stepped around her desk and her finger twirled in a circle as she searched the calendar. "It was right before I left for New York so it was two Fridays ago, on the 26th."

"That's right! You were a lifesaver," Clancy said, making her blush and stammer.

"Stop! It was just a few samples from the freezer. I'm glad they helped."

Clancy's smile tightened as he blinked at her. "You have no

idea how helpful they were," he said and Nelson coughed at his notepad.

"You didn't happen to see or hear about anyone else who's doing research with yew?" he asked quickly, distracting her.

"No..." She shook her head and he smiled reassuringly.

"What about opium? How easy is it for someone to grow poppy flowers in a backyard nursery and make opium in a kitchen?"

Nox wanted to clap as her eyes grew huge and she forgot all about the yew and Walt. "It would take a lot of skill and a very decent backyard nursery to grow and harvest the pods for the latex. And then you have to cure it and that takes time and there's some technique involved," she explained. Then, she slid Nox a suspicious look. "I hope you're not planning *that* kind of bachelor party."

"Gods, I wish I were. You are too good for Walt, you know," he said, letting her see that he meant it. "We're planning something safe and quiet," he promised with a completely clear conscience. "I bet his family is over the moon about this."

Her nose wrinkled as she cringed. "I'm afraid that Tony is all the family he really has left. Walt's mom is in a home but we haven't met yet. We're still working up to it. She doesn't know what's going on anymore and gets upset if he mentions me. She thinks Walt is his father whenever he visits her and she's always afraid he's going to leave her again, the poor thing."

"How tragic," Nox noted, earning a soft grunt from Nelson as he wrote everything down. "Does he know where his father is?"

"No. He left before Walt was born. Walt said it totally broke her. He's been taking care of Sheila and the house since he was a kid and she got worse when he went to school and moved out. That's when he had to get professional help. He was so afraid something terrible would happen if he wasn't there to take care of her," she told them in a sad whisper, sighing at a picture of Walt taped to her desk lamp. He was holding a fluffy orange cat but didn't look pleased at all.

Chapter Six

Nelson snorted at his notes. "He didn't want something terrible to happen. Makes sense," he said with a weak smile. "What about any other friends? Does he have some old roommates we could call up?"

"None that I can think of," she said, her lips twisting as she considered. She shook her head. "He kept me far away from his old place and his roommates when we first started dating. He said they were miserable pigs and he practically kissed my feet, said I'd rescued him from a dump when I asked if he wanted to move in."

"How romantic," Nox said flatly but she laughed it off.

"Walt's a dry guy and he takes some getting used to."

"He's alright," Nox said with a shrug and a playful wink, making her laugh again. "And I get that opposites attract." He tipped his head at Nelson and smirked when he blushed. "I'll probably invite some of my friends. Most of them are into witchcraft. Clancy says Sheila was Wiccan and passed her practice on to Walt. Do you two practice at home together?"

"Sure! He's taught me so much."

"Really?" Nox pretended to be surprised. "We've seen some dark magick lately. Maybe I'll pick his brain and see if he knows of anyone we should look into," he said, rubbing his chin.

"I doubt it! Walt keeps to himself, you know how he is. And most of our practice involves crystals and Tarot and moon cycles. He's a pretty peaceful witch!" She snorted to herself as she opened her purse and took out her wallet. "Here! I kept this from the first card he sent me." She unfolded a pink envelope and Nelson and Nox both leaned in to see the address. "You could see if any of his old roommates are there, but at your own risk. Walt said they were pigs," she repeated.

Nelson stopped her when she went to close her purse. "Could I..." He wrinkled his nose and pointed at a pencil, then held up the nub he never went anywhere without. "I keep meaning to replace this."

"Sure!" She took the pencil out and frowned when he pulled a tissue from the pack in his pocket and held it out. "Here you go," she said, widening her eyes at Nox.

He waved dismissively. "Nelson's just weird about pencils."

"I see." She bit down on her lips and nodded. "Nobody's perfect."

Nelson blinked at them. "I'm weird about pencils," he confirmed and smiled at her as he slipped the neatly wrapped bundle inside his coat and deposited it inside the chest pocket.

There was a soft cough from Clancy. "We'll probably skip his old roommates and keep it low-key for Walt's sake," he said, pushing away from the door and signaling that it was time to go. "You have labs to oversee soon. I'll make sure Nox doesn't bring any drugs to the party."

"You can send them my way," she sang under her breath, stealing Nox's heart.

"Hey, Aubrey," he said as he got up and swiped her hand, kissing her knuckles as he bowed over her desk. "You've been a tremendous help, with the party and the investigation, and we owe you."

"No! It was my pleasure," she protested but Nox hushed her.

"I was wondering if you would be interested in helping me with something else. But this would be something fun and right up your alley."

"Of course, professor! Anything I can do to help!"

"Brilliant," he said, smiling as he pulled his wallet from his back pocket. "Our friend, Howard, at Bippity Boppity Books has been having a tough time lately and he's been shorthanded after losing his son and his only other employee."

"Bippity Boppity Books? I know that place! I'd love to help," she said, nodding quickly as she studied the card.

"You're an angel," Nox said sincerely and delighted as a new plan came together. "Howard's had some help from another friend but he needs so much more. I bet you and Tony could turn that place around and be just the thing to cheer Howard up."

"Tony's helping too? Then, I am definitely in." She smiled

and Nox was pleased with the way her eyes and her aura lit up at the mention of Tony's name. They would need each other in the coming weeks and Nox was glad that she already liked and trusted him.

"Wonderful. The two of you will be good for Howard," Nox stated as he headed for the door. He felt better about lying to Aubrey and like they might have left her better than they found her after all.

They said their goodbyes and Nelson's frown was severe as they left the botany department. Nox waited until the three of them had the hallway to themselves again.

"What is it?" he asked Nelson.

"Walt's got someone else in the bureau," he said and snorted wryly at Clancy. "Someone other than you has been feeding him information."

"How do you know?" Clancy asked.

"Think about it," Nelson said as he flipped open his notepad and gave it a hard flick. "He knew before New Castle that Julian wanted to talk to us. I didn't know until that same Friday and I dragged my feet until I had to tell Nox on Wednesday, when we got called down to New Castle to check out Lonnie MacCrory's body and the shrine."

Nox's blood ran cold as he came to the same conclusion. "He asked Aubrey for the yew because he was ready to summon us and get rid of his accomplices."

"How did Walt know about Julian?" Nelson repeated, glancing at Clancy. "You didn't know so he didn't find out from you," he said and Clancy shook his head.

"I only knew that Julian Sherwood was your primary suspect. I wasn't being briefed on the case, aside from whatever you and Nox told me."

That earned a caustic snort from Nox. "And we weren't telling you very much because Nelson's gut kept telling him you were involved," he recalled with a hard look at Clancy.

"We know who's responsible for that now," Nelson

confirmed, silently chiding Nox. "I want to find out who Walt's other friend is. As far as I know, the only other person who knew Julian's lawyer had been in touch was Felton. So Walt's source is someone close to Felton and that someone is way above my head if he's getting that kind of gossip from the deputy director," he added.

Clancy offered him a half bow. "I'll see what I can find out," he said quietly and left them.

"Thanks..." Nelson frowned at Clancy's back, confused. "Why does he keep doing that, bowing at me?" he said to Nox, earning a soft chuckle.

He cleared his throat and stepped closer so he could whisper. "I think that technically, in the...spiritual scheme of things, you outrank Clancy and Merlin."

Nelson's frown deepened as he shook his head. "What does me being the harp have to do with this investigation?"

"Think about it!" Nox's whisper softened as he cradled Nelson's cheek. "I've tried to tell you from the beginning, the Uaithne trumps everything! Except the heir and the Dagda," he added with a dismissive swat, then tapped him on the end of the nose. "You're the gateway—the *gatekeeper*—and the right hand to both halves of the god. Who did *He* speak to first and who has *He* done business with the most?" Nox asked, his admiration obvious as he studied Nelson. "You met *Him* and...you withstood *Him*. *He* didn't get to you. You're impervious to *Him*!"

"You mean those nightmares that almost killed me and the throbbing panic attacks I get when we're apart?" Nelson asked, tempering his snarl into a dubious sneer. "I can't let go when we're...together or *He'll* snatch you out of my arms. That's *His* idea of doing business?" Nelson demanded and Nox crooned his name softly, smoothing his tie and the lapels of his coat.

"The gods have always cheated and played games. It's how they entertain themselves and each other. But we're getting the hang of it! And you haven't had the nightmares since we..." Nox reminded him with a wink. A hard grunt wafted from Nelson as he lowered his head and swiped his lips across Nox's.

"No. They stopped once I gave *Him* what he wanted," he said bitterly, then stalked to the Continental, leaving Nox wondering if there was anything he wouldn't risk or sacrifice for Nelson.

Seven

A few evenings later, Nox was still pondering that question as he and Merlin hunched over their laptops in the study. They were searching online archives for any mention of a Forsythe that came to America, with a connection to a noteworthy Irish family with magickal roots. Merlin wanted to see if Walt's claim that his family had been cheated might lead them to an ancestor, but they had yet to find anything of note about a single Forsythe.

Nox had found the line of Nelsons Merlin had mentioned and thought he might have discovered when *his* Nelson's ancestor had broken off from the heir and his three. They were originally MacNeighills out of Ulster. The prefix Mac meant son, the combination meaning son of a Neighill—eventually Anglicized to Neilson and Nelson. In 1712, Pádraig Nelson arrived in Virginia and moved to the Province of Maryland before he disappeared from the record. Then, in 1784, Pádraig's great-grandson, Fintan, returned to Maryland, joining the state's first night watch. A generation later, in 1813, a young lieutenant named Cormac Nelson served under General Perry Benson when his militia fought off British forces at the Second Battle of St. Michaels.

If Nox was correct, it was Pádraig who broke away but his

descendants returned to Maryland, remaining close to Georgetown and Nox's ancestors. They didn't understand why they were called to live there, but all of Nelson's ancestors served in night watches, militias, police departments, and eventually the FBI. All called to serve, protect, and hunt. Nelson said he never enjoyed killing animals for sport, but all the men in his family had been avid hunters and outdoorsmen with an uncanny aptitude for tracking.

All those generations of noble hunters, distilled into the perfect Nelson. Made just for Nox. It had to mean something. Why would the universe go to so much trouble to create such a perfectly matched pair just to let them fail?

It would be such a waste of good, pure love and Nox truly believed that he and Nelson were a force for good. And while Nox rarely looked to the universe to be "fair," they had given everything to the investigation and they deserved more than a handful of exhausted months before fate tore them apart again.

Merlin let out an exasperated curse and shut his laptop, snapping Nox out of his reverie. "We've been at this for hours and we've found nothing."

"Alright," Nox said, shutting his and sitting back. "We may have to accept that it's a dead end. Walt might have been lying about his family being cheated or he might not be talking about the Forsythe side of his family."

"Back to the drawing board it is," Merlin declared as he rose, then clapped his hands together. "It's been ages since we've pulled an all-nighter. Why don't we order takeout from that Middle Eastern place you love? I'll tell Nelson and brew a strong pot of coffee," he said as he turned to go.

For a moment, it was like the old days when Nox was studying for his exams and when he first began working for the FBI. He opened his mouth to suggest pizza instead, freezing when he remembered that it had all been an act before. Merlin wasn't helping Nox prepare for his future after school or build a reputation that would sustain him in a long and healthy career. It had all been a lie and Nox was always destined for this terrible task.

"I'll have to pass, I'm afraid," Nox said, rising to his feet and tidying the desk. "It's been a long day and Nelson gets fussy if I keep him up too late."

Merlin's shoulders sank and his gaze dropped to the floor as he nodded. "I...understand," he said weakly, then turned when Nelson strode into the study.

"I just got off the phone with an elderly gentleman named Roy Gardiner and it looks like Nox was right: Walt's been Bunburying," he said, making Nox pump a fist as he cheered.

"Which was fake? His piggy roommates or the sick mother in a home?"

"Both," Nelson replied and Merlin and Nox shared impressed gasps.

"You don't say!" Merlin said as he hurried to the board with Walt's name on it, prepared to copy.

Nelson chuckled wryly at his notes. "The address Aubrey's been carrying around in her purse isn't a residence. It's a butcher. At least, it used to be. Nobody buys their meats from an independent butcher anymore so the place went out of business a few years ago. I was able to track down the owner, Roy. He was very helpful. He said that Walt worked for him for about a year and had rented an efficiency unit Roy kept above the shop."

"Ha!" Nox tossed a hand at Walt's board. "He was being literal when he said his roommates were pigs. I want to like this guy, if he wasn't such a manipulative psychopath," he added flatly and Nelson snorted.

"I've noticed that Walt doesn't make things up from whole cloth. He stays close to the truth, just gives it a slight twist."

"It's how he's gotten away with it for so long," Nox said. "The best liars know how to turn the truth into a shell to hide a lie and how to use those shells to play their victims, like a trickster on the sidewalk."

Nelson pushed out a hard breath and waved his notepad.

"The shop was torn down and turned into a convenience store but Walt's childhood home is another story."

"Oh?" Merlin swung around, eyes alight and chalk poised to write.

Nox was alert as well as he prowled toward Nelson. "What did you learn about Walt's childhood home?" he asked, causing Nelson to humph in disgust.

"Roy said that Walt only lived upstairs for a few months. He was living with his mother over in Pennsville. I looked into it and the house isn't uninhabited at the moment. Walt's paying for the utilities there, including cable. I also did some research into Walt's mother, Sheila, and she isn't in any of the long-term care facilities that specialize in patients with Alzheimer's and dementia. I checked every facility in the Beltway and no one's ever heard of Sheila Forsythe but her mail is still being delivered to Walt's childhood home."

There was a dramatic gasp from Nox. "The plot has thickened and we've found Bunbury!"

Nelson nodded. "I'm working on a warrant. I have a feeling we're going to need one when we get there. I'm also looking into *her* background, because it's a little unclear about where Sheila came from, before she enrolled in Princeton in the '80s."

"Forsythe is an alias?" Nox sounded sincerely surprised and Merlin hummed knowingly.

"That would explain why we haven't been able to find very much about Walt or his mother or any of his ancestors. No one I've talked to or corresponded with has heard of a Sheila or Walter Forsythe but we know they're Wiccans and that they do practice."

Nox nodded. "Aubrey said Walt taught her a lot, she's rather competent herself so he couldn't be a novice."

"Definitely not," Nelson agreed. "We've seen how dangerous he is and how good he is at twisting the truth. My gut is telling me we need to be careful with Sheila and approach this house with caution. Walt's gone to a lot of trouble to hide both of them from the people he's closest to," he observed and Nox smiled.

"He has, hasn't he? All the breadcrumbs he's left have led back to me. He knows all about my past and has been clever about drawing us away from his." His brow furrowed as he stared at Walt's name on the board. "How much of New Castle was designed to lure and to *fool me*? How much of that was the MacCrorys and their dogma and what does Walt truly believe?"

Merlin's eyes tightened into a scowl as he shook his head. "Yet another shell he's used to hide his devious schemes. And that particular shell was already so ugly..."

"We're on to him, though," Nox said. "I want to check in with Howard tomorrow and see how his new helpers are doing, And then I want to get a look at Walt's childhood home and meet Sheila." His anticipation swelled as he calculated, but Nelson held up a hand, cautioning him.

"Walt could panic and get even more dangerous if we get too close, too soon. And my instincts tell me that we're going to wish we had a warrant once we get a look inside that place," he said as he widened his eyes at Nox, silently begging him to cooperate this time.

"I see what you're saying..." Nox nodded slowly. "We had better wait until *we* have a warrant to go in there. Any leads on Walt's father?"

"None," Nelson said but he cracked the smallest, most devious smile that Nox had ever seen grace those firm, frowning lips.

"What did you do?" Nox asked suspiciously and Nelson shrugged.

"I might have asked Bixby to do me a favor and test that pencil I found in Aubrey's purse."

"For what?"

"There were teeth marks and they were too big and wide to be hers," Nelson explained, but Nox and Merlin blinked back at him. "A man had been chewing on it," he added, yet they continued to stare at him. "Bixby can run it for DNA."

Chapter Seven

"But Walt's DNA isn't in any database," Nox argued and Nelson's smile grew wider.

"No, but his father's might be."

Merlin let out a delighted gasp. "Oh, that's brilliant, Nelson!" he said, clapping.

"Yup! Time to go, Merlin," Nox announced as he hooked his arm around Merlin's and rushed him toward the study door.

"What? Why?" Merlin asked, looking back at Nelson in confusion.

"Sex time," Nox informed them as he reached for Merlin's coat on the hook.

"Oh! Well, carry on, then," Merlin said as he took it and pushed his arm into a sleeve. "He certainly deserves to be rewarded after that."

"I thought so too, but this is mostly for my benefit," Nox said, then closed the front door behind Merlin, sending him on his way. "Because I have never wanted you more," he warned Nelson before running at him.

"Wait!" Nelson held out his hands but he caught Nox when he leaped and pulled his legs around his waist. "What about *Him*? We have to be careful!"

"I don't want you like that," Nox said as he gathered Nelson's face in his hands and showered it with kisses, then stopped. "I mean, I *could* if you want to take me upstairs and *ravish me*," he giggled and kissed Nelson's nose when it wrinkled, crooning softly as he nuzzled all over his face. "*My* perfect Nelson," he sighed with gratitude. He was grateful for Nelson and how soothed he felt after hurting over Merlin just a few minutes earlier.

"How many times do I have to tell you, I'm not perfect. I'm just a lot better when I'm with you."

"No." Nox shook his head firmly, his eyes locked with Nelson's. "You might have a holy dick, but *you* satisfy me, Nelson. Your heart, your honor, your selflessness... And your mind." Nox captured his face for a deeply intense kiss, letting Nelson feel how much his incredible brain and dry wit aroused him. "I love the way you know exactly how to love me, but I don't always need you to demolish my body and I know that you almost never need that."

"No. I like touching you and tasting you and making *you* happy. I never want to wear you out or demolish you," Nelson admitted and Nox sighed dramatically.

"That's something you're just never going to get, I'm afraid." He pressed a kiss on Nelson's forehead. "You're too damn chivalrous." Nox clicked his teeth at him before laughing and winding his arms around Nelson's neck, hugging him tight. "You are perfect and I'm so lucky. I love you, Nelson."

"I love you, too." His hands spread protectively, gliding up Nox's back. One speared into his hair, cradling Nox's head.

Perhaps, this was what Nox craved when he sent Merlin away, to simply do away with all the air and space between them and feel their bodies pressed together. He was so proud of his man with his quick, clever brain and his noble heart that Nox had to stop and cherish and revere him.

He was yet again grateful for Nelson's clarity and the calm he had provided. Nox would probably be balls deep in Nelson or riding him like a bumper car around the study if he gave into his wilder impulses. And Nox would have been too distracted by lust and the magickal chaos of dirty sex to bask in his pride and admiration.

Nox raised his head, touched when he found those same emotions glowing in Nelson's soft gray eyes. "Wow!" He kissed Nelson again and this time, desire radiated from Nelson as well, a gentle yet steady frequency. He craved the same intimacy Nox did but there was no throbbing urge to penetrate or the twitchy, gnawing need to be penetrated. It was a strong yearning to hold, touch, and to *love*. "Let's do it your way."

"My way?"

"Just like this," Nox whispered, tilting back his chin so

Chapter Seven

Nelson could suck on it. "Yes!" He gasped at the way he shivered and got hotter at the same time.

Instead of a wild, pulsing in his pants making him impatient, Nox was aware of Nelson's hands as they kneaded and caressed his back and shoulders and face. They held him like he was precious as Nelson licked and kissed, growling possessive words against his skin and into his ear, setting a different fire in Nox's core.

"Never stop burning for me, Nox. Burn forever, last forever like the sun."

He felt like his heart could burn forever, as much as he loved Nelson, and Nox knew an eternity wouldn't be enough. He would never find the end of his love for Nelson and his heart would always burn like the sun for him.

"I will," Nox vowed, his voice trembling as his nerves flared with warm, honey-like pleasure. None of it was in his groin, Nox noted with delight. It was his whole body and his soul, blooming with Nelson's as they kissed and clung to each other.

"Burn forever for me, Nox." Nelson whispered the command, his teeth scraping Nox's neck before he sucked.

"Okay," Nox managed as his eyes crossed and his toes curled in his sneakers.

"Mmmm..."

That rumbling growl rolled through Nox, causing his nerves to fizzle right up and he let out a strangled yelp as they imploded, his orgasm swelling outward from his center instead of bursting from his boxers.

"Did you...?" Nelson asked, leaning back and raising a brow at Nox.

Nox nodded jerkily, still dazed and tingling. "Yeah! And it was...*wow!*"

Nelson's eyes narrowed as they searched around them. "And *He* didn't take you?"

"I guess he can't when I'm too lost in *you*. Merlin said something about the significance of *you* and he was right. I can do anything if I put my faith in you and us," Nox boasted and tipped his nose back haughtily, truly feeling like a god as Nelson groaned and squeezed him tight.

"That's incredible. You're incredible, Nox."

"Nope," Nox stated, a wide smile spreading across his lips. "That was all you."

Eight

Nelson was already a tall man at 6'3, but he felt like he was a full foot taller the next morning. He didn't come with Nox in the study because he hadn't felt the urge to, but his senses had rejoiced and Nelson felt the same post-coital satisfaction and lightness as they went about their evening, talking, touching, and teasing as usual. They showered before bed, but Nox remained content and relaxed, nodding off quickly.

And like the brisk March morning, Nox had awoken refreshed and ready to attack the day with a new plan.

"It occurred to me that we haven't checked Walt's office and now's the perfect time to do it while he's away in Boston," he told Nelson as they enjoyed coffee and breakfast in the kitchen.

"We still need a warrant and what do you think he's hiding in his office?" Nelson looked dubious as he sipped.

"Meh. Clancy doesn't need a warrant," Nox said, waving dismissively. "Walt gave him a key and permission to use it if I remember correctly."

"*Oh.*" Nelson's eyes widened. "We don't need a warrant if we're just accompanying Clancy while he's dropping something off, if he has permission from Walt. But we can't go in with the intent to search or disturb anything," he added pointedly.

"Right. We will not disturb anything," Nox agreed and gave Nelson a firm nod, practically waving his bullshit flag.

"I'm going to let this be Clancy's headache," Nelson decided but gave his pocket a pat, making sure he had a fresh roll of antacids. The rest of the day, Nox was Nelson's responsibility while they were investigating, but Clancy had plenty of pull at Georgetown to cover his own ass and Nox's. Nelson would just go along to take notes and act as Nox's bodyguard.

Clancy was also dubious, when they met him in his office at Georgetown. "Walt's office? What do you think he's hiding in there?"

"Don't know. Yet," Nox replied, his finger straightening as he raised it. "But he can't hide very much at Aubrey's, can he? And his mom lives over in Pennsville, that's more than half an hour away if the traffic isn't crappy. Where else does he have a free place with a lock and a key to hide things around here?"

"Damn it, that makes sense!" Clancy conceded as he reclined in his seat and beat a knuckle against his lips, then shot Nox a hard look. "*You* can't touch anything."

"I won't!" Nox insisted and Nelson snorted as he flipped open his notebook.

"He's lying. Want to know exactly how many times I've told him not to touch something and how many times he said he wouldn't *and lied*."

Nox pulled a face. "What are you, the fact police?"

"Kind of."

There was a groan as Clancy rubbed a temple. "Is this how you two always work?"

"Unfortunately," Nelson said, sighing despite the twitching of his lips. It was hard not to smile as Clancy stared at him, looking baffled.

"I don't know how you haven't strangled him, Nelson. The only thing that stops me most days is Nox's mother and the fact that he still looks like he's six to me. You've only known him...like this," he said, glaring at Nox who smiled and smirked as he shoved his hands into the pockets of his jeans.

"That's how I know it's true love. He should have washed his hands of me after that first night in New Castle," he said, chuckling as he elbowed Nelson.

"Maybe." Nelson shrugged, returning to his notes. "I didn't and now I'm a harp. We should get going. Walt's supposed to return from Boston for the weekend and there's a cheap flight that leaves at 12:11 and gets in at 1:44 if he decides to make it a half-day."

Nelson didn't want to wash his hands of Nox and didn't see the point in pretending he'd have it any other way.

"I could say I was dropping off these reviews," Clancy said as he held up a stack of folders, then hunted in his desk drawer until he found the proper key.

The three of them proceeded to the other end of the department. Nox and Clancy's offices were larger and at the same end of the anthropology wing as the classrooms. The "working" end of the department—as Nox called it—was around the corner and through a set of double doors. The gleaming marble floors stopped and gray mid-century linoleum muffled their steps as they hurried down the beige corridor, past windowless doors with dry-erase plaques.

They reached Walt's door, his name neatly written in serious black ink. Clancy looked around before using the key to unlock the door and quickly waving them in. Nelson noticed that Nox flinched and hesitated at the door but he sniffed hard as he followed them in, silently closing the door behind him.

"Um..." Clancy's nose wrinkled as he took in Walt's office. "I'm not sure where he would hide anything. It's kind of..."

"Yikes! No wonder Walt's so bitter," Nox said with a hard wince at Walt's desk. It was little more than a metal table with a locked drawer and there was a short filing cabinet along the wall, as opposed to the classic, dignified elegance of Nox's and Clancy's offices. "This is rather depressing, comparatively," Nox added, making Nelson snort.

"Is this the first time the two of you have visited the 'working' part of the anthropology department?" he guessed and Nox nodded.

"Don't disturb *anything*," Clancy repeated, his hands splayed in front of him as he scanned the office. "Not that there's much to disturb. It has to look exactly like this when we leave or Walt *will* notice," he warned them and Nox gave him a thumbs up.

"Nelson, don't touch anything," he said out of the side of his mouth, earning a flat look from Nelson.

"I'll do my best."

"Then, we should be safe!" Nox said as he went around the desk and bent over it for a closer look at the calendar. He did a quick scan and took his phone out and got a picture. "We should probably check these appointments out in case he was off Bunburying," he murmured, then glanced at Nelson. He opened his mouth to say something but froze and a hard shudder passed through him.

"Nox?" Nelson asked and turned when Nox pointed, spotting a primitive-looking orange-haired doll on top of the tall white bookshelf behind him.

"Clance," Nox croaked as his pointed finger trembled.

Clancy turned and spit out a curse when he spotted it. "Cunús!"[1] He scrubbed a hand over his lips as he drew closer.

"What is it?" Nelson asked, leaning around Clancy for a better look.

"It's a poppet," Clancy replied in a husky growl. "Get back, Nox!" He waved and gestured at Nelson. "Do you have a glove?"

"I do..." Nelson said warily as he retrieved one from his outer coat pocket. "I usually keep one on me but I thought we agreed we weren't touching—" He stopped when he noticed that Nox was pressed against the door, pale and shaking. Nelson passed the glove to Clancy. "What's a poppet? Like a Voodoo doll?"

"No!" Nox gasped, shaking his head quickly and blocking his

face as Clancy carefully took the doll down. "Lots of cultures have poppets and they're often harmless and associated with white witchcraft."

"But this is an evil, cursed thing disguised to be an innocent totem," Clancy explained as he lowered the doll on his opened palms, cradling it.

Nelson's lip curled at the flame-red human-looking hair. "Do you think that's Elsa Hansen's?"

There was a tight nod from Clancy and Nox's hand clapped over his mouth to hold in an anguished sob. Clancy shushed Nox as he gently examined the doll. It was made of bits of cloth, string, a hairpin, an earring...

"It's made from pieces from all of the girls," Clancy explained, then raised it and sniffed. "And Nox's hair."

Nox covered his ears and mumbled something in Gaelic. "Burn it!" he begged them when he opened his eyes but Clancy shook his head.

"We can't. Not yet. He'll notice if it's not here."

"Nelson!" Nox was crying, his nostrils flaring as his chest heaved. "He can't keep it! He stole those things from us!"

"It's evidence!" Nelson argued, but Nox shook his head.

"Of what?" He flailed angrily. "Julian could have given him that doll. And we'll have to *wait* for it to be tested to prove it's even connected. Meanwhile, Walt or his mother destroys everything else that proves *he's* the mastermind and he blames it all on Julian and the MacCrorys."

Nelson was brutally and immediately torn. They *could not* take that doll. Not without a warrant and not without tipping Walt off. He would notice if his cleverly disguised trophy was gone and Walt would have no trouble guessing who had taken it. But loyalty to Nox and the deep need to satisfy him rose, buffeting Nelson's resolve.

"Hold on..." Nelson looked around and at the ceiling for anything that might help him. He squinted at the sprinkler above them, nodding as he worked through a plan. "I need a lighter or a match," he said, then reached for one of the cheap metal chairs in front of Walt's desk.

"What are you doing?" Clancy hissed as Nelson dragged it over to the shelf and stepped onto the seat.

"We need to call in a work order," he murmured as Clancy passed him a lighter.

"For what?" Clancy asked and Nelson smiled as he lit it and held it up to the sprinkler.

"You might want to get back, this one's about to malfunction," he warned and looked away, stretching his neck as he waited.

A few moments later there was a loud shriek from the alarm over Nelson's head as the heat from the lighter caused the sprinkler's glass bulb to burst and water sprayed around him.

"Nelson!" Nox clasped his cheeks as he laughed. "What are you doing?"

Nelson hopped down, flinging the water away from his face as he went to the bookshelf and pulled it out of the way, letting books and knick-knacks topple off.

"That's brilliant!" Clancy said as he sprang into motion, tucking the poppet inside his blazer before moving the other chair out of the way and unplugging everything on the desk. "We stopped by so I could drop off those reviews and peek at Walt's calendar for the bachelor party and we found it like this," he explained.

"I'll call it in!" Nox pulled the door open and ran into the hall. "We need some help in here!" he yelled, taking out his phone and dialing while Nelson and Clancy continued their destruction.

"Whoops!" Clancy picked up the wastebasket and used his arm to slide a stack of wet papers off the desk into it, then went to the bookshelf and began disposing of already soggy cards and blurring photos.

"Not Forsythe's office," a custodian grumbled as he rushed in with a bucket and a mop, skidding to a halt when he spotted

Clancy. "Let me take care of that, professor," he said and Clancy thanked him as he handed over the waste basket.

"Thank you. We tried to save what we could but some of this is clearly ruined." He dusted off his hands like he wasn't being drenched as well and stepped over a pile of spilled files. "We'll leave you to it," he said with a twirl of a finger, gesturing for Nelson and Nox to vacate with him. He kept his head down, offering terse nods as they passed other faculty and custodial staff on their way to help clear Walt's office. Once they were alone, Clancy removed the poppet and passed it to Nelson. "Merlin will know what to do with this," he said solemnly.

"Thanks, Clance," Nox said, his voice hoarse as he watched Nelson wrap it in tissue and slide it into his pocket.

Clancy waved dismissively. "It was all Nelson's quick thinking. I was prepared to drag you out kicking and screaming."

"I know and I will thank him when we get home," Nox replied and Nelson heard a faint sniffle. "But you went with it and I think you sold it back there," he said with a swing of his head toward Walt's office. Clancy denied that he'd done anything special and left them so he could change out of his wet clothes.

Nox held out his hand to Nelson. "Shall we?" His eyes shimmered and there was a warm, tender glow.

"Stop it. I didn't do anything but make a mess," Nelson muttered as he took Nox's hand.

Nox made a dreamy sound and stared at Nelson like he was made of crystals and moonbeams as they walked back to the Continental.

"You made a mess for me, though, and you stole evidence."

"No, I didn't," Nelson stated, shaking his head. "If anyone asks, I was tagging along to keep you out of trouble."

"You're very good at that."

Back at the townhouse, Merlin was on top of Nelson as soon as he stepped over the threshold.

"What is that? What did you find?" he demanded and pointed at Nelson's pocket as he rushed at him.

"We need you to destroy it. *Now,*" Nox said, nervously chewing a nail as Nelson eased it out of his pocket.

"Maleficium!" Merlin hissed and drew back but he collected the doll and took it out onto the back terrace. "Bring my bag, Nox."

They returned an hour later, both looking drained and frazzled. Merlin's emerald suit was rumpled and Nox's steps dragged as they trudged into the study and collapsed on the sofa.

"What a twisted soul," Merlin said and thanked Nelson when he handed him a tumbler of whiskey.

He had one ready for Nox as well, but he did little more than mumble a thank you and hug it as he sipped and stared at the French doors.

"I checked with Bixby while you were out there," Nelson said and Nox and Merlin raised their brows hopefully. "He didn't have anything yet. But he should in the morning." Nelson bowed his head apologetically. "It got too quiet."

"Such a twisted soul," Merlin repeated sadly. "I know it is typical for killers to keep souvenirs but that was..."

Nelson muttered a curse, scrubbing his face. "Walt is..." He considered everything he had learned about cult leaders, serial killers, and other dangerous narcissists and Walt possessed so many of the typical traits. But he was all the more dangerous and difficult to detect and catch because he cheated with dark magick and broke metaphysical laws as well. Walt was a terrible hybrid of both types of evil but Nelson was at a constant disadvantage, one hand tied behind his back because he had to play by the FBI's and the Justice Department's rules. "Walt is a fucking monster."

"He *loved* that thing," Nox whispered, suppressing a shiver. He took a large gulp from his glass and dragged his hand under his nose. "He bled in it and he came in it and he prayed to it. We burned a piece of his soul out there."

"His soul?" Nelson asked and Merlin nodded.

"He used a demon charm to bind himself to it and he'll know it's been destroyed."

Chapter Eight

Nox laughed shakily and needed another gulp. "Clancy will tell him everything was incinerated in case there was anything sensitive from the FBI and that they'll need to do some accounting to see what was lost. But Walt hedged his bets by selling a bit of his soul and we burned it."

"You can actually do that?" Nelson asked, earning a bark of wry laughter from Merlin.

"Pay attention the next time you're walking around the Hoover Building or the Capitol, lad. You'll find many with holes in their souls and those who have made pacts that haunt them."

"With demons?" Nelson didn't know why he was surprised. "Of course, there are demons. Why wouldn't there be if there are gods and monsters?"

There was a suggestive hum from Merlin. "How do you think so many ridiculously incompetent men manage to fail upwards with such astonishing frequency?"

"I assumed it was mostly corruption, nepotism, and systemic racism," Nelson replied and Nox laughed.

"That's how demons work. Weak hearts and weak minds are easy pickings and they're in abundance in politics." He stood and drained his glass as he turned from the room. "Let's go to bed, Nelson. I'm too sick to eat and I need what energy I have left for practice tonight. I'll see you in the morning, Merlin."

"We could skip it and just take a long shower. I can give you a back massage," Nelson suggested as he followed Nox from the study. Merlin had turned off the light and was heading for the front door.

"No," Nox said as he dragged himself up the steps. "We're not skipping it. I need you."

"I'll be right there," Nelson replied as he went to lock up behind Merlin.

Merlin's heart was in his shattered eyes as they followed Nox up the stairs. "That poppet did not burn easily," he whispered to Nelson. "I don't know where Nox found the fire to do it. I was certain we'd have to find a demon to break it first. Dark, dirty magick is extremely resistant, even to fire. Nox will be tired for a few days and will need all the nourishment you can give him. But he also needs to prepare for what comes after Walt. We only have—"

"I know," Nelson said gently, cutting him off. "We've been— We're working on it," he said with a suggestive look that caused his face to burn.

"Are you now?" Merlin chuckled as he put on his coat. "I don't know why I even worried. He's in good hands," he said to himself, bowing to Nelson as he left. "Until tomorrow."

"Have a good night, Merlin," Nelson said as he closed the door and locked it. "We will," he vowed, honored and humbled to be the one to care for Nox and share the burden.

---

1. **Cunús** (Coo-Nyoos) Dirty, foul thing.

Nine

Hell.

Nox didn't believe Hell existed and suspected it was the one thing nearly all religions got universally wrong. The earth teemed with evil and there were horrors all around, the devil didn't need an invisible, mystical plane to dwell and rule. The devil and his minions worked on the ground and out in the open, buying souls in dark deals and unleashing monsters amongst the innocent.

Hell couldn't be darker and hotter than Julian Sherwood's basement but if Nox had his way, Walt would roast for an eternity. Nox made his own forbidden vows in the shower, letting the hot water fall on his face, rinsing away his tears as he begged the Dagda for justice.

They had tried to burn the poppet with rare, ancient Greek fire, blue fire, and with Epsom salt and white fire. But the evil within the poppet protected it, leaving it cold on the terrace stones.

Merlin had begun to fret and was babbling about demons, so Nox tried using his own fire, figuring they had nothing to lose. Instead of calling forth a candle or a match flame or even one from the hearth in the study, Nox reached deeper. He called to the fire that burned in his core for Nelson, Nox's strongest and purest flame.

It only took a touch and just a spark for the doll to combust into a hissing *poof!* but it had cost Nox a dear sum. He could hear Elsa's howl, a memory trapped in her hair that Walt had cherished. That shredded, tormented scream now resided in Nox's heart, in place of the bit he'd sacrificed to burn Walt's sick treasure.

"Can I join you?" Nelson's gentleness saved Nox, quieting Elsa's pain.

Nox turned from under the water, filling his lungs as he reached for Nelson. "Please."

Again and again, Nelson proved himself to be worthy of being Nox's keeper—his guardian and his guide. It had been his noble heart and quick, clear mind that had saved them in Walt's office. And it had been Nelson's love and the parts he'd claimed within Nox that had given him the power to burn the poppet.

"You're so tired. Do we have to practice tonight?"

"Yes." Nox's arms slid around Nelson and he was content to hold him under the water until it started to get cold. "I'm tired, but I feel strong right now."

Nelson had already replaced the piece Nox had surrendered and was filling his heart with more loving magick. How could they possibly lose?

It didn't take long for Nox to ascend, once they were in bed and Nelson had his hands on him. His steady, devoted touch and calm patience breathed new life into that fire in Nox and made him desperate.

"Oh, gods! I love you, I love you, I love you..." Nox held on for dear life, his fingers tangled in Nelson's hair and his heels digging into the mattress. Nelson's face was pressed between Nox's asscheeks, his tongue thrusting and swirling skillfully. He had mastered the art of rimming and was destroying Nox. "Wait!" Nox cried when he heard buzzing and the plucking of a harp.

Chapter Nine

"Go ahead and let go." Nelson's low, lazy rumble didn't help, creating a new cascade of goosebumps.

"I can do this!" Nox insisted with a tap on Nelson's head, signaling that he was ready to try again. He had named it his "Nelsonspace," that safe, warm place within him. Nox believed it was a source of incredible power and could shelter him from the Dagda if he could access it at will during sex, the way he had with Nelson in the study.

"If I must," Nelson said with a dramatic sigh, settling in again. He parted Nox's cheeks and growled softly as he sucked at the tender, puckered flesh.

"Fuck, fuck, fuck... I can do this," Nox panted as his eyes crossed, whimpering when Nelson chuckled, the deep sound and soft huffs of breath making him shiver.

"I love when you swear. I'm the only one who ever hears it."

Nox's teeth scraped his lip and he nodded quickly. "I never need to unless I'm with you." A finger pressed past the tight ring of Nox's ass and he fought so hard to reach that sacred place where Nelson resided. "I love you, I love you, I love you..." He could stay with Nelson and keep the Dagda out if he could just keep his pleasure and his orgasm from blooming too quickly in his groin and overwhelming him.

But Nelson was too good. Nox was no match for his slow, slick strokes, gentle growls, and the hot lashing of his tongue.

"Fuck it!" He grabbed hold of Nelson's head with both hands and writhed against his tongue, giving into the warmth and rejoicing when he heard a harp. "Don't let me get too close," he told Nelson.

"I won't."

Nelson was true to his word, whipping Nox into a hot frenzy and sending him soaring only to snatch him back at the last second. He was devastating with his mouth and fingers, pleasuring Nox but keeping him ruthlessly on the brink of release. The room was spinning and Nox's legs were shaking when Nelson rolled onto his back and pulled him on top.

"See how high you can fly without touching *Him*," Nelson dared Nox.

"I'm learning," Nox huffed, his head bobbing loosely as he rocked back and forth. His hands were planted on Nelson's chest, the firm, unyielding strength supporting Nox as he allowed his senses to sink, sink, sink until he was caught up in the heady pleasure spilling through his veins and making his soul lighter. "There it is!" Nox laughed when he felt the exact point where it began to detach from his body.

It was like the edge of a sneeze. When he was small, his mother had said it was fairy dust tickling his nose. Nox knew he could find that fairy dust feeling again, the way he'd found the quiet place where the Dagda couldn't hear him. Nox was learning how to access the safe place where Nelson made him strongest and he could find his way back to this too and touch the Dagda when it suited *him*.

"Come back, you're getting too hot," Nelson warned as his hands locked around Nox's hips, lifting him off. He was stunning, Nox's brave and mighty Uaithne. In his sensual haze, Nox could see Nelson the way the Dagda knew him, with long waves of ash blond hair, a proud, braided beard, and Pictish tattoos across his brow and cheeks.

"My Uaithne," Nox whispered in awe, tracing the harp stings tattooed under Nelson's beard and the crown on his brow. His silver eyes glowed with cunning and loyalty as he guarded Nox's soul and his heart from the Dagda. "My beautiful Uaithne," he said, breathlessly taken with Nelson as he kissed him.

"You're mine," Nelson said, his fist tight in Nox's hair as he rolled them. He filled Nox with a brutal, rolling thrust, forcing the Dagda out. "You will stay here with me," he commanded as he hooked Nox's leg around his waist. "Du thabairt dorais du glé, for mu muid céin am messe."[1]

"Yes!" Nox nodded frantically, fully under Nelson's enchantment. He was enthralled and possessed, but not by glorious, blinding rapture. His entire body sang with the joyful pleasure of

Chapter Nine

two souls communing and fusing, not one soul consuming the other.

"Du thabairt dorais du glé, for mu muid céin am messe." His hips pumped hard, swift, steady, carrying Nox with him as Nelson repeated his sacred chant.

"Keep going," Nox urged, his arms and legs tightening around Nelson. "Take me with you."

Nelson nodded, his sweat-streaked brow pressed against Nox's as they panted into each other's mouths. "Du thabairt dorais du glé, for mu muid céin am messe."

Their tongues lapped and their fingers curled into claws as they fought to get closer and deeper, defiantly fighting back a god as they tipped into ecstasy.

"Nox!" Nelson's ragged, primitive roar ignited that flame within Nox, creating an inferno. They came together, crying and laughing as their bodies flickered with pure, loving radiance.

"We did it," Nox whispered, as he burrowed into the corner of Nelson's neck, sated and utterly spent.

"You did it," Nelson said with a yawn. "I just helped."

"I couldn't have done it without you."

Nelson's chest shook as his fingers trailed up and down Nox's back. "Sure, you could."

"Maybe with toys," Nox pondered and Nelson's hand stopped.

"Could I watch?" he asked, surprising Nox.

"Would you enjoy that?"

That got another chuckle out of Nelson. "Probably. I liked when we tried them."

They had taken Nox's 'secret' box out of the closet a few times to try out his toys. There was an assortment in the black hat box because Nox used to get adventurous when it was just him and he'd had a dry spell. Nelson was perplexed by the array of dildos, vibrators, beads, plugs, rings... There were even a few E-Stim options but Nelson had closed the box and put it away from him when Nox explained what they did.

"Why would you want to shock your—?" he had asked, looking genuinely concerned.

"The tingles are kind of nice on the lower settings," Nox had explained but Nelson shook his head.

"Add that to the list. I don't want to play with those."

Nox had added electro-sex to the list of hard limits and they had stuck to using mostly vibrators, when Nelson wasn't in the mood for penetrative sex but still wanted to be involved.

Just as Nox was nodding off, it occurred to him that with the help of a little black silicone cage, he might be able to be more like Nelson and access his Nelsonspace more easily. He chewed on his lip as he considered the box in the closet. That particular accessory had been a whim and hadn't worked for Nox *at all* in the past. But it could be just the thing to contain Nox's particular demons and keep the Dagda at bay.

"I like it!" Nox whispered, grinning wickedly at the closet.

Nelson yawned again, his limbs getting heavier as they tightened around Nox. "What?"

"You'll see..." Nox would let that be a surprise and see if Nelson noticed a difference. "I think I might know how to tap into my inner Nelson."

"Hmm... It's late and I don't think I want to know."

"Probably not but I'll show you later," Nox said, a plan coming together as he drifted off to sleep.

---

1. **Du thabairt dorais du glé, for mu muid céin am messe** (NA): I am the knowledge and the door, turning the darkness into light.

Ten

The next morning, Nox's secret silicone experiment was yielding rather interesting results. He was incredibly focused and more relaxed once he settled into wearing the chastity cage. There was some protest from his nether regions in the beginning because Nox was usually randier in the morning, but he'd shut it all down by the time he and Nelson had finished their breakfast and Merlin arrived.

It was so easy once he reminded himself that Nelson was in charge of *that* now as well. "Do me a favor and keep this in your wallet for me today." Nox smiled brightly as he slid the small, slim metal key across the work table to Nelson. "I'll need it when we get home this evening and it would be a headache if I lost it."

He shrugged, obediently taking out his wallet and tucking it behind his credentials. "Is it for a safe?"

"Sort of," Nox had said as he sipped his coffee, then used Merlin's arrival to distract Nelson. "You're just in time," he said when Merlin strolled in, bowing at them elegantly. "I had some thoughts about where we might look for these mysterious Forsythes."

"So did I!" Merlin said as he rubbed his hands together. "We associate the name Forsythe with families from Northern Ireland, but I remembered that many of them hailed from the de Fersiths out of Scotland."

"Exactly! We focused too much on *Irish* Forsythes and our monster might come from Scot stock," Nox said, offering Nelson a wave as he steered Merlin out and into the study so they could get to work.

They hadn't gotten very far into their search when Nelson walked into the study looking deeply perplexed.

"What is it?" Nox asked as Merlin set down his laptop and rose.

"Is everything alright, lad?" he asked Nelson.

"I know who Walt's father is. I just got off the phone with Bixby. He's emailing me the RAP sheet."

"RAP sheet?" Nox asked, alarmed and Merlin made a worried sound as he went to the board and picked up a piece of chalk, ready to copy.

Nelson had his laptop opened and was logging in. "Walt's father was a custodian at Princeton. He's serving at East Jersey State Prison after this third strike for...Jesus," he muttered under his breath as he read. "He's tried his hand at a little bit of everything but this last bust for dealing in a school zone sent him away for the rest of his natural life."

He printed out Jacob Trenton's entire criminal record and the three of them scrutinized everything they could find on him for any hint of practice or a connection to any other known witches or magickal practitioners. Three hours later, Merlin threw up his hands.

"I've placed calls and searched every roster and record at my disposal and there is no mention of a Jacob Trenton in our circles," he declared and Nelson sighed at the pages on the desk in front of him.

"As far as I can tell, the custodian position at Princeton was the last decent job Trenton held before falling in with his con brothers. They ran various scams, committing some B&Es—one got out of hand and Robert Trenton pistol-whipped a man after he walked in on them—bad checks, all shades of assault, robberies, and those drug charges. Jacob Trenton was just a common, low-level thug who earned himself a lifer at East Jersey."

Nox hissed as he scrubbed his hair. "Two very important questions: does Walt know who his father really is? And was his conception consensual?"

"Oh, dear," Merlin said sadly, glancing at Sheila's name on the board. "Did she lie to Walt to hide her shame?"

"That is my fear as well," Nox said distantly. "I need to know if this woman was a victim and if Walt has used her broken soul as another shell to hide his misdeeds. Or if she turned Walt into this because she wanted revenge."

"I'll see what I can find out from Trenton," Nelson said, taking out his phone and heading for the terrace again. "He might be willing to talk if it'll earn him some points with the feds or I can swing a few extra privileges."

"Nothing too nice," Nox called after him, making Merlin chuckle as he wrote.

"He does seem like a rather unsavory individual." The piece of chalk tapped against the board before he turned back to Nox. "Is this nurture or nature? Did Walt inherit this darkness and duplicity from his father or was it nurtured by his mother and the many disappointments he must have experienced as a young man..."

Nox chewed on his lip, curious as well. "It would depend on if Walt knew, and what part his mother played. If Walt truly doesn't know who or where his father is, then I suppose that would be a good case for nature. We couldn't really say if Walt did know, whether he was taking after his father or motivated in some way by shame or resentment of him."

Nelson returned as they were discussing how Trenton might have shaped Walt's life and nature despite his incarceration.

"Let's go ask him," Nelson suggested. "I called East Jersey and talked to the warden and he said it wouldn't be a problem to arrange an interview. Trenton's on kitchen detail this morning and he's a moderate behavioral risk but usually cooperative."

"Excellent!" Nox said as he rose to leave, but Merlin halted him.

"I had hoped you'd give yourself a few days before you charged back into the fray. Don't overdo it, my boy," he pleaded gently.

Nox waved him off and went to get his coat. "I'll be fine."

"I'll look after him," Nelson told Merlin as they left. "He's trying. They're both trying," he scolded Nox once they were in the car.

"So am I," Nox replied with a forced smile. "I find myself loving them again and it feels better, until I remember how much they lied to me. And I know now that my father's last moments were filled with terror—for me—because he was left to face the Dagda alone." He pushed out a slow, cleansing breath, keeping his thoughts quiet and private.

Nox silently thanked his father for giving him a way to protect his sanity. He no longer worried which thoughts were his own and if the Dagda was tampering with his memories. Having the cage and giving Nelson the key had added even more reinforcement and ironically, helped Nox feel *more* in control of himself.

"I'm sorry." Nelson's hand curled around Nox's giving it a squeeze. "Are you okay?"

Nox raised a brow. "Me? Aside from the crushing disappointment and dread?" he asked, earning an apologetic wince from Nelson.

"I know you're hurting, but you're...really quiet. Did something happen?"

"I'm quiet?" Nox bit down on his lips so they couldn't stretch into a grin and give him away. "In what way?" He was genuinely fascinated to know.

Nelson frowned at the windshield as he took the New Jersey Turnpike and I-95 North. "You're usually...friskier in the morning," he said with an awkward, blushing grimace. "Did I say something or—?"

"No!" Nox did not want Nelson worrying that he'd done *anything* wrong. "Not at all. I'm trying a new thing to help me focus during the day."

"Okay..." Nelson cast him a quick glance before nodding at the road. "That's good."

"So far," Nox said and reached for his bag and Trenton's folder. It only worked if he didn't think about the cage. If he did, he felt it more and then it made him antsy. "What's the plan?" He held up the file, distracting Nelson again.

They discussed what questions they needed answered and which approach was best and Nox was pleased with how tuned-in he was to Nelson as they parked in front of the prison.

"It's really going to depend on Trenton, isn't it?" Nox predicted as he closed his door and walked with Nelson to the first checkpoint. "He's only going to cooperate if he thinks there's something in it for him."

Nelson nodded along, halting Nox before they were searched at the gate. "This is the most important thing: we don't want Trenton defensive about whatever happened with Sheila Forsythe. If he thinks we're here to add a rape charge to his sheet, he'll shut the interview down."

"What if we tell him the truth?" Nox asked, holding up a finger. "He may be happy to learn he has a son or he may want to cooperate if he learns that Junior is about to face charges."

"Good point. We should probably steer clear of the cult and the serial nature of the poisonings," Nelson said as he held out his arms and was patted down. "We don't want Trenton thinking there's more in this for him than some extra time outside of his cell. I'm not interested in giving him anything more than a few extra hours of fresh air and sunshine."

"He doesn't deserve much more than that, from what I read," Nox replied, wrinkling his nose at the overcast sky. "It's going to rain soon. We should get inside."

It began to pour as soon as they were buzzed into the prison's west wing. "That was convenient," Nelson noted and cast Nox a suspicious glance out of the corner of his eye.

"I told you, *He* wants justice as much as we do."

"I seriously doubt that," Nelson replied, leaving Nox so he could sign them in and hand over his service weapon. "Agent Nelson. I called earlier," he told the guard behind the desk and thanked her for the clipboard.

Nox watched the rain as he waited, happy to follow quietly as Nelson was briefed on Jacob Trenton's guests, commissary purchases, and behavioral violations by one of the guards. She was brisk as she read through the details, then handed him a Manila envelope.

"I've provided copies for your records. He keeps with 'the Brotherhood' when he's not in solitary confinement," she told them with a hesitant wince at Nox. "Are you sure you two don't want some Plexiglass between you? He's low risk but he can get nasty if you rub him the wrong way."

"We'll be fine," Nox said cheerfully as they were let into an empty visitation room.

Nelson let Nox pick and he chose a table by the window, enjoying the view of the sky over the guard tower and the parking lot beyond. There was a loud buzzing and Nelson turned as four guards led a tall, lean man in through the double doors behind them. Nox recognized Trenton from his most recent mugshot, noting that he was limping as he shuffled, his ankles tethered together by chains. Aside from the limp, Trenton was in impressive shape for a man in his mid-fifties. He had wide, well-muscled shoulders and a broad, sculpted chest stretched the front of his orange scrubs. His hands were bound as well and Nox sat with his fingers interlocked on the table as Trenton's restraints were secured to the seat across from him.

"What the fuck are you?" Trenton asked, leaning forward and squinting at Nox.

Chapter Ten

Nox looked down at himself, then raised a brow at Trenton. "I *know* the tattoos aren't weirding you out."

Trenton was covered in swastikas, lightning bolts, and shamrocks, including his face and shaved head. "Nah," he snorted, his neck stretching to see around Nox's. "They said I was seeing a professor, but you don't look like no fuckin' professor. You Irish, punk?"

"Yeah!" Nox said excitedly as he sat forward, his eyes glittering as he studied Trenton. "Go ndéana an diabhal dréimire de chnámh do dhroma ag piocadh úll i ngairdín Ifrinn!"[1] he said, smiling sweetly at Trenton as he waited for a response.

The older man's tongue pushed against the inside of his cheek as he eyed Nox down. The hostility in his aura was almost palpable, but Nox sensed that Trenton wanted to be entertained. "I bet you think you're smart," he said suspiciously.

"I am," Nox replied, nodding as he held Trenton's belligerent stare. "But that doesn't mean that you aren't. You might even be smarter than me," he challenged.

"What is it you want?" Trenton asked, throwing a quick glance at Nelson but couldn't keep his eyes off of Nox.

"Congratulations!" Nox whispered. "It was a boy," he said and Trenton's head pulled back.

"What's a boy?"

Nox grimaced awkwardly at Nelson before offering Trenton a wince. "That forgettable was it?"

Trenton's befuddled frown could have made for a masterclass in running circles around an idiot. "What?" he asked and risked another glance at Nelson. "What's he talking about?"

Nelson flipped open his notepad, pretending to check something. "You had a son in 1989 and I believe the professor is referring to the evening ten months prior."

"Prior to what?" Trenton asked, making Nox whistle loudly.

"You might not be smarter than me."

"Hey!" Trenton objected and held his hand up as much as the

chains would allow. "Fuck you, you freak. But, what do you mean, I had a son in 1989? I didn't have no girlfriend in 1989. I got popped for two robberies and spent all of '89 and '90 locked up."

Nox hummed, barely stifling his disbelief. Walter Forsythe fell very far from the paternal tree. "What about '88?" he attempted with a hopeful raise of his brows.

"'88..." Trenton's head swayed from side to side. "There were a few. You might have to be more specific," he boasted

"It would have been in the fall, just before the holidays," Nelson said and Trenton laughed.

"That weird hippie girl from the school?" He pinched the bridge of his nose, wheezing as he giggled. "She had a kid? Bet that little fucker's messed up."

"Why would you say that?" Nox asked softly. Nelson glanced up just as the lights lowered and smirked as he watched Trenton.

There was a soft chuckle as Trenton's eyelids lowered. "Dawg, that's nice. What is that?"

"Why would her son be messed up?" Nox repeated, his voice low and lulling Trenton.

"Oh, she was real messed up. Always talkin' to herself and followin' those professors around like they were all Jesus. Especially that one, Patches."

"Patches?" Nox asked and Trenton laughed, dreamy and far away as he tapped his elbows.

"He always wore them preppy blazers with the stupid elbow patches."

"Let's go back to her," Nox said, waving faintly because he had an idea of who "Patches" was. "What else was messed up about her?"

"I heard some rumor about her dad and she had that crazy thing with her eyes. You can always tell when a girl's been touched by her daddy," Trenton told Nox, his gaze unfocused as he pointed at his own face. "Their eyes are always a little too wide and they stare weird."

"Is that all?" Nox asked, his tone trembling as his nostrils flared with disgust. "What about the night you had sex with her? Did she look at you weird?"

"She was drunk," Trenton replied.

"Was she willing?" Nox shushed Nelson when he tried to object. "Was she willing, Jacob?"

"Shit, yeah! She was waiting for me when I got off work. Sitting on the hood of my truck, drunk off her face on Mad Dog. Offered me some and said she was mad at her man so I did her in the parking lot behind the bowling alley on J Street."

"I'm sure she had a lovely time," Nox said, his face pinching.

"Dunno." Trenton shrugged. "Got mine, didn't I? What's he done?"

"Who?" Nox asked and Trenton laughed as he pointed.

"Who do you think, smart ass? This kid of mine."

"Not really a kid anymore," Nox countered. "He did you proud," he said as he stood, gesturing to Nelson that it was time to go. "He doesn't know anything else. He's of no use to us."

"Is that it?" Trenton objected and Nox snorted.

"That's what she said."

Nelson tapped his brow in salute, turning to follow Nox out. "The bureau thanks you for your cooperation."

"What about it? What do I get?" Trenton called after them.

Nox laughed, turning so he could walk backward. "A son, you racist dipshit."

"Come back and say that to my face!" Trenton shouted as he was pushed toward the other door by his escorts.

"You really don't want that," Nelson said loudly, then thanked the guard who got the door for them.

Once outside, Nox stormed to the Continental, grateful to feel the rain on his face. He'd felt like he was withering in that room with Trenton and was keen to get home and thoroughly scrub and rinse the experience away.

"What?" Nelson asked after he started the car and turned the heater. "You can't tell me *that* got to you."

"No." Nox shook his head, hugging his chest as he stared at

the prison. He'd hoped to feel illuminated after the interview but he had only found more darkness. "Part of me wants it to be Trenton's fault that all of this happened. Not because I need to forgive Walt or explain how he was capable of so much evil, but because *I* need an explanation for how anyone could be capable of what Walt's done. And then, I'm conflicted because I wouldn't wish that man on my worst enemy and am almost glad Walt never had to endure Jacob Trenton."

"I'm not so sure he didn't," Nelson said as he started the car. "They may have never met and Sheila may have lied to Walt, but *she lied* because she was ashamed of Trenton or unstable when she was with him and that would have affected her parenting. It certainly affected Walt."

"We just don't know if Walt knew his mother had lied and if he had discovered why she lied as well."

"I think it's safe to say that Walt didn't get his brains from his father," Nelson said, making Nox chuckle. He relaxed and slid across the bench, so he could lean against Nelson's side once they were on the highway and the prison was behind them.

"He certainly did not. If anything, Walt's managed to do a lot with the measly hand fate dealt him."

They settled into thoughtful silence and Nox gave himself a pinch when he nodded off. He was still imagining a long, hot shower and possibly some Kung Pao Chicken and they were nearly to Georgetown. "Are you alright?" Nelson asked, giving Nox's arm an affectionate knead.

"Great!" Nox stretched and scooted back over to his side. "I can't wait to get the stink of Trenton off of us and update Merlin. We still don't know if Walt knew and was nurtured or driven by the knowledge of who his father was. But this makes a stronger case for nature if he didn't know."

"He did tell Tony that he was lucky to have had a father to protect and provide for him," Nelson said and Nox gasped.

"That's right! Who did he resent more? Tony for having a dad, Trenton for not being there—whether he knew about him or not—or his mother for failing to find a decent partner to have a child with?"

"What if it's like Tony said and a little bit of all three?" Nelson suggested, voicing Nox's very thoughts.

Nox made an exasperated sound as he grew frustrated all over again. "Merlin might be getting his all-nighter after all. We answered one question about Walt's past and his parentage, but it's gained us nothing but more questions."

"More information is never a bad thing," Nelson said but Nox could see that he was just as aggravated.

Sheila Forsythe was the key to unlocking the truth behind who and what Walt truly was. And the only way they were going to unlock that truth was to get a look at Sheila and Walt's childhood home.

He glanced at Nelson, already anticipating an argument but Nox would spring it on him later. There was no point in giving him more heartburn this late in the day and ruining his evening.

---

1. **Go ndéana an diabhal dréimire de chnámh do dhroma ag piocadh úll i ngairdín Ifrinn!** (NA) May the devil make a ladder of your backbone while picking apples in the garden of Hell!

Eleven

Nelson was having a hard time putting his finger on it, or why it was bothering him so much, but Nox was definitely different. He insisted he was fine and chattered excitedly about visiting Bippity Boppity Books as they ate their breakfast the next morning. And Nox seemed content and incredibly focused as they discussed their observations on the way to Adelphi.

"Is something wrong?" Nelson asked after he parked the Continental, turning to Nox and catching his chin.

"No. Why?" He slid close and pressed a kiss to Nelson's cheek. "You haven't done anything wrong," he promised, then kissed him again before getting out and closing the passenger door behind him.

Nelson stared after Nox. "You haven't said one inappropriate thing about my appendages or made any lewd suggestions this morning."

He told himself he was being ridiculous and that Nox was just extra focused because they were so close to catching Walt. It was a good sign and Nelson was just imagining the strange wall he sensed between them.

"This is so much better!" Nox said when Nelson got the

shop's door for him, gasping and clasping his cheeks as he looked around for Howard.

Nelson nodded as he scanned the shelves and displays on the tables. There wasn't a speck of dust and candles glowed invitingly while the scent of smoky, earthy patchouli plumed from incense sticks scattered around the store.

"Much better," Nelson agreed.

Howard came hurrying from behind the counter, looking revived as well. His silver hair was styled in a tall, dramatic quiff and his aubergine suit included a dapper cape. "Hello and welcome! It's so *good* to see you again," he said, leaning on an elegant gold cane and opening his arm to Nelson and Nox for a hug.

They each accepted his embrace, Nox gushing as he kissed Howard's cheeks. "It's so good! The shop looks wonderful and you're looking so much better than last time."

"Well, it's all because of you! You sent two angels and look at the miracle they've worked here!" He took out a handkerchief and waved it around him before wiping his eyes. "You blessed this place when you left last time and I have had nothing but good fortune since then."

"No, sir," Nox said, shaking his head as he set Howard away from him and wagged a finger. "None of this should have happened to any of you but we've found the culprit and we're going to fix as much as we can."

"You've already worked a miracle here," Howard said to them and waved for Nelson to come closer. "I wasn't sure about that Tony at first. He's a little…" Howard twirled a hand by his ear. "But I don't know what I'd do without him now."

Nox laughed, soft and fond as he nodded. "Tony only *seems* like he doesn't have a clue. He runs my life at the university like clockwork and he's in love with learning and teaching. I knew the two of you would hit it off."

"Oh, it's been a joy to have him here!" Howard said sincerely. "He asks the most delightful questions and went right to work on all those boxes and sorted out the shelves in just two days. And you wouldn't believe how much Heidi laughs now, thanks to him."

"He's a sweet soul," Nox confirmed.

"That Aubrey is a delight too! So bubbly and smart. She did all the new displays and I've never met anyone who knows more about plants. She's a wonder!"

"I had a feeling they'd be a good fit here," Nox said absently, distracted by a tarot deck on the counter.

"You had a feeling?" Nelson raised a brow at Howard, indicating his skepticism.

The office door opened and Tony backed out, carrying a box and groaning loudly. "I'm not betting you again. You always cheat."

There was a maniacal giggle as Aubrey followed carrying a basket. "Hello, professor! Agent Nelson! This is a lovely surprise."

Nox grinned at her as he shuffled the cards, his clever, tattooed hands and deep purple fingernails momentarily distracting Nelson. Nox had several decks at home and would shuffle his favorites while thinking over a problem and would do a spread whenever he needed extra guidance on a personal matter. Nelson liked watching Nox shuffle and found it arousing, the way he handled his decks and respected them as if they had personalities of their own.

"I'll take this one," Nox told Howard, waving the deck. "It feels nice."

"It's on the house," he replied but Nox made a *pfft!* sound.

"It is not." He shook his head, ending the matter and smiling at Aubrey. "I wanted to see how Howard was doing and how the two of you were settling in here."

"I am having the time of my life!" Aubrey declared as she went to kiss his cheek.

"Oh! What are these?" Nox asked, poking at the small, colorful organza bags in the basket. They had drawstrings and were decorated with silver moons and stars.

"I thought I'd make some little crystal bundles to keep by the register. The purple bags are for stress relief, the blue are for clarity, the yellow are energizing, and the pink are what I'm calling our 'reading magick' bundles! They have fluorite, sodalite, amethyst, hematite, and clear quartz."

"Nice! Fluorite is amazing for boosting clarity!" Nox said as he went with Aubrey to the register, happily chatting about crystals and his new tarot deck.

Nelson raised a brow at Howard and Tony. "Anything I can do to help? Have you two had any trouble here or with...anyone lately?"

"Can't think of a single thing!" Howard declared with a pat to Nelson's lapel before taking himself off to join Nox and Aubrey.

Tony winced at Howard's back, then shook his head at Nelson. "I don't think he wants anyone to worry, but I think he's sleeping in the store. I found clothes and toiletries hidden in the storage room and there was an eye mask under the sofa when I came by to help him open yesterday."

"Is he having trouble with his finances?" Nelson wondered out loud but Tony snorted.

"I doubt that. Howard is way too trusting and logged me right into his bank account so I could order whatever I wanted for the store and pay bills."

Nelson recalled that Julian used to drive Howard home every evening and help him up to his apartment. "Damn it! I don't think he can go home by himself," he whispered to Tony and explained Howard and Julian's old routine.

"Why didn't he say something?" Tony groaned, tossing a hand at Howard.

"I suspect he didn't want to be more of a burden," Nelson replied and Tony made a knowing sound.

"I'll make sure he gets home in the evenings and talk to Heidi and Aubrey about picking him up in the mornings. I didn't even think about *why* he was staying and I had no idea he's on the second floor."

"We should see about finding him someplace more suitable so he doesn't feel so dependent on us," Nelson mused out loud, noting how much better it felt to care for and help Howard, than pity and worry about him. And Nelson noted how caring for Howard and helping at the store had helped Tony. He was in much higher spirits and looked just as relieved to have something useful to do in the face of so much pain and tragedy.

Nelson watched Nox, laughing with Howard and Aubrey. *Healing* with Howard and Aubrey. He hadn't forgiven Merlin and Clancy, or himself, but Nox was healing and helping Walt's victims grow their own support system. Nelson knew that he was seeing a *good* god at work. Instead of playing tricks like the Dagda or manipulating like Clancy, Nox's preferred forms of magick were caring and kindness and he craved peace and joy instead of power.

"Professor Mac's the best," Tony said, nudging Nelson. "Looks like you two are pretty serious."

"We are," Nelson confirmed, then looked away, blushing when Nox glanced in their direction.

"That's cool!" Tony gave Nelson's arm a friendly, encouraging punch. "I wouldn't call the professor a player, but he was…restless before he met you and he seems a lot more grounded now and like he knows what he wants."

Nelson blinked at Tony, picturing Nox levitating in one of his Dagda trances. "I wouldn't say he's grounded, but he has a good idea of what he wants."

"I need to put these away then see about a lunch run," Tony said as he bent to pick up the box. "Will you two be sticking around? We're getting food from the deli on the corner and they have the best homemade pickles."

"I'll ask Nox."

Nelson waved him off and went to the store's front window. Walt was back in town but Clancy was keeping him busy doing an inventory of all the files that had been lost due to the sprinkler "malfunction." But Nelson's hackles were still up as he searched the parking spots along the street and the lot diagonal from the bookstore.

"He's not here," Nox said quietly as he wandered over and Nelson nodded.

"I know. Do you think we've done enough to protect them?"

"Isn't that one of yours?" Nox asked, pointing at the dark sedan parked in the lot and facing the store. There were two agents in the front seat but Nelson hadn't forgotten how deceptively warm and welcoming Bippity Boppity Books could look from the outside. No one would have suspected that Julian Sherwood had drugged his father and Elsa Hansen, then carried her unconscious body out of the back door.

"We can only hunt the monsters we know about and make our friends strong enough to fight and defend each other. And I think we're doing that."

"I hope so." It was times like these when Nelson had to rely on faith and mysticism that he felt most out of his depth. Julian had taken the fall and died while Walt was still pretending to be the respectable professor-in-training, fiancé, and caring son.

Unfortunately, Nelson's hands were tied until they had viable legal evidence to act on.

"We're getting closer," Nox murmured, reading Nelson's mind, then turned when Aubrey marched over.

"I wanted to give you two a...heads up," she said, sniffing hard and tipping her chin back. "Tony told me about Walt. He told me everything and I know that it was him. He was the one who..." She squeezed her eyes shut, sucking in a shuddering breath. "I can do this! I swear!"

"Oh, gods! I'm so sorry!" Nox said as he rushed to her, cradling Aubrey's head as he pulled her into a tight embrace. "We were trying to shield you from as much of this as we could."

"I know but he used me to hurt all those people and I can't let him get away with that!" She leaned back in Nox's arms, her voice shaking angrily as she looked at him and Nelson. "I can't believe how stupid I've been but I am done being his fool. Tony said he's been helping you and feeding Walt disinformation and I want in."

Nelson groaned as he rubbed his temple. "She wants in," he said under his breath, then opened his mouth to warn her off but Nox stopped him.

"I think she should be in and I think Tony needs to stick to her like glue until this is over," he added, waving for him to join them.

"Why?" Nelson asked warily and she nodded.

"Not that I mind, but why?"

Nox hummed seriously as he studied Aubrey. "Tell me, Nelson: does she remind you of anyone?" He asked and gestured at her. "Imagine she was average height and a bit curvier with longer hair," he said, stopping Nelson's heart as he imagined her tied to an antler altar. He swore as he whipped out his phone.

"I want someone with you at all times. I'm arranging for another agent—a woman—to keep an eye on you until this is over. But I agree, it would be a good idea for you and Tony to stick together."

"What's going on?" Tony asked as he arrived with a cardigan for Aubrey, draping it over her shoulders and earning a pleased humph from Nox. Nelson was glad to see that Tony was already looking out for her. They had a message from Clancy warning that Walt was "in a state" about the destruction of his office and asking a lot of questions. No one expected Walt to buy it hook, line, and sinker, but Nelson worried he could become even more dangerous when rattled and confused.

"We think it would be a good idea for you to stay close to Aubrey," he said and she raised a hand.

"You still haven't explained why, beyond the fact that I remind you of someone who might be taller and have a banging body," she said, making Nox laugh.

"Guard her, Tony! At all costs," he added as he sobered. "She is very similar to our murder victim and the girls who were kidnapped. I'm worried that Walt might have been saving her for something terrible," he said quietly.

Tony's expression hardened and there was a fierce glint in his eyes behind his glasses. "I won't let him near her," he vowed, sliding an arm around Aubrey.

She leaned into him, but she was still defiant. "We all know what he is now and we won't let him hurt anyone else."

"Good girl," Nox said with a smile for Tony. "You'll have your hands full but I think you can manage."

"I won't give him too much trouble," she said, smiling up at Tony. "I wanted to die when he broke down and told me about Walt, but we promised we were going to get through this together. Tony's kept me going and he saved me last night after Walt came home. Tony took me to his mom's place but we told Walt I was staying with my friend, Amy. Walt thinks she's going through a bad breakup and doesn't want to be alone," she added with a shudder.

"Poor Amy," Nox said sincerely as he gave her arm an affectionate knead. "She has an amazing support system, though, and we're all going to help her get through this." He squinted at her, searching her face before he let out a thoughtful grunt. "Something's bothered you for a while and you'd like to tell us."

Her head pulled back and she reeled for a moment. "I might... But it's kind of..." Her nose wrinkled and she looked away as a rash crept up her neck.

Nelson could certainly sympathize. "There is *nothing* you could say that would offend or shock us."

She laughed softly and nodded. "I had a feeling but it's really..." She rolled her eyes and her laugh turned watery. "I thought there was something wrong with me but...*wow!* I'm so glad we never..." She widened her eyes at Nelson and Nox suggestively.

"Oh," Nox said and nodded as if he was taken aback. "When you say you thought it was you, do you mean you weren't attracted to him in that way or was it him?"

There was a hard snort from Tony. "If there was a problem, it was him."

"Stop!" Aubrey whispered as she elbowed him. "I thought it was kind of sweet, at first. Walt said he wanted to wait until we were married because I was the first girl he's ever loved and wanted to be with like that."

"He's a virgin?" Nox asked and sounded extremely dubious, earning a hard snort from Nelson.

"Maybe sex just isn't his thing," he countered.

Aubrey looked mystified as she held up her hands. "I assumed it was nerves or he was demisexual and needed more time. Which was fine but I was getting more and more concerned as the wedding got closer because he was so...sexless with me. I was afraid he'd never warm up, but I caught him once and he was sweating and swearing up a storm so I told myself it was a good sign."

"You caught him?" Nox prodded and Nelson noticed that Tony was hanging on her every word too.

She covered her face and groaned. "It was so weird, in hindsight. But I have always wanted a sweet nerd of my own to corrupt and Walt can be very sweet."

"He's incredibly manipulative," Nox said, making her laugh again.

"I'm seeing that now. But I got off work early one evening and hurried to the grocery store and back to our place so I could surprise him with a home-cooked meal. When I got home I found him...in the kitchen. He was...*finishing* in a copper bowl. I couldn't make out most of what he was saying but there was a 'Just like that!' in there that sounded like he had a good idea of what he wanted."

There was a knowing sound from Nox before he offered her an apologetic wince. "Is there a reason he might suspect that you're a virgin?" he asked carefully but a louder laugh burst from Aubrey and she covered her mouth to catch it.

"I made it very clear that I was not," she stated with a firm nod. "But Walt said that as far as he was concerned, I was, and that our first time together would feel like a true first for both of us."

"Ew!" Nox said, then cleared his throat. "I mean, that's very interesting. And ominous. You stay away from him, alright?"

Nelson snorted in agreement, sharing a quick nod with Tony. "Just find a way to stay away from Walt this weekend. We'll have Clancy send him back to Boston on Monday and keep him busy all week and hopefully, that'll give us enough time to find everything we need."

"It's almost over," Nox told them and both Tony and Aubrey looked relieved.

A woman with three teenage daughters came into the shop and the two sprang into action, leaving Nox and Nelson. Nox was looking particularly happy and confident as he hugged his new Tarot deck and watched them so Nelson decided to test something.

"We should go by Howard's place and talk to the landlord about his lease. Howard needs a ground-floor unit with easy access. Maybe an extra bedroom in case someone has to stay with him at night."

"Brilliant thinking." Nox took out his phone and started tapping on the screen as he headed to the register. "Let's say goodbye and see if Merlin's found anything."

"Alright," Nelson said as he followed, slightly concerned that Nox hadn't pounced on the opportunity to make a joke about his own nightly needs or bedrooms. He waited until they were in the car to try another test. "It's getting close to lunchtime. Want to make a detour and maybe grab a pizza?"

"I'm not that hungry yet," Nox replied, distracted as he read something on his phone. "Or we could have it sent to the house. Merlin thinks he may have found someone who knew a Forsythe who ran with some witches around Worlds End."

"Worlds End?" Nelson asked, making Nox chuckle.

"It's a state park in the wilds of the Pennsylvania Appalachians. Beautiful, rugged country that belonged to the Iroquois[1] people," he said, placing his hand over the center of his chest.

"Okay. Let's go home in case Merlin finds something," Nelson murmured as he steered out of the parking lot. "Are you sure you're alright?"

"Me? Of course. Why?" Nox raised a brow at Nelson, his arm stretching across the back of the seat.

"No reason. You just seem..." Nelson squinted at the road as he tried to put his finger on the difference. "You're...different but I can't explain it. Did you find the tea?"

"No, I didn't find the tea," Nox chuckled while giving Nelson's shoulder a reassuring squeeze. "I promise, I'm fine. But would you say I'm not as...cocky lately?"

"Maybe..."

---

1. **Iroquois** (Ir-ah-Koy/Ir-oh-Kwa) Native Americans of northeast North America and Upstate New York. They were known during the colonial years to the French as the "Iroquois League", and later as the "Iroquois Confederacy". The English called them the "Five Nations", including the **Mohawk** (Mo-Hawk), **Oneida** (Oh-ny-dah), **Onondaga** (On-on-dah-gah), **Cayuga** (Kay-yu-gah), and **Seneca** (Sen-uh-kuh). After 1722, the Iroquoian-speaking **Tuscarora** (Tus-cah-ro-rah) from the southeast were accepted into the confederacy, which became known as the Six Nations. The Confederacy likely came about between the years 1450 CE and 1660 CE as a result of the Great Law of Peace, said to have been composed by **Deganawidah** (Day-Gon-Na-We-Dah) the Great Peacemaker, **Hiawatha** (Hi-Ah-Wah-Thah), and **Jigonsaseh** (Gee-Gon-Saw-Say) the Mother of Nations.

Twelve

"Can you handle the rest of this?" Nox asked as he passed Nelson his dishtowel. They had shared a quiet dinner in the kitchen and Nox had yet to make a single sexual insinuation or improper offer.

"Sure. Everything alright?"

"Everything's alright," Nox insisted. "I want to pop back into the study and see if Merlin's already looked into Walt's dating history before Aubrey," he explained, handing Nelson the last plate to dry.

Nelson frowned and nodded as he took it. "Okay. You're sure everything's alright?" he asked, receiving a shrug from Nox.

"Fine. Why?"

"No reason. We usually go upstairs after dinner. Do you want me to join you?" he offered, but Nox shook his head.

"I won't be long but don't wait for me. Go ahead and get ready for bed." He offered Nelson an easy wave as he left, leaving more confusion than assurance in his wake.

"Okay..." Nelson called after him, but Nelson wasn't sure if everything was okay. He waited for the soft pounding of drums or an itch of restlessness and frowned when he felt *nothing* from Nox. "Is he broken?" he wondered out loud as he went back to drying, then glanced toward the study. A deeper frown furrowed his brow. "Are we?"

Nelson didn't have any past relationships to compare them against so he had no way of establishing a baseline or knowing if he had cause for concern. Perhaps Nelson was overreacting, but it wasn't like Nox to keep his hands to himself. It was rare for them to eat a whole meal without Nox finding an excuse to lick Nelson, yet he had remained engrossed in the conversation and hadn't made a single lewd remark.

It seemed churlish and a little childish to be upset about *not* being objectified for an entire day. But Nelson's concern only deepened as he climbed the stairs alone and undressed by himself in the bathroom. Was he too controlling the last time they "practiced"? Perhaps the shift in their power dynamic had become a turnoff for Nox or he wasn't feeling as enthusiastic about their "practice sessions" anymore.

Could that explain Nox's sudden increased attentiveness to the case? Was he less distracted by Nelson and was that a bad thing? They had been together for almost four months and it was normal, from what Nelson had read and observed as an investigator, for couples to cool off after they became more comfortable and familiar with each other.

In Nelson's case, he was *more* attached and enthralled. He had never felt anything akin to interest in another person's body before, but Nelson had grown to cherish the strange sensual connection he and Nox shared. Nelson reveled in the joy of touching and exploring Nox's body in ways he had never experienced with his own. And Nelson now understood Nox's body and his desires just as instinctively, if not better.

In fact, Nox's desire was *all* he understood or cared about and had become the core of Nelson's being—both sexually and emotionally. His life—personal and professional—was a gray hunk of clay before Nox and the Dagda had shaped him into a man with a real and *good* purpose. And Nelson's purpose was to love and serve Nox.

He showered and paced in a robe until Nox wandered into the room. It hadn't been a half hour but Nelson was nervously chewing on his thumbnail, afraid that he'd damaged or broken their bond by being too assertive and aggressive.

"Uh oh..." Nox said as he headed for the closet, unbuttoning his shirt. "What have I done this time?" he asked, making Nelson snort as he followed.

"I think it was me." He leaned against the doorjamb while Nox dropped his shirt in the hamper and stepped out of his jeans. "I don't want to say that you've been distant because we've been together all day but you haven't..." Nelson scrubbed the back of his neck and swore at his bare feet. "This is going to sound ridiculous but *you're* different and I think it's because I went too far last time," he said and a startled laugh burst from Nox.

"Too far? You were brilliant," he insisted, reaching to strip off his socks before he straightened and pushed his boxer briefs down. "So brilliant and I think my little experiment is working." His neck craned as he offered his lips. "Better than I expected, actually."

"What kind of experiment?" Nelson asked warily. They kissed and he groaned in relief as Nox slid an arm around his neck, drawing them closer.

"I wondered if I might be able to keep *Him* out of my head and our bed if I was more...*chaste* like you."

"Chaste?"

"Mmmhmm..." Nox took Nelson's hand and guided it lower and between them.

Nelson's knuckles and then his fingers brushed against something hard and smooth instead of hot, straining flesh. "What is —?" He leaned back, then gasped at the small black cage nestled against Nox's groin where an erection usually resided. "What did you do?" he demanded as he pulled Nox out of the closet and into the bedroom where there was more light.

"It's a cage," Nox said simply, but Nelson shook his head, growing more agitated.

"What if you break...it?" he asked, waving at Nox's caged penis, then sweeping a shaking hand through his hair in distress.

Nox laughed. "Break it? We're just keeping it in time-out for a while by restricting the blood flow so we can see what happens."

"No." Nelson shook his head, then grunted when he was shoved and fell back on the bed. "Take it off, Nox."

"Shhh! Hear me out and I can't, you still have the key."

"That's what it's for?" Nelson tried to roll and run for his wallet but Nox straddled him.

"Stop and listen!" Nox braced his hands on Nelson's chest, easing him back onto the bed. "You were on to something with the mystical edging and I thought I'd take it one step further and try a little magickal chastity during the day. I'm trying to stay in my Nelsonspace."

"Your Nelsonspace?" He had so many questions but Nelson's brain was short-circuiting as Nox flicked the halves of the robe out of the way and slid lower. Need and heat swelled as Nox licked and nibbled his way down Nelson's chest, nipping and sucking on nipples and squeezing and scratching his ass and thighs. "We should slow down," he said, but Nelson moaned and nodded frantically when Nox gripped his hard-on.

"I don't think we have to now, you see," Nox murmured, his lips gliding over Nelson's skin. His tongue swirled around Nelson's navel and he gasped when Nox's teeth dug into his side. "I'm not at all a sub in the bedroom, as you've probably noticed," Nox continued silkily, rubbing his lips in the neatly trimmed hairs at the base of Nelson's now painfully erect shaft. "But I bought a few cages a while ago to see what they were like." He inhaled deeply, making a euphoric sound as his nose trailed up Nelson's length. "They *did not* work before! They made me *nuts*, not being able to touch myself and I felt like I had this...void where my twitchy dick was supposed to be. That freaked me out—then— because I didn't have a reason or a partner I trusted enough to submit to like that. The last few days have been totally different. I handed you the key and everything was...quiet. I knew I could trust you to let *it* out of its cage when the time was right, so I could focus on everything else."

"You trust me? I barely know—" Nelson stopped when Nox shushed him.

He lapped at the head of Nelson's cock, groaning in delight. "I trust you completely and I realized that we might be able to work around *Him* by embracing your soft Dom instincts. Which then inspired me to engage in a bit of role reversal by exploring my inner Nelson. And it had occurred to me that while the cage and chastity might not be *my* kink, it was yours."

Nelson stared up at the wrought iron branch canopy, attempting to untangle his thoughts as Nox's lips and tongue wreaked havoc on his ability to concentrate. "How? I've never worn one and I don't have a chastity kink. I didn't have *any* kinks before you," he babbled, earning an amused chuckle from Nox as he sucked.

"You don't need a cage because you exist in a state of natural chastity when I'm not poking at you and winding you up. Now, I can be like you and exist in that Nelson-like state of mental clarity, thanks to this cage. It isn't nerve-wracking this time because I trust you implicitly, Nelson. I barely felt *Him* intruding on my thoughts because *He* couldn't use my libido and my feelings to manipulate me. The cage blocked most of that and I was able to focus while learning what it feels like to keep *Him* out."

His lips tightened around Nelson's length as they lowered, making it difficult for him to process everything he was learning. But that was the point, he realized as Nox's head bounced slowly and Nelson's concentration and control crumbled. "I think I get it... Your brain worked better because your dick was in a cage. Are you sure that won't have long-term—?"

"There are men who live like this for months at a time and only take them off to bathe or when they're going through metal detectors. I'm not planning to make this a permanent addition to my wardrobe. I love you and I love learning more about who *you* are in here when we're alone," Nox explained in a low, sultry purr before taking Nelson deep into his throat and scrambling his brain anew.

"Fuck! That's—!" Nelson gasped and thrashed on the mattress.

"Mmmm...." Nox sucked hard as he raised his head and released Nelson's cock with a loud *pop!* "I can feel the frenzy building in you and it's so sexy. I'm aroused, but I don't feel the same wild need to get off. I'm more focused on *you* and my desire to satisfy your needs. That has nothing to do with *Him* and I don't think *He* can touch us if I find my Nelsonspace." He rose on his knees and crawled to Nelson's lips for a languorous, intoxicating kiss.

"What does that mean?" he panted when Nox reached for the lube.

"The subspace is a state of deep, blissed-out emptiness that some subs can achieve, like a submissive sex trance. All they exist for is pleasing their Dom—being the means and the receptacle of their pleasure."

"That, I understand," Nelson said raggedly. "Not the blissed-out part, but I was empty before you and now I just want to please you." He smothered a curse as his cock was coated with a generous amount of lube.

Nox guided the head to his hole and slowly sat back, wrapping Nelson's shaft to the hilt in slick, gripping heat. "Not empty." Nox whimpered and rocked forward on his knees. "So, so full of you. That's all I feel and it's really good, Nelson. It's just *you*. It's the Nelsonspace."

"Okay." He nodded jerkily as he held onto Nox's hip and bucked off the bed, making them both gasp and swear. "I like that. You're sure it's safe?"

"Oh, I hope so. I couldn't pull off more than a weak, ruined orgasm while wearing one of these before, but that's what I'm hoping for this time."

Nelson's hands locked around Nox's hips, halting him. "Ruined?"

"It's fine! I promise!" he said, planting his hands on Nelson's chest and setting a faster, slapping pace. "Really fine," he said with a drunken giggle, his head bobbing loosely as he nodded. "It's about the build-up and the build-up and the build-up with *you* and then skipping the bang. Because the bang is where *He* gets me. And I don't think *He* can get me if I'm hiding in the Nelsonspace."

"Nelsonspace."

The idea that such a space could exist within Nox touched Nelson deeply and sparked a wildly possessive urge within him to claim and protect it. He didn't understand BDSM, but he didn't have to because Nox was creating new terms and kinks to fit *their* unique chemistry and needs. He was doing it to give them more control and freedom from the Dagda and Nox had trusted Nelson with the physical key to his sexual pleasure.

"I like the sound of that," Nelson said as he rolled them and wound both of Nox's legs around his waist. "And you'll tell me if we get too close, if you start to hear bees and harps? Because I might not be able to stop, Nox." He captured Nox's lips for a kiss, starved after just one day of good behavior.

"I'll tell you. I *want* you to lose control, Nelson." Nox held tight, his fingers twisting in Nelson's hair so they were nose-to-nose, their ragged breaths synchronized as he kept them locked together. "Do your worst. Or, your best," he amended with a swat to Nelson's flank.

"I will," Nelson vowed, pulling Nox hard onto his cock.

A high, tight squeak burst from Nox. "Fuck!"

"Are you okay?" Nelson went to pull out but Nox's heels dug into his ass.

"*Yes.*" He gave Nelson another slap on the back. "Now, don't stop unless I scream about the bees."

"Got it," Nelson said and rolled his hips, grinding deep and hard.

That was where he longed to be and it wasn't long before Nelson was lost in the slick slide of his body, driving into Nox's.

He was tight and hot and Nelson cried at how good and right it felt when it was just them. For the first time since Nelson had set eyes on Nox, they were truly alone and there was no reason to hold back.

"Nox!" He lapped at Nox's tongue, drunk on the taste of *his* lips, not the heady euphoria of kissing a god and floating into golden rapture. "Nox, Nox, Nox..."

"Yes. *Your* Nox," he promised Nelson, his arms strong and his voice steady as they held him and urged him on.

Nox was lucid and solid, so Nelson gave into the warm flickering of his nerves and the pleasure pooling in his core. He sank into Nox's mouth as his hips thrust faster and Nelson was pulled into a different bliss when he shattered. He closed his eyes, tears spilling down his cheeks as he spilled into Nox, a hot, joyful tide that rushed from Nelson's soul.

"Nox, Nox, Nox, Nox, Nox..."

There was simply nothing else and Nelson had never felt happier or lighter as the last of his tremors faded and his breathing settled. Nox was still clear and so beautiful, flushed and sweating as he chanted soft, loving words, praising Nelson for his performance and for trusting *him* in return.

"Can I get the key now?" Nelson asked, raising his head and pushing off the bed. "I want to lick you clean and let you fly."

"I'd like that," Nox replied as he calmly traced Nelson's cheek. "If you think we're ready."

"We're ready."

Nelson made sure it was the last calm thought Nox had that evening and that he wouldn't be able to walk or sit without feeling a twinge the next day.

Thirteen

Am I any better than Clancy and Merlin?

Nox felt a whiff of guilt as he sipped his coffee and prepared to ruin Nelson's morning. His aura was so light when he awoke and Nelson's lips kept tilting into the most adorable smiles as he shaved and dressed.

"Get over yourself." Nox had overheard Nelson grumble to his reflection after whispering "Nelsonspace" to himself. It was magick, watching Nelson blush and stammer every time their eyes met and their hands touched. But Merlin had yet to hear back from his source about a Forsythe at Worlds End and Nox was done waiting. He knew Walt's mother was the key to understanding who he was and how he had become so twisted.

"I want to visit Sheila Forsythe today," he announced when Nelson had finished his coffee and whole-grain toast with peanut butter and fresh berries.

"Come on, Nox," he groaned as his head fell. "We don't have a warrant and Walt will know we're on to him if we—"

"*We* won't," Nox said pointedly, widening his eyes at Nelson. "I have a plan but you're going to have to trust me."

Nelson's brows fell as he nodded. "Of course, I trust you but *she* could be dangerous and there's no telling what's in that house that might hurt you. My instincts are telling me that it's the last place Walt wants you poking around and where he's set his worst traps."

"I know," Nox said, smiling as he came around the table so he could kiss away Nelson's frown. "But he's no match for me. I'm in my Nelsonspace and I've never felt stronger."

"Is that so?" Nelson leaned back and searched Nox's eyes and his face. "I *think* you mean it and it isn't bullshit," he mused out loud.

"I'm ready, Nelson," Nox stated clearly. "I can do this without upsetting her and giving us away."

Alright." Nelson relented, but he made several attempts to change Nox's mind as they drove across the bridge to New Jersey and Pennsville.

"That's the place," Nelson said, pointing at the windshield and the small, white two-story house at the end of the street. The paint was dingy and peeling and the screened-in front porch sagged ominously.

"Drive around the corner and let me out," Nox whispered as he dug in his pocket for a length of red thread and tied it around his wrist.

"It looks like she's home. Are you sure you want to do this?"

"Don't worry. She won't remember," Nox murmured, searching the property and taking stock of all the warding. He could see that something had recently been buried by the mailbox and on the other visible corner of the lot. Crows' claws, feathers, and beaks had been hung from the tree in the front yard and were strung around the porch.

"I don't think you should go in without me," Nelson stated firmly, but Nox flashed him an apologetic wince.

"Have to. Her hackles will definitely be up if she sees a federal agent on her doorstep and I can't shield the both of us," he said with a shrug, ignoring Nelson's twitching eye and jaw muscle. "I'll be fine and I won't be long."

"Aside from the procedural nightmare you could unleash, could we take a moment to review all the reasons why this could be uniquely dangerous for *you*?" Nelson asked calmly. "I don't like whatever it is that you're about to do."

"I'll be fine." Nox shook his head as he studied the house. "He booby trapped this place like Julian's and I can tell she's even more batshit than he is. But none of this crow business scares me," he said with a dismissive wave at the house. "That's like putting out a welcome mat, as far as I'm concerned. Sheila Forsythe's magick is just as twisted and ridiculous as her son's but I think she's the key. *She's* the start of all of this, mark my words," he said as he held up a finger.

Nelson stared at it for a long moment, then flicked Nox a hard look. "You had better not be bullshitting me, Nox. My instincts are screaming that this isn't good for you. I don't want to have to carry you back to Merlin to fix."

"I'll be fine but I'm afraid there's nothing for it," Nox said with feigned regret, then sat forward so he could get the black salt he had stashed in the glove box. He opened it, slid the original manuals and maps aside, and found the small vial with the cork stopper.

"What's that?" Nelson leaned and checked to see if Nox had anything else hiding in there.

Nox closed the glove box and pulled his father's pocketknife from his jeans. "It's better if you don't know."

"You're doing dark magick," Nelson realized as he slowed the Continental and sidled along the curb.

Nox nodded, scanning the windows on the side of the house. The back of the property faced acres of state-owned forest that acted as a buffer between the neighborhood and the highway.

"I'm going to show Walt how it's done and why intent

matters," Nox murmured, then pointed. "They have a lot of privacy."

"That's why my gut's screaming." He had a roll of antacids out and thumbed a lozenge into his mouth. "Who knows what they're hiding in that rundown house and on that land. Most of this is getting torn down and a new subdivision is going up," he said, gesturing at the lots across from Sheila's with the remainder of the roll. "She's the only holdout. The house on the other side of hers has been empty and on the market since the owner died four years ago."

"Lots of privacy," Nox amended, then slid across the bench and pressed a kiss to Nelson's cheek. "Shouldn't be more than ten, fifteen tops," he promised and slid back and out of his door before Nelson could stop him. "Take a few laps around the block," he suggested as he closed the door and offered Nelson a jaunty salute.

Nelson followed until they reached the corner and Nox turned on the sidewalk. He silently ordered Nelson to relax and have faith, then used the knife to nick his left palm. Nox squeezed as he jogged up the walkway and climbed the porch steps. Turning his back to the street, Nox quickly tapped black salt onto his bloody palm and shoved the empty vial into his pocket. Then, Nox focused on his fingertips on his right hand, summoning heat. They grew warmer and warmer until they burned and a spark jumped from the tips. He touched the small flame to the blood and salt in his left hand, creating a loud hiss and a thick black plume.

"I sall gae intill smoake," Nox whispered and blew the smoke and ash at the door. He pressed his palm against it and repeated the charm. When he removed his hand there was a print that would fade when Nox passed through it again. "I sall gae intill smoake," he said, smiling as he gave the doorbell a good press.

The door cracked open a moment later and a small, frail older woman with long salt-and-pepper hair squinted up at Nox from under the chain. "Can I help you?" she asked, sounding wary and confused. She was bundled protectively in a clean, but faded and ratty mauve housecoat.

"Sorry! Walt didn't tell you I was coming by?" he asked cheerfully as he retrieved the empty vial. "He wanted me to show you this," he said and she frowned as she eased the door shut and took it off the chain.

"What is it?" she asked as she opened the door and reached for the vial.

Nox set it on her palm and clasped their hands together. "The first handis that handles thee, the devillis blind thy mind to time and me," he sang as if he were telling her a lullaby.

"What?" She attempted to pull her hand away but Nox held on.

"The first handis that handles thee, the devillis blind thy mind to time and me," he repeated again, even softer.

"Oh..." she said, nodding dazedly.

"The first handis that handles thee, the devillis blind thy mind to time and me," Nox said once more as he turned her and opened the door for them. "Why don't you make us a pot of tea?"

"Alright." She nodded again but didn't take her eyes off of Nox's face as they walked. "Have we met before?"

"Possibly!" Nox replied, giving her shoulder an encouraging pat as he looked around the dark, cluttered house. "Not again," he whimpered at the waist-high piles of magazines and mail clogging the entryway, searching through the dusty dim for the kitchen. There wasn't as much rotting food and the plumbing worked as far as Nox could smell. Nox would point that out to Nelson when they came back, to cheer him up. The tote bins, boxes, and stuffed trash bags were typical in a hoarder's house and would be a challenge, but Nox drew back at all the dead, stuffed birds in the living room. "The first handis that handles thee, the devillis blind thy mind to time and me," he said and waited to get a closer look until Sheila paused and blinked at the kitchen, as if she couldn't remember why she was headed there.

Nox made his way through the living room, grimacing at the

sofa, sinking under the weight of all the boxes and bins piled in a mound on it. He reminded himself that taxidermy was an art as he scanned all the crows on the built-in bookshelves and the mantle. There were dozens, draped in cobwebs like frozen sentinels, creeping Nox out as he went to get a closer look at a rather mediocre painting of a dark woman and a battle crow over the mantle. Nox's head tilted as he searched for the artist's name and rolled his eyes at the signature.

"Walt painted this? You must be so proud," he said, earning a faint, dreamy hum from the kitchen.

"He's my pride and joy," she mumbled.

"Did he collect these birds too?"

"No. They're mine. My daddy taught me to collect them and keep them. But Walt knows they're magick."

"Did you teach him magick?" he asked, turning away from the painting and making his way around the room to the stairs.

"Some," Sheila said with a faint, distant chuckle. "But he found my daddy's books and taught himself most of it."

"Your daddy?" Nox asked, propping himself against the banister and crossing his ankles. "Who was your daddy?"

Her smile was wide and uneven and her eyes took on an even dreamier haze. "He changed his name to Cathal [1]Forsythe after they tried to ruin him, but he was Cathal O'Casey. He was a *great* sorcerer and he had his own coven but he was too powerful and he knew too much so they tried to destroy him."

"Cathal O'Casey... Why do I know that name?" Nox wondered out loud, making a note to ask Merlin later. "Is he the one you learned from?"

Sheila shook her head. "No. Daddy died when I was just a girl. We kept his things but my mama didn't want anything to do with them. She joined another coven after he died and that's where I learned. And from Walt. He's taught me so much, my brilliant boy."

"I can see how proud you are of him. What about Walt's

father?" Nox asked and there was a marked change in her demeanor.

Her face twisted into a scowl, shedding the dreamlike haze. "That...*man*," she spat. "He might have forgotten about us, but Walt knows his father."

"Easy," Nox murmured gently as he drew the bitterness from her and searched her aura. "The two of you got along just fine without him, didn't you?" he whispered, making her smile again.

"Yes, we did," she replied as she slipped into another happy memory. "Walt taught me more than he ever could and my little boy is going to be a king."

"A king?" Nox asked, feigning wonder. "He must be powerful, indeed."

"Yes!" She nodded jerkily, her eyes misting over as she trudged toward the back door. "He is wedded to the mother goddess and is her earthly consort."

Nox's brows jumped at her dreamy delight. "Oh? And how did he wed her? On Samhain?" he guessed and received another jerky nod as Sheila pointed at the door at the end of the short hall.

"We've always worshiped the mother goddess on Samhain."

"How?" Nox whispered as he pushed away from the stairs and went to get a look at their ritual site.

A faded laugh fluttered from Sheila as she clutched her breast, fondling it through the housecoat. "The way we always have."

"I see..." Nox grimaced at her as he passed and glanced at the kitchen. Like the rest of the house, it was packed with just enough room to get to the sink and the refrigerator. From the looks of things, Sheila didn't believe in throwing *anything* away except food waste. There were stacks of flattened cereal, frozen dinner, and Kraft Mac & Cheese boxes filling nearly every flat surface. No thought was given to decoration, save for what was necessary for Sheila's practice. And Sheila's practice was not kitchen or hearth-based like Nox's. She practiced in secret—in the shadows—so her workroom was where he'd find it. "Our tea," he reminded her, earning a slow nod.

"It'll just be a moment," she said as she left him in the hall and headed for the kettle on the stove.

"Take your time," Nox insisted. "The first handis that handles thee, the devillis blind thy mind to time and me."

He left her stuck there as he stepped outside and Nox was immediately aware of the stench of bad magick. There were echoes of old chants and he could see wisps of smoke as the day grew dark around the house and the lot. Nox covered his face, blocking the skunky fumes as he skipped down the back porch's rickety steps.

"Nocht,"[2] he commanded, his hand sweeping at the yard around him and Nox was surrounded by smoking torches, while a Key of Solomon was carved and burned into the middle of the lawn. Nox shuddered at the bed in the center, fashioned from pallets and an old mattress and draped with white sheets and cheap lace. "No, don't show me," he said, covering his eyes and turning back to the house. "And we thought the MacCrorys were bad?"

Nox chuckled as he climbed the kitchen steps and let himself in. The only thing separating the Forsythes from the MacCrorys was better plumbing and college degrees. "How's the tea coming along?" he asked Sheila, shaking her from her deep trance so she could talk. "Can I give you a hand with something?"

"No. It'll just be another moment."

"That's fine. Take your time," Nox repeated, keeping his voice as gentle as his intentions. He was there only to learn, not to take anything or to do any harm to her.

"Alright," she said and paused to look out the back window, so Nox left her to take a peek upstairs.

Walt had the larger bedroom at the end of the hall. It was obvious that it was his from the chill and the soft hisses Nox heard as he eased the door open. Unlike the rest of the house, the room was immaculate aside from the school medals and trophies on the shelves. There wasn't a trace of dust in the room. The simple white sheets and blue comforter were clean and free of wrinkles, ready for his next visit.

Gray smudges blurred various spots around the room, hinting at layers upon layers of fading charms throughout the years. "What could you possibly have to hide in here?" Nox mused as he went to the desk.

The drawers were empty and Nox sensed that it had been cleansed to hide the residue of Walt's dark tinkering. A quick scan of the closet revealed some older suits and shoes, but nothing of interest. There was nothing under the bed or in the bedside table either so Nox went to check out Sheila's room.

"Whoa." Nox whistled as he strolled into the smaller bedroom. "So unhealthy," he said, his eyes wide as he took in all the pictures of Walt. They covered the walls, obscuring the room's dimensions and disorienting Nox. He felt like he was in a teenage girl's room in the 80s or the 90s. Framed photos of Walt covered the dresser and the table next to the twin-size bed.

A quick check of the drawers, closet, and under the bed revealed very little of interest but Nox stopped when he spotted a familiar face in two of the pictures on Sheila's bedside table. "What in the...?" Nox pulled his sweater's sleeve down and used the cuff to cover his hand as he inspected both pictures of Sheila and Clancy, too stunned to process what he was holding.

In one photo, Clancy had an arm around Sheila and he was holding an award and the other was of the two of them in what appeared to be an art gallery. "Now what have you done, Clance?" Nox groaned at the sour twisting of his stomach as he looked around. They were the *only* pictures in the room that weren't of Walt.

"Or are they the first pictures of Walt?" Nox wondered out loud as he put them back and got his phone out to take a picture. He'd show Clancy and get an explanation. "Now, where's their workroom? They have to have a permanent altar somewhere," he predicted, leaving Sheila's room as he found it.

In the hallway, Nox listened as he searched the ceiling but it was completely still overhead. The attic space would be small and vaulted and not dark enough for their purposes, so Nox headed back downstairs.

"It's supposed to be warmer this weekend," he said to Sheila as he passed the kitchen. She was still at the window and nodded.

"The bluebells are already blooming."

Nox spotted the basement door on the other side of the refrigerator and slipped past Sheila without disturbing her, then paused. "Tell me…" he started, his hand on the door's knob. "What college did you go to and what did you study?"

"Me?" She frowned at the window. "I went to Princeton and I studied anthropology."

"Did you know Darach Clancy?" he asked quietly, but she still flinched and blinked at the glass.

"That's not what he called himself when he was at Princeton."

Nox sucked in a startled breath. "I see. Blind thy eye…" he said soothingly, tracking the heaviness of her gaze as it drifted back to the kettle. "That's it. You were making tea."

"I was making tea," she agreed flatly.

He made sure she was lost in the task before opening the door and silently slipping around it. He ducked to check that the steps were clear before flipping the light switch. It looked like a normal basement with a simple cement floor until Nox came around the wall.

"Now, we're talking," he said as he took out his phone and began documenting the sigils and symbols spray-painted on the walls and on the ceiling. Much of it was dedicated to the Badb, but it was interspersed with themes common to Hecate worship.

Nox was intrigued by the smatterings of Satanic symbology but drew back when he saw the triskelion with horns on the basement's south wall. There were numerous pictures of the girls, but Nox was drawn to the picture of himself in the center, under the painted swirls. His eyes had been blacked out and red X was drawn over his mouth.

"Weird," Nox said as he turned from the photos, then snorted at the washer and dryer and the shelves under the stairs.

The shelves were lined with jars of herbs and dried flowers. He recognized several common tinctures amongst the labeled vials and humphed in approval at the array of crystals and sands. Sheila kept a well-stocked pantry, at least.

Everything else was so...random and sick. The basement, the ritual in the backyard, and the warding around the house was a curious melange of Hellenic and druidic magick with a sprinkling of dark, Satanic magick. Nox could see how the different threads had been woven together, but the connections were so tenuous and the intent so clumsy and selfish, it was a wonder that any of it had worked for Walt.

"Spite," Nox reminded himself. Spite could be powerful but it was brittle and fickle. He took one last look around Walt's sanctum, memorizing every detail because nothing in the basement was unintentional. Walt kept complete control of the basement and his room and he kept his mother hidden and trapped in her cluttered house, delusional and obsessed. "I've seen enough," he said and headed back upstairs. "You'll only be needing one cup of tea. You're all alone. No one was here," he told her, receiving a dazed nod as Sheila trudged to the cabinet by the sink. She opened it and removed one mug from the precarious collection of dishes crammed behind the door.

"There's no one here but me," she said and he watched as she prepared her tea and shuffled into a small den by the back door. He leaned so he could see her lower into a rocker and swaddle herself in an afghan blanket.

Nox showed himself out, filling his lungs with fresh air as soon as he reached the sidewalk. The Continental pulled alongside him and Nelson took off as soon as Nox was inside and buckled.

"Are you alright?" Nelson asked, throwing quick glances at Nox as he drove.

He nodded, his gaze stretching past the windshield as he

considered everything he'd learned. "It was a piece of cake. But we have to get back to Georgetown. I need to talk to Clancy. *Immediately.*"

---

1. **Cathal** (Co-Hull) Irish name meaning vigilant.
2. **Nocht** (NhocT) Reveal

Fourteen

"I have to talk to Clancy."

That was all Nox would say during the forty-five minute drive back to Georgetown. He chewed on his nails, mumbling names and dates, shaking his head and saying "she" had to be wrong.

"Why do I know the name Cathal O'Casey?" Nox asked when they strode into the study and Merlin spun away from the board. Clancy was seated behind Nox's desk and looked up from his laptop, frowning as Merlin let out a belligerent snort.

"Cathal O'Casey? Please don't tell me he's somehow involved." he sneered and Clancy humphed in agreement.

"The man was a dangerous charlatan," Clancy said and went back to typing.

"He was, indeed," Merlin said. "Tried to pass himself off as a... magickal Manson and was building himself a little family in the country out by Worlds End in the 60s. But there were whispers of dark rituals and there had been some squabbling about the number of wives Cathal had taken."

That got a chuckle out of Clancy. "Too many wives has been the downfall of many cults and kings throughout the ages."

Nox nodded in agreement. "Speaking of, did you, by any

chance, have sex with Sheila Forsythe in the late 80s?" he asked, making Clancy jump and splutter as he reared back.

He shook his head, looking offended. "I didn't have sex with *anyone* in the 80s."

Merlin hummed knowingly. "I cannot tell you how many times I wish he had gotten laid. An unbearable decade, let me tell you."

Nox's lips twisted as he considered what he had learned at Sheila's, then gasped when he remembered the pictures. "What about these?" He got out his phone and quickly tapped at the screen until he found the pictures of Clancy and Sheila.

Clancy snatched the phone and stared for a moment, then let out a startled "Oh!" He gave Nox a loaded look. "I do know who that is but I *did not* have sex with that woman. She was an assistant to one of the other professors when I taught at Princeton and went by Patrick Darby. But I *barely* knew her. I don't think I even knew her name at the time."

"This is Walt's mom, Clance! She knows that *you* changed names and moved to Georgetown so no one would notice that you weren't aging."

"She was Walt's mom..." Clancy stared at the picture, shaking his head at the photo. "It was time for me to move on but I thought I was leaving before matters got out of hand. But I didn't pay any attention to her. I didn't want to encourage her in any way. You know how some students and assistants get, Nox. They take everything you say too seriously and too literally and they start turning up in places they shouldn't."

"Like stalkers?" Nox suggested and Clancy hissed as he shrugged.

"I didn't think she had reached that point. I *never* gave her any encouragement and I thought I had disappeared from her orbit before she could become fixated."

"She was definitely fixated and I don't think it got better when she realized you were living another life just down the road in Georgetown."

Merlin chortled as he made the applicable notes on Sheila's half of the board. "You could still get away with that in the 80s, before the internet. It helped that Clancy lived like a monk and spent much of his time in the field with Nox's grandfather. He'll have to retire now and lay low or get better at makeup."

"Or I could go away and age with Ingrid," Clancy countered. "That was always the hope, when Nox no longer needed me," he added with a cautious look at Nox.

Nelson cleared his throat and held up a hand, requesting a turn. "Does your wife know about...?" He gave Clancy a pointed look, earning an amused chuckle as he nodded.

"Her family has been in this area for as long as we've been here and they keep their own vow," Clancy explained and Nelson shook his head.

"That doesn't surprise me. Is it only Irish families and Celtic gods?" he asked, earning a titter of laughter from Merlin at the board.

"Of course, not. Most cultures have their own practices and gods. And like ours, their gods sleep because Christianity took most of their followers or drove them underground."

"Strange that Christ never came back when he had most of the world on his side and that the Dagda is stirring as Christianity grows more unpopular..." Nelson said, earning a bemused snort from Clancy.

"Strange or telling?"

Merlin made an impatient sound as he waved his arms. "Nothing could be more boring or pointless than Christianity at the moment. Why did you want to know about Cathal O'Casey? He would be far more interesting of a topic if he's somehow relevant to the investigation."

Nox's eyes took on a wild glow as he went to the board. "I have a feeling he's a lot more relevant than Christ, seeing as he was Sheila Forsythe's father."

That got a loud, long gasp from Merlin and Clancy's face was red as he rose from his seat. "Walt's grandfather was Cathal O'Casey?"

"Yup," Nox replied and nodded at them.

Merlin quickly turned the board around like he was assisting on a game show. "We definitely need a family tree and this will require a great deal of research because Cathal O'Casey was known to be a liar and a snake oil salesman when it came to his history and his dogma," he began as he wrote Cathal's, Sheila's, and Walt's names on the board. "I had suspected that O'Casey was an alias and I can see why his wives and children would have dropped it."

There was a chuckle from Clancy as he joined Merlin and tapped on Cathal's name. "It's basically Casey O'Casey or Cathal O'Cathalsaigh. They mean the same thing: Vigilant of the Vigilant."

"He was anything but vigilant," Merlin replied, sniffing in disdain at the board. "He was a conman and a trickster who knew just enough about dark magick to be dangerous," he said, and Nox nodded.

"We've seen his strange dogma and how Walt tried to splice it with ours in New Castle," he said, shaking his head at their names. "Sheila said that Walt learned from her father's old books..." He stared into the distance, then shook his head. "Walt probably has them hidden away and I doubt he'll give me a reading list," he said and Nelson cast him a dubious look.

"You seem to be doing fine without them and we don't have time to search for copies of ancient books so you can cram before your face-off."

"You're right, of course," Nox said with a saucy wink. "I don't need to hit the books to beat Walt, but we know *who* he is now and we have a better understanding of what he knows."

Nelson nodded slowly as he held up his notepad and reviewed his notes. "He's the delusional grandson of a known conman, who was raised by a delusional woman, who thinks he's Clancy's son, *and* a descendant of the Badb."

"He *is not* my son," Clancy stated emphatically and Nox grinned.

"You sure about that?" He wiggled his brows at him but Clancy grimaced at Nox.

"Am I sure? Nách mór an diabhal thú!"[1] he said, throwing a hand at Nox and making him laugh. "There was no one before Ingrid for...centuries. I didn't see the point until the prophecy and the vow could be broken."

The smile faded from Nox's face as he regarded Clancy. "You want out. You want to grow old and die," he said and Clancy nodded, his eyes shimmering.

"That's all I've ever wanted for us. But I can't—won't—age and die unless I leave you and I can't do that as long as we're bound together by the prophecy."

"I'm so sorry, Darach," Merlin said hoarsely, coughing to recover his voice. "I was very wrong. I accused you of being a brutal, ruthless cunt who would sell out his own family to protect Nox and the MacIlwraiths but that couldn't have been further from the truth."

Clancy shrugged it off. "I'm sure I've accused you of worse over the years. We both did what we thought was right and made an almighty mess of it."

"I understand now," Nox said sadly, then glanced at Merlin. "What about you? Have you been trapped too?"

Merlin's head pulled back and he laughed. "Gods no, lad! I'm rather content and happy to serve the MacIlwraiths, for the most part," he said as he batted his lashes at Nox, then gave him a hard look. "When they listen and avoid flying too close to the sun."

"You're sounding like Clancy again," Nox warned, wagging a finger at Merlin and making the older man sigh at him.

"The *only* burden I have ever carried was the loss of my charges, *my children*," he added heavily. "It has never been easy to let go but every member of this family has been a blessing and it's been an honor to care for you all through the ages."

There.

Nelson nodded as he shut his notepad and tucked it into his coat's pocket. Those were the *true* reasons behind Clancy and Merlin's betrayal. He couldn't fathom—no matter how much they explained or how rational their reasons seemed—how or why they would do it when there was no denying how much they loved Nox.

But both men were fighting to save a beloved child and to hold onto their families. Clancy wanted to hang on to the life he'd built and age with his wife and daughters and Merlin was struggling to protect the last of the MacIlwraiths—his family.

"I'm sorry," Nelson said simply, crossing his arms over his chest as he regarded them. "I came into this with nothing to lose, looking for something to live for. But the stakes couldn't be higher for you three," he said and Nox's eyes narrowed as he considered, then shook his head.

"Not as high as they were for those girls. Whatever your intentions were, Walt hijacked them and we have to deal with the consequences of that before we can forgive each other."

Nelson made a weary sound as he turned to the board. "Nox is right. We know his motive now, too. Walt came to Georgetown ready to present himself to his father only to learn that Clancy already had a son—a son he'd never replace."

"So he came up with a plan to replace me once he figured out who we were and that Clancy was using him to do his dirty work and grow the cult," Nox continued, his face pinching as he shook his head at Walt's name. "And he decided to teach Clancy, me, and my three a lesson."

"Such a shame..." Merlin clicked his teeth. "He might have made something good of himself if he hadn't been lied to and warped by his mother and her awful father."

"Oh!" Nox's finger shot up and he tapped his forehead when a memory tickled the corner of his brain. "Dad said something to me during our tea party!" He scrunched his face harder, then gasped as he smiled at Merlin. "Dad said *'Ask Merlin why the Ó*

Murchadha[2] were chosen all those years ago when the MacIlwraiths had that one magickal girl.'"

Merlin smothered a shaking, watery laugh. "Lucas! You brilliant, brilliant boy!" He was crying as he hurried across the study and searched the bookshelves. "Where is it?" He sounded frantic as he hunted, then hopped and pointed. "Up there! Would you be so kind, Darach?" Merlin asked Clancy. "That gold one in the middle," he said excitedly as Clancy reached for an ancient-looking leather-bound book from the top shelf.

"I haven't seen this in ages," Clancy said, taking it down and carefully passing it to Merlin.

"What is that?" Nox asked as he followed him to the desk.

Merlin used a sleeve to smooth any dust off of the cover, his hands shaking. "This is the history of the MacIlwraiths, going back to the fourth MacIlwraith, Aodh[3] MacIlwraith. Everything before that was passed on by word of mouth, but here we have an unbroken account of all the MacIlwraiths since Aodh in 226 BC."

"*BC?*" Nelson confirmed as he yanked his notepad from his coat. He had to write it down because he'd doubt himself and his sanity later.

"Indeed!" Merlin said with a quick nod.

"Open it up, let's get a look," Nox urged with an impatient wave.

"Let me see..."

Merlin patted his pockets and removed a pair of white satin gloves, then pulled them on before easing the book open. He took his time, scanning and lifting pages as Nox watched over his shoulder.

"Here we are!" Merlin announced and tapped the top of a page. "Domhnall MacIlwraith, born in 822 *Anno Domini*," he clarified with a glance at Nelson, then gave Nox a sparkling wide-eyed look. "Who had that one magickal daughter." His fingertip slid down the page. "Eithne[4], who was married to... Glaisne[5] Ó Murchadha!" He stopped and went to the back of the book, gently flipping until he let out a giddy sound. "Here they are! The Ó Murchadha!"

"They have their own section?" Nox asked, making Merlin giddier.

"Yes! Because of this!" He turned the book and gestured for them to move in as he pointed at the top of the page.

"Ríonach[6] Ó Murchadha 420 BC," Nox read, then he swore as he leaned in for a closer look. "This line is...matrilineal?" he asked Merlin, earning a pleased hum.

"It *always* has been and it has been unbroken since Ríonach and that line only produced one boy— Glaisne. And would you like to guess why *that* particular line remained matrilineal and why it was so venerated in the old, old country?"

A loud laugh burst from Clancy. "Is that why you picked Sorcha for Lucas?"

"No!" Merlin shook his head as he turned to Clancy, practically dancing. "I forgot about that bit of old lore!" He reached for Nox's hand, he was so excited. "I left your father with Clancy when Lucas was a child because I heard there was an Ó Murchadha girl who was close to the right age. I stayed with Sorcha and her people until she was ready to meet Lucas because I had read that the MacIlwraith and Ó Murchadha heirs were always more powerful. Sorcha's grandmother, Orla, and I both agreed that the omens foretold a great and *good* child who would be blessed by the gods, but I forgot why!"

Nox and Nelson exchanged frustrated looks. "Why?" they asked at the same time and a beatific smile spread across Merlin's face as he stared up at Nox.

"Because they were believed to be descended from the Morrígan." He shared a tearful glance with Clancy. "Now we know," he said and Clancy nodded.

"Now we know."

"Know what?" Nox asked them and Clancy sighed at the book.

"Old families like ours... We don't always know what kind of vows they're keeping. Her family could have been Tuath Dé and hiding until you returned and summoned them. Or, they could be descended from any number of gods. We never asked Sorcha what the nature of her family's vow was because it was always forbidden. For everyone's safety."

A dry snort huffed from Nelson. "That makes perfect sense. The only way these interconnected secret societies could exist in the Beltway was if they didn't know about each other. It's how successful terrorist organizations work. One cell can't lead investigators to the other if it's captured and interrogated."

"Investigators or inquisitors?" Nox countered. "Perhaps I need to study this book," he decided and gestured for Merlin to hand over the gloves. "Shame on you for just showing me," he said but Merlin gave him a belligerent glare as he tugged each finger free.

"When have you ever been amenable to discussing *your* family's history? *That* has truly been the curse of the MacIlwraiths. You're all obsessed with history and the teaching of it but will not look at your own."

"Well..." Nox's head tilted from side to side. "It has been pretty grim for us, but Mom's side of the family tree sounds promising."

"Promising?" Clancy parroted, blinking at Nox. "There's a very high likelihood that *you* are a descendant of the Badb on your mother's side, just as much as you're descended from the Dagda."

Merlin laughed loudly, his emotions getting the better of him as he reached for Clancy. "Don't you see? Our Nox is exactly what Walt dreams of becoming. *He* is the union of the Tuath Dé and the Morrígan—half glorious light and half immortal, eternal night!"

"*No.*" Nox closed the book and set it away from him, shaking his head as he backed away. "*Our* Nox is *human* and being a descendant of the Badb is useless unless you can tell me how it proves Walt was behind the abductions and Elsa's death. Or, how it helps me defeat the Dagda," he stated, stalking around the desk and toward the door. "Nelson, get us a warrant so we can properly search Sheila's house and property. Walt's murder wall is in the basement and it proves he's behind all of it. And we'll find traces of those Samhain rituals in the backyard that will match New Castle."

"On it," Nelson answered, trading wary glances with Merlin and Clancy as Nox left.

"He's still resisting," Merlin said with a sad sigh, but Nelson snorted dismissively.

"He isn't resisting. Nox is searching for ways to buck the system and regain control. He's afraid of losing himself to this, so backing him into another corner with his incredible destiny might have been too much," he guessed and shrugged. "But he'll come around."

"He's talking about it now, at least," Clancy pointed out, earning a heavy hum from Merlin.

"That was always the problem with the MacIlwraiths, especially poor Lucas. So very inflexible about his nature and his potential because he was afraid of what it could cost him."

"Can you blame him, though?" Nelson asked, somewhat incredulously and Clancy shook his head.

"Not at all," he said softly but his tone was heavy with regret. "But *we* forgot what we were when we went into hiding and assimilated. We became so enamored with humanity and being human that we forgot what our missions were and what we were protecting."

Merlin nodded as he picked up the book and passed it to Clancy. "We weren't put here to fall in love and live happily ever after. We're here to ensure the Dagda has a way back and an able heir to carry *Him*. We've managed to hold the line while keeping *Him* dormant for over two thousand years, but our time is nearly up. *He* is almost ready to return and all we can do now is make Nox as strong as possible."

"And you think we have a little more than a month?" Nelson

asked and Clancy shook his head as he went to return the book to the top shelf.

"It isn't set in stone and the prophecy only mentions the return of the sun, but there is a reason why Christ rose and we celebrate Easter with bunnies and eggs on the equinox. Much of what Christians celebrate now is taken from pagan traditions that coincide with the cycles of the sun and the moon, not random events in any one deity's life. During the March equinox, the earth will be covered in equal parts day and night. The ancient druids revered that day and they called it Alban Eilir[7], which means 'the light of the earth' and they believed it was when *He* would return," Clancy explained, causing Nelson to hunt for his notepad.

Merlin chuckled as he returned to his boards. "It could not be a coincidence that our Nox was born on the spring equinox. And he would get so wild around his birthday. Tell him, Darach," he said, making Clancy smile as he headed for the decanters.

"He'd get absolutely feral." He chuckled, looking over his shoulder at Merlin and Nelson and checking if they wanted a drink.

"Please," Merlin said, but Nelson shook his head.

"He was feral?" Nelson prodded and Clancy laughed as he poured.

"Practically climbing the walls the whole week so we'd take him out where he could run and climb and play as loud as he wanted. And Sorcha would need to rest and recover," he said with a nod at Merlin.

"Poor child would be so drained. I'd spend the week making her soup and tonics and pampering her. Lucas encouraged her to go abroad more for work and insisted he preferred being the stay-at-home dad."

"He loved every moment of it, but it hurt Lucas to give up so much time with her," Clancy said gruffly as he handed Merlin his drink, then took a long sip from his own glass. "He didn't want that for Nox, but Nelson doesn't seem to be any worse for the wear. Yet," he added with a raise of his glass to Nelson.

Merlin tittered into his whiskey. "Oh, he's extremely drained and Nox is riding him ragged. But thankfully, Nelson appears to be built for this very purpose," he said, toasting Nelson.

He shook his head at both of them, as he went to see what Nox had gotten himself into while they were gossiping about him and his parents. "Goodnight, gentlemen. Lock the door on your way out."

---

1. **Nách mór an diabhal thú.** (NA) You're the devil.
2. **Ó Murchadha** (O-Murra-khoo): Old Irish surname and origin of the surname Murphy.
3. **Aodh** (AY) name meaning fire and traced back to the worship of the druids.
4. **Eithne** (Eeth-nah) meaning "kernel" or "grain."
5. **Glaisne** (Glash-ne) name meaning calm or serene.
6. **Ríonach** (Ree-Uh-na) name meaning royal or queen.
7. **Alban Eiler** - (AHL-bahn eye-ear) Druid name for the festival of the spring equinox, which means "The Light of the Earth."

Fifteen

They *were not* talking about Nox's mother. Nelson had tried to comfort Nox and get an idea of how he was processing everything they had learned, as they prepared for bed and after they made love. Nox had worn the cage and asked Nelson to help him forget for a while. But after, Nox had refused to talk about the *Ó Murchadha*, saying he didn't need to be more confused about who *he* was, that it could wait until after they had dealt with Walt.

Nelson had a new appreciation for Merlin and how much he was able to teach Nox about the history of the MacIlwraiths, given how stubborn he could be when it came to his family's destiny. But so many years of secrets and denial were bearing down on them and Nelson couldn't help but notice that Nox was running from all the things that Walt craved. Every time they unraveled another one of Walt's lies or delusions, they found a matching truth in Nox's family tree.

In the morning, Nox seemed more intent on their face-off, as if he needed somewhere to direct his frustrations and his fury. They received a call from Tony as they were eating breakfast and discussing their next steps in the investigation. Tony was frantic when Nelson answered the phone, warning them that Walt had taken a "sick day" to spend some "quality time" with Aubrey and that he had sounded strange.

"We need to get to the bookstore." Nox was adamant and impatient as he hustled Nelson out of the house and into the Continental. "He has to know we're closing in on him and I don't want him getting close to Aubrey. Tony's covering my lectures so we have to cover Aubrey and the store."

"I have a unit parked out front and she has an agent with her now too, but we'll be there soon," Nelson had promised.

When they arrived, Nelson was pleased to get a thumbs up from the agent behind the wheel of the unmarked sedan in the parking lot across the street. And he got an assured nod from a young woman dressed in overalls and a tie-dye tank top by the display of pendulums by the register once they were inside. She looked like a college student but Nelson recognized her from the Hoover Building and one of the surveillance teams.

"So far, everything's been perfectly calm and quiet this morning," Howard said when he greeted them. But Aubrey was pale and shaking as she rushed over.

"He's messaged me four times asking where I am. I told him I was running errands and would get back to him when I had a minute. I didn't want to tell him I was here," she whispered nervously.

"Good thinking," Nelson said. "We'll stick around until Tony can pick you up and I'm arranging for the two of you to stay in a safe house tonight. Walt's not getting close to you without plenty of protection," he promised her.

"What was the plan for these?" Nox asked, gesturing at the forgotten box of beeswax candles in her hands.

"These?" She laughed as she looked around the store. "I was going to switch out all the candelabras and sconces. We're decorating the store with bees and flowers and rabbits for Ostara," she explained.

"How perfect," Nox said hoarsely, a hard smile stretched across his face. "Let me give you a hand with that."

While they decorated, Nelson made all the arrangements for a team and a safe house for Aubrey and Tony until they were able to apprehend Walt. The morning remained quiet until Aubrey hissed at Nelson and Nox from the register.

"Walt's here!" Aubrey whispered and pointed at the windows. "That's his Civic!"

Nelson shushed her and grabbed Nox's sleeve before he could make a beeline for the door. "Let's see why he's here and what he knows first," he said as he pulled Nox to the back of the store and pushed him down an aisle and out of sight. "Just ask him what's going on and act as normal as possible. We'll be right here," he told her and cleared his throat at Howard. "Do not let him know we're on to him. Be cool," he advised quietly.

Howard offered him a stubborn nod. "I won't let you down," he said, holding up a thumb and Aubrey sniffed hard and nodded.

"I can do this," she stated with a defiant tip of her chin. "For those girls," she added in a shaking whisper.

"You've got this," Nelson said with a wink for her, then stepped behind the bookshelf when he spotted Walt jogging toward the shop's door.

Nelson and Nox exchanged loaded looks when they heard the bell over the door chime, announcing an arrival.

"Hello! How can we help you?" Howard asked, sounding perfectly calm and professional. Nelson let out a silent, hopeful breath as he listened.

"Oh! Walt!" Aubrey sounded delightfully surprised. "What are you doing here?"

"I...um..." Walt stalled. "I took the day off and thought I'd surprise you but you weren't playing along. Your texts were... evasive so I checked your phone's location and tracked you here."

Nox's brows jumped as he traded wide-eyed looks with Nelson. "Creepy!" he mouthed and Nelson nodded in agreement.

Aubrey laughed it off, thankfully. "You should have just called. I've been giving Howard a hand until he can find someone permanent to help around here. I ran some errands for him and we've been decorating," she explained.

"I didn't realize you knew about this place," Walt said, making her laugh.

"Did you? How could you keep this a secret from me?" she asked and there was a slight edge to the question.

Walt laughed but it was weak. "It must have slipped my mind."

"Have we met before?" Howard asked, earning a dubious hum from Walt.

"I don't believe we have..."

"Maybe you just have one of those faces..." Howard said.

There was another laugh from Aubrey. "Never mind! I wish I had known you had the day off, I would have rescheduled with Howard but I can't leave him hanging today. And I've had big plans for that window display," she informed him.

"I see..." Walt replied and Nox grabbed Nelson's arm when they heard his voice coming closer. "And it's just the two of you here today?"

Nox swiped a book next to his shoulder and gave the cover a quick scan, then flipped it open. He signaled for Nelson to follow as he headed around the shelf, pretending to read.

"It's right here, Nelson. It says that you want obsidian for that kind of work," he said and jumped when he almost walked right into Walt. "Hey, there!"

"Professor!" Walt froze, then reversed, looking behind him nervously. "What are you doing here?"

"Me? I stop by pretty often to check on Howard and see if he has anything new I might need."

"Yes! The professor and Agent Nelson have become regulars!" Howard boasted and beamed at Nox. "I don't know what I would have done if they hadn't been here to help me pick up the pieces," he said, his tone hardening.

"That's...wonderful," Walt replied but his eyes tightened as they swung to Aubrey. "How did you find this place?"

"I recommended it," Nox said as he passed the book to Nelson and advanced on Walt. "I thought Aubrey could use the distraction and make new friends. You never know when you'll need a new support system," he added, making Walt flinch.

He nodded and swallowed hard. "You never know," he agreed. But Nelson could tell by the way his nostrils flared that Walt was feeling cornered and didn't like it. Walt held his hand out to Aubrey and smiled tenderly at her. "Just lunch. I'll bring you right back after we're through," he said with an innocent flutter of his lashes.

"I'm sorry." She shook her head as she stared at his hand. "We just placed an order for Chinese food and it should be here soon. Raincheck?" she suggested, earning a hard snort from Walt.

"Sure. I'll see you at home, then," he said as he backed toward the door but Nelson was on him.

"Hold on, Walt. There's something I've been meaning to ask you," he said as he followed, but Walt turned and dashed to the door, throwing it open and racing down the sidewalk.

"Damn it!" Nelson took off after him.

He sprinted past pedestrians, mumbling apologies as he bumped shoulders and almost knocked over an elderly woman in his haste to catch up with Walt. But Nelson lost sight of him when Walt ducked into a narrow alley on the other side of the old bank.

"What the...?" Nelson found a dead end and turned to see if there were any doors Walt could have used but there was nothing but brick walls and a tall fence behind the dumpster at the far end. Nelson went to take a look, but Walt wasn't hiding in or behind it and he hadn't gone over the fence. Unless he'd taken a flying leap and vanished on the other side. There was no way he could have climbed it fast enough and Nelson was baffled when he returned to the store. "I lost him. Is he into parkour?" he asked Aubrey, making her laugh.

"Walt? That's the most I've *ever* seen him run and I know he's afraid of heights."

The rest of the day was quiet but Nelson's nerves were on edge by the time Tony arrived and Howard was ready to close up. Nelson handed Tony and Aubrey over to their newly expanded protective detail and he and Nox took Howard home.

"I will be fine and you have done enough!" He shooed them away when Nelson offered to check the apartment first and Nox suggested they have a cup of tea.

"Call if anything feels strange or you get bored," Nox said and made Howard promise before they left him and headed back to Georgetown.

They were just around the corner from the townhouse when Nox got a text message. "It's from Bixby," he said, sounding concerned. "Someone at the FBI requested copies of everything he has on New Castle."

"From the FBI? I'll make some calls and see what that's about," Nelson replied, then slowed the car as they came around the corner. "What the fuck...?"

Cars and vans lined the street in front of Nox's townhouse and people in suits and coveralls rushed out with boxes of evidence bags.

Nox blinked in horror at the site and was frozen in his seat while Nelson parked. "All those people...in my house."

They saw Merlin hurrying after a tech who was wheeling one of his rolling boards down the lawn and Nelson swore as he got out. He scanned until he spotted Agent Benson and stalked in his direction, ready to fight.

"What the hell do you think you're doing?" Nelson demanded and the other agent gulped and looked around in fear.

"Sorry, Nelson," he said, averting his eyes. "We got a tip and someone sent in some pictures of the professor. Felton told us to search every inch of the professor's house and we found all kinds of occult shit that matches the scene out in New Castle," he explained quickly, earning a furious snort from Nelson.

"Come on! Anyone who practices witchcraft is going to have

the same things in their home," he argued, then groaned when he saw a tech carrying a box of various antlers that had been tagged.

"We found an item belonging to Elsa Hansen in one of the guest room closets," Benson added and Nelson whipped around.

"What?" he growled, causing Benson to jump.

"It...was a necklace. In a tin of dirt."

"In one of the guest rooms?" Nelson verified and Benson nodded.

"Nelson!" Merlin cried as he raced across the lawn. "Put a stop to this immediately!"

"I'm working on it," he said, but Benson cast him a skeptical look before Merlin gasped and pointed at Nelson's car.

"Stop them!" Merlin ordered.

Nelson swore and his blood pressure jumped as two agents handcuffed Nox and read him his rights. Nelson saw red and was on his way and ready to fight, but Felton's cackle caught him off guard.

"We got him, lover boy," he said as he strolled down the lawn dangling an evidence bag. "Already got confirmation from the Hansens that this belonged to Elsa."

"We've never seen that before," Nelson stated and reached for it, but Felton pulled it away and clicked his teeth.

"Not a chance, Nelson. You're on suspension until we've made heads or tails of this."

"Suspension?" Nelson laughed in disgust. "We're in the middle of an active investigation and our main suspect is on the run. Do you think this—!" he waved wildly at the chaos on Nox's lawn. "Do you think this is a coincidence?" he shouted as he scanned around them for any sign of Walt. "I'll rip his fucking arms off," Nelson muttered under his breath, then cast Felton a furious glare. "This isn't going to end the way you want it to," he warned but Felton's lips tilted into a crooked smirk.

"I'd like to see the both of you behind bars. But I have a feeling he's been playing you and the best I'll get for you is a dishonorable discharge," he predicted and Nelson's head cocked in dismay.

"You've executed a search warrant on one of your own consultant's houses with what sounds like a bullshit tip and hearsay," he said, earning a snide chuckle from Felton.

"What I got was a lot more than a bullshit tip," Felton replied as he sidled up to Nelson, looking him up and down in disgust. "I've got pictures of that little freak that prove that *he* was the inspiration behind that nightmare in New Castle. Just wait until it gets out that the sketchy professor was poaching coeds..."

"No. *That's* bullshit and he'll come at you for defamation if this blows up his reputation at the school. What pictures?" Nelson asked and Felton shook his head, looking smug.

"We've got pictures of that *freak* out back, naked and eating cereal in his pajamas," Felton said as he pointed in the direction of the townhouse's terrace. Walt must have been watching them after New Castle and Felton was ready to pin it all on Nox. A wild, hot rush of fury erupted within Nelson and he tensed to lunge at Felton.

"Don't call him that!"

"*Stop!*" Merlin hissed, grabbing Nelson's arm. "We are in Walt's trap and this is what he wants," he said slowly, then offered Felton an imperious tilt of his chin. "You, sir, are at the end of your fucking around era and are about to enter a long period of finding out," he predicted with a withering glare.

"Whatever," Felton said dismissively, then squared up to Nelson. "You're either stupid or you've sold your soul to that freaky demon and this ugly little troll. You can't tell me you missed that he's covered in the same bullshit that was all over your crime scene."

"There's a reason for that and you're playing right into our suspect's hands now."

Felton made a knowing sound as he shook his head. "That witch boy's got some kind of hold on you, Nelson. His pussy's that good?"

That was when Nelson would have hit Felton but Merlin beat him to it.

"Oof!" Felton doubled over and cupped his groin after receiving a swift punch from Merlin. "You son of a—!" he wheezed weakly.

Nelson covered his mouth to hold back a laugh, then groaned when two agents came over to handcuff Merlin.

"Come on! This is getting out of hand," he said, but Merlin shushed him.

"Have Jeff call my attorney. It's too late to do anything this evening, but he'll have us out first thing in the morning. I'll stay with Nox." He gave Nelson a firm nod before presenting his wrists to the other agents.

For a moment, Nelson considered advising them against keeping Nox and Merlin in the same facility. But he suspected that hitting Felton was a tactical move on Merlin's part and his way of staying by Nox's side and taking a bullet for Nelson. Because Felton had it coming.

"Okay." Nelson nodded slowly, eyeing Felton down. "I'll produce copies of the break-in we reported here almost two weeks ago and statements from *unimpeachable* witnesses putting Nox at the school or the Hoover Building or in different states when Sherwood and the MacCrorys were poisoned," he said, knowing that his word or Clancy's wouldn't be enough this time. He smiled when Felton flinched and Nelson caught a flicker of fear in his eyes. "I'll have them on the Attorney General's desk by morning and you can explain why *your* expert consultant is in custody while the main suspect in *four murders and six abductions* is at large. And you'd better hope the AG doesn't find out that our suspect is the source of your 'tip.'"

They stared each other down until Felton's lip curled and he snorted.

"My gut's been telling me that VanHalfass has been twisted for years. We found cult shit all over the study—"

"Because we're investigating—!" Nelson attempted but Felton laughed.

"What about the rest of it? There's witch shit all over the house. Just like Sherwood's and your boy has their symbols tattooed all over his fucking body. It would have to be a pretty big fucking coincidence. My gut says he's behind this and that he's been playing you."

"Ready to stake your career on it?"

"I'm not staking shit," Felton said with a toss of his chin in Nox's direction. Nox was in the back of a black, unmarked SUV. He held up his cuffed hands and waved cheerfully at them and Felton's snarl intensified as he swung back to Nelson. "I saw the pictures of that little asshole and I got a look at his study and the kitchen. I know he's involved in this. Question is: how stupid are you, Nelson? Has he been playing you for a fool this whole time or are you in on it too?"

Nelson counted down from ten, reminding himself that he couldn't help Nox and Merlin or clear their names if he torched his career by attacking the deputy director.

"I don't know how that necklace ended up here, but I can promise you that I'm not the one being led by the nose. *Sir*," he said, excusing himself. "I've got evidence and statements to gather."

His gaze locked with Nox's and Nelson heard and felt a command: *stay calm, stay close.* Nelson braced his hands on his hips and pushed out a hard breath, willing himself to focus.

Nelson's first priority was to make sure Nox went to the Hoover Building for questioning. Nelson could get a lot more work done there than in the parking lot of the county jail and the less time Nox spent in "official" custody as a suspect, the better for his career. The university would not be happy about their star professor being arrested and Georgetown would cut him loose the moment he turned into a liability.

"Let's see what Jeff and the Attorney General can do," Nelson said as he took out his phone, shaking his head. He couldn't fathom a reason he'd ever need to contact the AG when Nox added the number to his phone, now it was a godsend. And Nelson wondered if he was high again as he searched for Merlin's Bentley and Jeff.

Nelson spotted the elegant black luxury car and there was no mistaking the strapping blond in the black suit, nervously twisting a driving cap. He watched from the other side of the car and returned Nelson's nod as he approached.

"Merlin said to contact his attorney," Nelson said. "Tell him he's got two clients headed to the Hoover Building,"

"Yes, sir!" Jeff looked relieved as he pulled his phone from his pocket and got to swiping and dialing.

"Now, I just need to figure out how to explain this to the Attorney General of the United States," Nelson said, his palms sweating as he tapped on the number and said a prayer.

Sixteen

"This is intolerable!" Merlin declared, hugging his chest and glaring at the two-way glass.

"This is an inconvenience," Nox corrected as he folded his arms on the table and rested his head on them. "I'm going back to sleep."

"How can you sleep at a time like this?"

"Well... If you'll pipe down, I'll show you."

"Where's my attorney? He should have been here by now."

Nox groaned as he sat up and scrubbed his face with his hands. "It's 1:00 AM. He's probably at home, sleeping, because there's nothing he can do until later," he guessed, but Merlin tutted and shook his head.

"I don't keep him on retainer so he can sleep while I rot away in this dungeon."

"Would you calm down," Nox said, laughing. "We're lucky we're not at the county jail. I think they use this room for training and not for actual suspects," he mused and squinted up at the long LED bulbs above them, beaming bright soulless, artificial light. Nelson and the Attorney General were keeping their presence and detention in the Hoover Building as unofficial as possible and Merlin and Nox had yet to be processed.

Chapter Sixteen

There was a knock before the door opened and Clancy was let in, balancing two styrofoam coffee cups and an assortment of vending machine pastries on a stack of folders. "The observation room is locked and the cameras are off. This is the best I could do until the cafeteria opens," he grumbled while he laid everything out for them like a disgruntled waiter. "Nelson's managed to create a rather impressive paper trail detailing *all* of your movements for the last few weeks, including your phone logs. Your alibis for all the poisonings should be airtight without corroborating witnesses, but he'll have those too once it's decent to call people," he continued and Nox hummed dreamily as he sipped, then gagged.

"Ew. That's dreadful. But I knew Nelson would fix Felton's little red wagon. I'm almost happy to have a front-row seat for this," he said with a wry smirk. The deputy director had taken a big bite out of a particularly poisonous apple and Nelson would see that the consequences were swift and vicious.

"Meanwhile, we don't know where Walt is," Merlin complained and Nox shrugged.

"It would appear that we've backed him into a corner and he's unraveling," he said, earning a dubious snort from Clancy.

"I hope that's true, but from my vantage point, it looks like we're pinned down until morning."

Nox's fingers danced over the selection of plastic-wrapped pastries before he chose the mini crunch donuts and sat back. "Nah. He's desperate and this is his Hail Mary. That necklace—that untainted and undetectable necklace muffled by hallowed grave dirt—and this frame-up was his smoke bomb, in case he needed to make an escape." Nox gave Merlin a loaded look because they had both searched the house and missed it.

"It must have been taken early on and hidden away," Merlin said angrily. "We would have felt it if she had worn it while she was suffering or if Julian had made it a memento of his twisted obsession."

Nox nodded in agreement. "She probably left it at the bookstore and Julian kept it and showed it to Walt. Walt must have taken it when he realized how valuable she was to Julian. Saving it to curse or plant as evidence was just good sense if you're a magpie. And Walt certainly is," he added and Clancy humphed as he flipped through one of the folders until he tossed a picture of the necklace and the tin on the table.

"I used to tease him about being a kleptomaniac because I thought he was just absent-minded. He'd walk off with my pen, or even my glasses once, and would say he hadn't realized he'd even done it or that he thought they were his," he said, making Nox wince.

"You might want to have Merlin cleanse your aura and bleed you in case Walt's cursed you or been poking around in your house as well," he warned.

Clancy's eyes widened with shock and a red rash swept up his neck. "That's probably a good idea," he said quietly, making Merlin roll his eyes.

"You and your ridiculous hubris, Darach. You always assume that everyone is beneath you, and mark my words: he's exploited that...fatal flaw to goodness knows what end," he said and clicked his teeth.

"Yes, yes, I'm an arrogant fool," Clancy said as he bent and offered Merlin a regal bow.

His facetiousness offended Nox. "Tell me, Clance, what was it you said about those who refuse to learn from their mistakes?"

Clancy's blush deepened, his shame sincere this time as he hung his head. "That they were the devil's best helpers."

"And look at how well you helped this particular devil by underestimating him," Nox scolded.

"I'm sorry," Clancy said, as he shook his head. "I won't do that again."

"I'm glad to hear it," Nox said, popping a donut into his mouth and chewing. He washed it down with the cheap, weak coffee. "How many times was he in your home with all those picture albums and keepsakes?" He raised a brow at Clancy, picturing his elegant home study. It was practically a shrine to the past and Nox's parents with numerous framed photos and knick-knacks from their adventures. "He was only in my house once, as far as I can tell, and look at how much he made of that."

There was a thoughtful hum from Merlin. "We'll see to it as soon as I'm free from this oubliette," he said, making Nox and Clancy groan and snort.

Nox suspected that Merlin was trying to lighten the mood and chuckled as he elbowed him. "Stop being so dramatic. Clancy brought sweets and...that," he said with a wave at their cups. "Pretend it's coffee and eat something. You're not as much fun when you're hangry."

"How can you eat that garbage?" Merlin asked.

Nox's shoulder bounced. He tossed another donut up and caught it with his mouth. Barely. "When in Rome."

"I see..." Clancy said, exchanging pointed glances with Merlin. "What's the plan, after we get you out?" he asked Nox.

"Sheila Forsythe. Walt has nowhere else to go but home now. I want to talk to her and see if he's gone home to mother and if that draws him out," he said and Clancy nodded.

"He knows that we're on to him and that he's lost Aubrey."

"He won't go far," Nox predicted. "Not without Sheila and Nelson's got a few junior agents watching her place."

Merlin shuddered and sneered as if he smelled something rotten. "She'll never leave that house, mark my words. It's her temple and it holds her fondest memories, from the sound of things," he said, causing Nox to grimace.

"Her mind is gone and she is lost in halcyon days there. Walt *can't* move her and there's too much evidence of their practice to leave the property. That's why he went to such great lengths to convince everyone she was in a home and too fragile to meet his fiancée and closest friends."

"He's been living a double life, essentially," Clancy summarized. "We all thought he was spending his weekends being the dutiful son and keeping the house from falling apart until he could sell it."

Nox shook his head. "He can't sell that house and she can't be trusted not to ramble about him and her father so Walt *can't* put her in a decent care facility," he summarized and smiled. "He won't go far."

"That's what I'm afraid of," Merlin said heavily. "He's out there regrouping and he knows we're on to him now. This might be his Hail Mary, but Walt is smart and he's dangerous. We should take care with what we eat and drink until he's been dealt with."

"That's probably a good call," Clancy confirmed with a nod at their cups. "They only taste miserable. It's from the machine down the hall so it's instant and there won't be any grounds to read."

"In the mood for a little divination?" Nox asked him and Clancy shrugged.

"I'm certain the omens are in our favor but we're blind at the moment," he said, casting a quick glance at Merlin who chuckled and nodded.

"I've been scrying," he boasted as he tipped back his chin. "I spent a few hours peering into my bullán yesterday and saw many encouraging signs."

Clancy's brow notched. "Encouraging? Is that it?" he asked and Merlin spluttered in offense.

"The omens are in our favor, I'm certain. We must merely be cautious, is all," he replied, earning dubious looks from Nox and Clancy.

"What did you see?" Clancy prodded and Nox jabbed Merlin with his elbow.

"Out with it," Nox ordered.

Merlin pulled a face. "I saw a crow rising with the sun. Among other things," he added pointedly.

"Oooh!" Nox said, rubbing his hands together dramatically. "Place your bets, gentlemen! Who do we think the Badb favors? Me? Or Walt?" he said as he rolled his eyes. "I can't speak for the

Badb and I haven't heard from her recently, but I have a feeling she's not pleased with Walt either." He was being completely facetious because Nox didn't need to ask to know that Walt's behavior and use of the goddess's name was an abomination. "I've had the Dagda's blessing and that's more than enough."

"And you're sure you can trust that?" Clancy asked warily.

Nox chewed on his lip as he considered. He didn't trust the Dagda to play fair and *His* intentions were extremely dubious. But Nox did trust his father and his own instincts and it didn't make sense for the Dagda to allow anyone or anything to harm *His* last heir or bring shame to *His* name.

"Yeah." He nodded, completely certain. "*He's* almost ready to rise and this mess that Walt and the cult made is ugly and dirty and it's not what *He* envisioned. That was not *His* glorious light and *He* does not appreciate Walt messing up *His* entrance," Nox said distantly, momentarily distracted by the rush of warmth and euphoria, then nodded. "We just want a minute alone with Walt."

"*Nox!*" Merlin barked, making him jump.

Nox frowned up at Clancy who had come around the table and was looming over him and glaring. "What?" Nox asked.

"Fuirich air falbh on grian!"[1] Clancy shouted at him.

Merlin made a soothing shushing sound as he turned Nox. "You must resist!" he pressed the back of his hand to Nox's forehead, then cradled his cheeks. "But remember where that warmth and voice sprang from so *you* can call it forth when the time is right!" Merlin urged tenderly.

"I'm working on it," Nox snapped, leaning away. He didn't want to be comforted like a child anymore. Not from Merlin. "It's easier when Nelson's here."

"Of course," Merlin rasped and nodded jerkily.

Nox sensed that the rejection had stung. But Nox didn't trust his intentions anymore and wasn't sure if he'd ever truly been Merlin's "sweet boy" or if that had been a lie too.

"It's taking a little time," Nox admitted as he rose, then cleared his throat, warning Clancy when he hesitated to get out of his way. "I'm feeling restless now and I'd like some space," he said slowly, despite his simmering temper. Clancy offered a deferential bow and murmured an apology as he stepped aside so Nox could pace in front of the long window. "I've worked hard to figure out which of the voices in my head are mine and how to silence *Him*. But it hurts whenever I wonder if it's safe to trust *you*," he explained, allowing his bitterness to rise. "I need Nelson."

"He's doing everything he can to get you out of here and your name cleared by morning," Clancy said gently, but Nox sighed at the clock.

"He's the only one I can trust now." Nox didn't feel safe without Nelson. Even in the Hoover Building with Merlin and Clancy at his side and that made Nox's heart hurt worse. "You were right, Clance," he murmured sadly. "I've always been on my own and I'm alone now while I fight my hardest battle."

"You are not," Merlin argued, but his voice shook and he was crying as he watched Nox and waited to be forgiven.

"I did appreciate that right hook to Felton's junk, though," Nox said to him and winked, lightening the mood. His heart might be broken but Nox wasn't good at stewing and he didn't want to sit in tense, awkward silence until Nelson rescued them.

"Did you see that?" Merlin asked, straightening in his seat and attempting a watery smile.

"Bravo." Nox nodded and clapped quietly. "Saw it from the back of that SUV and it was extremely satisfying. I've wanted to do that to Felton for close to two years," he confided, earning a knowing hum from Clancy.

"I think everyone wants to punch Felton in the junk but we're all too tall and too worried about our asses to do anything about it," he grumbled, making Nox and Merlin laugh.

"I was happy to be of service," Merlin declared with a roll of his hand.

"He said 'junk,'" Nox said, smothering a giggle. He recalled Lucas's warning and that Nox had to forgive them *soon*. "Dad told me he was wrong and he wants me to listen to you," he whispered as he recalled how safe and *good* he'd felt when Lucas had touched his face.

"You really talked to Lucas?" Clancy asked, his voice cracking, but he was hopeful as he studied Nox.

"Yeah." Nox nodded, certain that he had talked to Lucas or had tapped into a place in his psyche that truly understood and mirrored his father's spirit. "He knows that you were right and he should have listened. And I'm doing my best to listen and do what he'd want me to do," he continued, but shook his head and snorted wryly. "It's a lot easier said than done when I remember why he isn't here. But I'm working on that too. It's just one of the many, many battles I'm fighting right now," he told them and Merlin pushed out a hard breath and nodded.

"We will do whatever it takes to regain your trust and I will heal this family," he vowed with a determined hump.

"As will I," Clancy said sincerely.

"Good," Nox replied. "Then, something positive will have come from this little diversion of Walt's. This night won't have been a waste and a mere inconvenience," he said, his smile stretching into a menacing grin. "But if Nelson has any say in the matter, it will be the end of Felton. He's underestimated and abused Nelson for years and Felton's about to get what's coming to him."

---

1. **Fuirich air falbh on grian!** (Fwirr-ick err voliv on gree-an) Stay away from the sun!

Seventeen

It wasn't the longest night of Nelson's life. He'd had some doozies after New Castle. But the hours that Nelson spent pacing in front of his desk, begging anyone he could get on the phone for help and feeding reams of paper into the printer had been a marathon through clerical Hell.

And Nelson had the paper cuts and the bags under his eyes to show for it when he delivered *a box* of files, detailing nearly every move Nox had made since the two of them had been handed the first two files on those "nuisance cases" the prior fall.

"It's all here, sir," he told the Attorney General as he placed the box on the desk in front of the dignified older man. It was the first time Nelson had ever been face-to-face with an attorney general and it had been nerve-wracking, requesting a meeting first thing in the morning and explaining why Nox had been taken into custody. "Professor MacIlwraith was nowhere near any of the locations when any of the crimes were committed. I've detailed his whereabouts and corroborated them with phone records, receipts, and provided contact information for witnesses. Not only that, but I've provided documentation that proves that Walter Forsythe, our primary suspect, *not only* had access to the rare poison used to kill most of our victims, he also had access to them and had abused his position within the bureau to cover his activities."

"You did all of that in one night?" The older man looked bewildered as he regarded Nelson from behind his desk.

"Yes, sir." Nelson took out his notepad. "I write everything down. It's all here and we've been gathering evidence for weeks."

"That's astounding, Agent Nelson," the Attorney General said, rising and offering his hand. "Go get our boy and take him home. You don't have to worry about Felton anymore. I'll have his resignation by the end of the day. Just for starters."

"Thank you, sir. About Felton," Nelson said with a hesitant grimace. "I realized someone in the bureau—in Felton's office—has been helping Forsythe. He knew that Julian Sherwood had requested a meeting with the professor before we did and someone put those photos of MacIlwraith's tattoos directly in Felton's hands. Someone who knew Felton was looking for a reason to take us down."

The Attorney General whistled loudly, rocking on his heels. "There's a mole in Felton's office?"

"It's his secretary," Nelson said as he turned to leave. "Her son's a Ph.D. candidate in History at Georgetown. I suspect we'll find that Forsythe's been doing his papers for the last two years. I've already confirmed that Forsythe recommended him for a fellowship."

Felton was waiting when Nelson pushed through all the agents loitering in the hall outside the room Nox and Merlin had been kept in. They were hoping for a showdown and to get a look at the "sketchy professor."

"This isn't over," Felton said but he had no choice but to let Nelson pass.

Nelson nodded at Agent Benson, guarding the door. "Sorry, Nelson," Benson whispered as he opened it.

"Nelson!" Nox ran right to him and threw himself into Nelson's arms, disregarding Felton and the other agents in the hall.

"There's nothing to worry about." Nelson held him tight and pushed his face into Nox's hair, breathing him in. "Your alibi is bulletproof and the AG's promised to take care of Felton. I wouldn't be surprised if he's out and Merlin was deputy by the end of the day."

Nox shook his head, nuzzling into the corner of Nelson's neck. "Score one for Walt, but I wasn't worried. I missed you," he whispered and Nelson's face was hot as he released Nox and fixed his tie.

"I missed you too," he said quietly, then nodded as Felton joined them. The deputy director would be singing a very different tune after a panel of FBI attorneys reviewed all the proof and Nox's alibis were corroborated. "I asked the AG to request an emergency OPR panel to examine the claims against Professor MacIlwraith. I'm more than confident they'll find that there was no cause to detain him *whatsoever*," Nelson added pointedly.

There was a hard laugh from Felton and his lip curled as he watched Nox with open hatred. "You'll never convince me he's not behind this. He's covered in the same symbols and *his* hair was at the second crime scene down in New Castle. There's no way all of that's a coincidence," he argued.

Nox opened his mouth to set him straight but Clancy cleared his throat loudly as he shoved his hands in his pockets, strolling between them.

"And I'll explain to the panel that the triskelion is almost as ubiquitous as the cross," he informed everyone loudly. "As well as the prevalence of horned deities and serpents in numerous religions. I'll also explain that Professor MacIlwraith's practice is personal and is protected in the same way all religious practices are in this country under the First Amendment of the United States Constitution. At the moment, there are no laws against being a practicing witch but there are still those that would scapegoat and burn them." He raised his brows at Felton, daring him to dig himself into a deeper hole as more people craned their necks and peeked around the corner.

"How do you explain what we found in the professor's house?" Felton countered, making Clancy laugh.

"Your *tip* led you right to it! I saw the transcript from the call and he told you to check the guest rooms. How lazy and stupid could you get?" Clancy asked him, then laughed as he looked around. "Please, go collect that evidence I planted!" he said sweetly and clasped his hands while batting his eyes, creating a ripple of titters and snickers.

"I thought you had more sense than this, Clancy," Felton said, then shoulder-checked Clancy as he stormed off. They watched him go and Nox waited until everyone went back to minding their own business to nudge Clancy with his elbow.

"You realize you're probably going down with him when we bring Walt in," Nox whispered out of the side of his mouth. "There's no way Walt doesn't drag you into it and the FBI is going to want your head on a platter because he was your assistant."

"I don't care," Clancy stated, shaking his head. "It won't matter if I never step foot in this building again once Walt is brought to justice. I don't care if I have a career after that as long as I know Walt can't hurt anyone else and you're safe *and free*," he added and then left them so he could make some calls.

Merlin had scolded his attorney for being useless and excused him. He looked thoughtful as he joined Nelson and Nox. "You know, no one will be as severe in their judgment and punishment as Darach Clancy will be with himself," he predicted as he stared after Clancy. "He has the heart of a general and that is vastly different than the heart of a warrior or a cleric," he said as he glanced at Nelson and then at Nox. "You see the human toll and fear for the soul while Clancy sees the battlefield and prepares his strategy. And it's so easy to forget that for Clancy and myself, a childhood and a career pass like the blink of an eye when you've been guarding a secret for centuries."

That caused Nox to rear back and his face twisted. "That doesn't make their lives less valuable," he said, waving around them. "If anything, it makes them even more precious. They don't get centuries to screw up and infinite do-overs until they learn from their mistakes. Clancy might have the heart of a general, but he's a bit of a fraud if you think about it. He puts his nose in the air because he knows so much but he's not smarter than everyone else, he's just had *way* longer to grasp the things ordinary people learn in the blink of an eye."

Merlin let out a belligerent humph and squared up to Nox. "Now who's underestimating whom?" he challenged. "You may be wise, my lad, but you are a thimble compared to that ocean of knowledge. I do not excuse Clancy for losing sight of how fragile lives can be, but I do understand how easily it could happen when one has reenacted the same family tragedy dozens of times over the centuries. And I am complicit. We were both so desperate to see the cycle finally broken that we became careless."

Nox blinked at Merlin. "The cycle that the two of you broke by...letting Dad fall off a cliff?" he confirmed, causing Merlin to suck in a gasp.

"Nox," Nelson chided, but Nox held up a hand.

"No. He wants to plead Clancy's case and his own by extension. He wants to be absolved, but *how* can I absolve them of something that makes no sense to me? I am trying," he said, his eyes glistening as his gaze locked with Nelson's. He stepped closer until their noses nearly touched. "It hurts not to love them and I want to forgive them. But I just can't understand how they could do it or how they could live with themselves."

"You've seen how, what it's done to them. Let's go home," Nelson said softly. He could do something about how lost and lonely Nox looked at home. A tear rolled down Nox's cheek, nearly bringing Nelson to his knees. "Please," he rasped. "You need to eat something decent and get some rest."

"We should talk to Sheila firs—"

"Tomorrow," Nelson interrupted. "She's not going anywhere. Just give me until tomorrow to make sure you're fully recharged."

"Tomorrow?" Nox pouted loudly. "What am I going to do until tomorrow?"

Chapter Seventeen

Nelson cleared his throat and lowered his head so he could whisper in Nox's ear. "You could practice some sex magick," he suggested.

"Yes! Sex magick!" Nox pumped his fist excitedly as he hopped, his mood recovering. "That's an excellent idea. Let's go home!" he decided as he headed for the exit, leaving Nelson with a beaming Merlin.

"Excellent, indeed," he said and held out his arm so Nelson could escort him from the building. "You always know just what he needs."

"I do my best," Nelson murmured dismissively, ignoring the other agents' curious stares. In the past, Nelson had craved their approval and respect. Now, he no longer cared about his peers' opinions. The inter-office politics and jockeying for better desks and assignments seemed so petty and pointless after all that had happened in New Castle. Nelson pitied them for their lack of purpose and dedication to anything outside of themselves and their careers.

"Now, I have every confidence in your abilities, but if you could keep him home and...otherwise occupied it would give me some time to see if my sources have heard anything about Walt. And Clancy will need some time to do a little damage control at the university. You've nipped this in the bud here at the FBI but the news will have spread around campus by midmorning. We must make it clear that this was nothing more than a misunderstanding and that Nox is completely innocent."

"Keeping a low profile for a few days is probably a good idea," Nelson agreed, then winced. "How? I might be able to keep him... occupied for the day and maybe most of the night, but he's going to be in attack mode when he wakes up tomorrow," he whispered, making Merlin chuckle.

"I'll talk to Clancy and see if we can create a diversion. We can't have you worn out and busted when it's go time," he said under his breath.

"And you still believe that Ostara, the 20th, is when it should happen?" Nelson verified but Merlin shrugged.

"I believe that it could occur at any time of Nox's choosing and that the higher power is enticing him. But this business with the cult and the Badb was a complication *He* couldn't overcome. Too much of Nox's will is bent on avenging those girls and giving them justice. And if our Nox is to be believed, *He* is deeply offended and wants to see *His* name cleared as well."

"That's reassuring," Nelson muttered and Merlin stopped him.

"Yes! *It is*," he stated, his voice wavering. He looked around before leaning in. "If *He* wants us to love *Him*, then that suggests that *He* intends to keep us around. Does it not?"

Nelson's eyes widened as he grasped what Merlin was saying. "He wouldn't bother waiting and letting us do damage control if he was going to wipe out everyone who might care..."

"There is more danger for *Him*, the longer *He* waits," Merlin whispered so quietly, as if he was afraid the Dagda might hear him. "The stronger Nox gets, the better his chances are of besting *Him*."

"You think he'll be strongest on Ostara?" Nelson confirmed in an equally quiet whisper, but Merlin let out a giddy, mirthful laugh.

"Oh, yes!" He clapped a hand over his mouth, stifling a giggle as he looked around them. "Just you wait! He will be glowing and bursting with magickal energy the entire week, he always is. Nox can barely sit still or help himself, he's so enchanting and he will radiate so much heat that he'll leave little burned fingerprints on whatever he touches." Merlin's fingertips danced in the air and on Nelson's sleeve as he suppressed a titter. "We've always had him take leave. He tells the university he's using the time to work on his book and calls it his annual writing retreat."

"His book?" Nelson frowned when they reached the elevator, looking around for Nox.

"He's probably waiting outside. He hasn't seen the sun or the moon in over twelve hours or felt the breeze on his face," Merlin predicted, setting Nelson at ease.

He nodded as he pressed the call button. "I got him out as fast as I could, but he's behaved surprisingly well considering how long he's been down here."

"He has," Merlin agreed as the doors opened and they stepped inside. "Perhaps you should let him off that leash—or whatever it is you two have done to keep his libido in check—until one of you sprains something?" he suggested with a loaded hum.

"I... Can that be plan C or D? Or maybe our Hail Mary? Because Walt's a runner and I might have to chase him again."

Merlin hushed Nelson and patted his arm soothingly. "It's all for a good cause and I have faith in you."

"Thanks," Nelson said flatly, frowning at the doors as they closed. The elevator bounced as it began its ascent and Nelson's stomach did a little somersault. "The week of Ostara is...a little more than a month away. What's the plan?"

"We're supposed to go up to the cabin the weekend prior, on St. Patrick's Day. He hasn't mentioned it?" Merlin looked troubled as Nelson shook his head.

"I've brought up his birthday a few times and he keeps saying we don't need to make a big deal about it."

"He never wants to. Not since we lost Sorcha," Merlin said sadly. "But I think he might be afraid this time."

"Because he thinks it's going to be his last?" Nelson's voice broke and he grunted at the sharp ache in his chest and the rising panic at the thought of losing Nox.

"He told me to make the arrangements, but I can see how badly he doesn't want to go. You know how he is when he has to do something he doesn't want to do," Merlin said with a weary sigh.

Nelson groaned as the elevator doors opened and they were greeted by the morning rush. They had to part and make way as agents and attorneys crowded into the elevator. The lobby was packed but Nelson breathed a sigh of relief when they stepped outside and spotted Nox resting against the side of Merlin's Bentley next to Jeff, eyes closed and basking in the sun.

"I'll put in for leave that week," Nelson said, halting Merlin. "But we have to get him to talk to us about this. We need to make a plan."

"I agree," Merlin said and nodded quickly up at Nelson. "What would you suggest? Because after almost twenty-six years, I can't get him to do anything but plug his ears and ignore me."

Nelson's shoulders dropped and his heart sank as he watched Nox, feeling extremely pessimistic. Taking down Walt and the Dagda? No problem. Probably. But a battle of wills with Nox?

"Fuck."

Eighteen

"Purge and cleanse, Merlin," Nox said as he climbed the stairs in the townhouse, grateful to his toes to be home and able to wash the stink of the last night off of him. "It's going to take a few days to get all my stuff back but I don't want to feel these strangers in my house."

"I'm on it," Merlin said as he hung his coat and pushed up his sleeves.

"I'll be in my room. Come along, Nelson. I need a shower and to get laid and you need to rest."

He was right behind Nox as they jogged up the steps. "You should rest too."

"I did nothing but rest in that stupid little room," Nox complained, turning so he could catch Nelson's hand. He walked backward, kissing Nelson's knuckles. "But I'll rest with you."

"Thank you," Nelson said as he gathered Nox in his arms and danced them into the bedroom, past the bed, and into the bathroom. "It wasn't as bad as New Castle but last night was awful. I just want to get naked and fall asleep with you in my arms."

"You promised me sex magick and I need to get this cage off. I've never worn it this long and it's starting to get to me," he admitted. "It wasn't as effective this morning, without you there."

"Do you still need it? Can't you block *Him* and find your Nelsonspace on your own now?"

Nox smiled as he wound his arms around Nelson's neck so he could whisper in his ear. "I think I can and I was dying to take it off when I was struggling to pee last night. But you have the key."

"Nox!" Nelson pushed him away and yanked open his coat. "Why didn't you say something sooner?" His hands fumbled as he flipped open his wallet and found it.

"I figured it out and I survived," Nox said with a shrug.

He reached for the key, but Nelson pulled it away. "There's something I want to talk to you about before I let you out of the cage," Nelson said, tracing Nox's pouting lips with the key.

"Oh? Is this something serious or sexy?" Nox's brows jumped and he searched Nelson's face for hints.

"It could be serious but I'd like to make it sexy, if you'll help me," he said softly.

Nox nodded, holding onto Nelson's tie because he had a feeling he'd need something to hang onto. "What's up?"

"I'm taking a week off for your birthday. I'd like to talk about the trip."

"Right..." Nox's grip was suddenly sweaty around the tie and he was dizzy. "I figured Merlin was handling it and he'd fill you in on all the details. We're just..." He shrugged, flinched, laughed, and flailed vaguely, his gaze darting around the bathroom as he blinked back tears. "It's not a big deal," he croaked.

"Nox." Nelson cradled his face and shushed softly as he kissed him. "I want to celebrate the birth of my love, mo anam cara,"[1] he breathed, his lips clinging to Nox's reverently, making the hairs on his arms and the back of his neck stand.

"Gods, Nelson," he panted, shivering against him despite the soft, seductive warmth swirling in his chest and the front of his boxers. The cage held the throbbing need at bay, so Nox could cherish and revere the sensual heat of their souls as they burned hotter for each other. "You don't know what it does to me to hear you speak like that," Nox said as he angled his head and lapped at Nelson's lips and tongue. He sipped and became intoxicated by the minty taste of Nelson's mouth and the slide of their tongues as they swirled around each other.

"Wait." Nelson paused to catch his breath. "I want you to listen to me, first." He shushed, tapping their foreheads together so Nox would settle and focus. "This thing that may or may not be the calamity you're afraid of doesn't have to be the *only* thing that happens. We're going up for the whole week, right?" He waited until Nox nodded and pressed a kiss to his lips, rewarding him. "I've already done a little research of my own and I thought we'd leave early Sunday morning. I planned a few romantic detours, starting with breakfast at a diner in Altoona. They serve pancakes as big as your face and something called 'the mess' that's made with fried potatoes that's popular, according to the reviews."

"Pancakes and fried potatoes?" Nox laughed, a shaky watery burst, suddenly delighted and excited. He'd dreaded this year's birthday trip because it had become a big, dark question mark that Nox didn't want to face. He was so afraid that it would be the end. Not for him, but for him and Nelson. Before Nelson, Nox had been simply defiant, determined to live as much and go as far as he could before he reached the end of his journey. Now, Nox wanted to put it off and hold onto every moment with Nelson he could before his time was up. "That's perfect," he said, sliding an arm around Nelson's neck. His legs were shaking but he was the happy kind of lightheaded. "I can't wait now."

Nelson rumbled in agreement as his hands kneaded and caressed Nox's neck and back, making his legs even more useless. "There are some falls and a few wildlife viewing areas, one with an easy hiking trail by a place called Drift Wood. I thought we'd ditch the dysfunctional duo so we could go on a romantic walk. I'm hoping we can time it right so I can...do the thing with my mouth," he added in a mumbled rush.

"Fuck," Nox said hoarsely, licking his lips so they'd work. "I love it when you talk dirty, Nelson."

He blushed and swore into the corner of Nox's neck. "I'm trying."

"No!" Nox leaned back and yanked Nelson's tie loose. "I love the way *you* talk dirty because I know exactly what you mean by 'the thing' with your mouth." He took Nelson's hand and guided it to his fly and the cage waiting under the zipper. Desire throttled, tempered by molded silicone. But Nox shivered in anticipation. Those shocked, over-sensitized nerves would sing once it came off. His senses would be heightened as his nerves and his uncaged cock stretched and unfurled. "Dear gods, what that mouth can do..." He groaned raggedly, already drunk on the thought of Nelson on his knees in the forest. "We'll have days out there before the equinox," he realized with a wavering laugh.

"Mmmhmmm..." Nelson nodded, distracted as he flicked the button at Nox's waist open with his thumb, then slowly unzipped. "Days for me to do lots of...things to you in the woods. And by the lake. Merlin said there's a lake."

It would be too cold to go swimming, but Nox's Pisces-Aries cusp heart beat faster at the thought of fooling around by the lake up at Coudersport. The only thing Nox loved more than nature was when you added water to nature. His soul practically sang when he was on that lake and felt the sun on his face, it was that magickal. It was probably a good thing they couldn't go swimming, Nox would probably combust and make the lake evaporate if Nelson put his hands inside his swim trunks.

"Oh, there's a lake alright," Nox murmured dazedly, laughing as Nelson pushed his jeans and boxers down and lifted him.

"How do you feel about glamping?" Nelson asked as he set Nox on the counter and whisked them off. The jeans and boxers were tossed at the closet, along with the last of Nox's worries.

"Glamping?" Nox blinked at Nelson, too in love to make sense of what he was saying.

Chapter Eighteen

"I found a company that rents fancy tents and they come out and set everything up for you. There's a glamping package that comes with everything—a bed, linens, a little outhouse with a shower and toilet. Everything runs on solar but there's a backup generator. I didn't have a lot of time to do much research but I thought it might be a good birthday gift and fun," he explained with a vague shrug that set Nox's heart ablaze.

"You did?" He pulled Nelson to him, crying as he covered his face in wet, giggling kisses. "I love you, I love you, I love you. And I can't wait to go glamping. *Thank you*," he said, then kissed Nelson with every bit of gratitude and joy he could muster. "I haven't been this excited about my birthday since I was a kid. I really haven't felt like celebrating since I lost my parents. It didn't make sense without them, but I have a new reason to now." He was crying as he plucked at the buttons on Nelson's shirt with clumsy, trembling fingers and pushed it over his shoulders.

"You are the best thing that's ever happened to me, my... A chuisle mo chroí,"[2] Nelson said in his low, tender rumble, bringing fresh tears to Nox's eyes and making him ache. Nelson was so shy about practicing Gaelic but he was *learning* and it made Nox's insides turn to jelly every time Nelson tried. "You're the best thing I've ever had, Nox. Before you, the only thing I had that I could love was my car. Nothing will stop me from celebrating *you*, mo anam cara."

His lips slanted over Nox's, claiming them and stealing his breath. Their fingers fumbled and tangled as they wrestled Nelson's belt through the buckle and attacked his zipper. Nox swallowed Nelson's frustrated swears, as he kicked away his trousers and did his best to tug off his socks without breaking their kiss.

"The key," Nox reminded him when Nelson picked him up, ready to move to the shower.

"Right!" Nelson set Nox back down and had to release him to reach for the key. "How could I forget?" He clicked his teeth, scolding himself as he lowered and took a knee in front of Nox. "When I've been looking forward to this for days," he said, parting Nox's thighs. His confession causing goosebumps, whispered and kissed against Nox's trembling skin as Nelson deftly turned the key in the tiny lock.

Nox was dizzy as he watched, panting. "Have you?"

"Mmmm..." Nelson's tone was lazy but his gaze was fierce and starving when it flicked to Nox's, a wolf ready to devour his prey. "Time to set you free," he said in a beguiling growl.

"Yes!" Nox begged, ready to be released and ravished. Old, old wounds had been healed and Nelson had given Nox an early birthday miracle. His heart burned with pure joy for Nelson as he eased the cage off of Nox's compressed flesh, crooning softly and nuzzling tenderly.

"I miss this," he whispered, the hot huffs of breath against Nox's sac and swelling shaft made him shudder and whimper in relief. "I miss feeling you need me."

"Me too but this feels so..." Nox's eyes rolled as Nelson's tongue curled around his cock. The pounding, flashing pleasure from nerves that had been pressed and smothered was intoxicating and excruciating. "Nelson!"

He took Nox's semi-flaccid length into his mouth and sucked slow and hard, coaxing it to full length as his hands stroked and teased.

"Come for me now," Nelson ordered in his low, deep growl and Nox's body reacted immediately, cum bursting from his straining erection in a thick rope that landed on Nelson's chin and chest. The flash of bright, pulsing pleasure startling Nox, as he held onto Nelson's head and the counter.

"Oops!" He was unsteady and drunk with lust and love as Nelson hummed happily and gathered the cum from his skin, licking his fingers clean.

"I meant to do that," Nelson said with a cheeky grin as he rose and backed Nox into the shower.

Nox laughed as he reached behind him for the faucet. "Did you?"

"Mmmhmm... Want to see how many times I can do it again?"

---

1. **Mo anam cara** (muh ann-imm carrah) my soulmate, my soul friend.
2. **A chuisle mo chroí** (A quish-leh muh kree) my treasure, my beloved.

Nineteen

"Oh...my god." Nelson had never been so sore in his life. He had managed to keep Nox home and distracted for three days but Nelson had pulled something in his left thigh and his ass was raw from what Nox was calling his "jail beard."

"Nope. It's Nox!" He cheered as he crashed onto the bed next to Nelson and rolled him over. "Want me to kiss it and make it better?"

Nelson cracked an eye open and shook his head. "You haven't shaved yet and I'm raw...there."

"Here's the thing!" Nox whispered. "I tried to but my shaving cream keeps melting because I made it out of beeswax and shea butter. I tried yours and it turned to liquid too and spilled right out of my hand."

"It melted?" Nelson verified slowly. Nox hummed as he took Nelson's hand in his and pressed their palms together. Nox's hand was *hot*, burning against Nelson's cooler skin. "Nox!" Nelson grabbed Nox's wrist and checked his hand to make sure it wasn't blistering.

"I know." Nox's lips fluttered as he shrugged. "It usually

doesn't get this bad until a few days before, so I usually ask Merlin to shave me or I let my beard grow out until I get back."

"I can do it," Nelson offered. He regretted it almost immediately.

"You have to hold still!" he complained half an hour later, after nicking Nox's jaw by his ear. He'd cut Nox a few times but he didn't seem as troubled about it as Nelson.

"I'm trying!"

"No, you're not. You won't stop wiggling."

"What if we did it outside on the terrace? I want to go outside."

Nelson shook his head. "I don't want to risk more pictures. Walt could be watching us."

"To hell with him!" Nox's shoulders drooped as he pouted loudly.

Nelson grabbed the top of Nox's head, pinning him. "Be still!"

It took several more requests but Nelson was eventually able to complete the task. He was already worn out as he rinsed the blade and wiped down the counter and it wasn't even 8:00 AM yet. And they still had *three weeks* until the beginning of Ostara.

"Not too bad," Nox said while admiring his reflection. "We're a little behind this morning so let's get breakfast on the way," he suggested, heading into the closet.

"On the way?" Nelson asked as he followed.

"To Sheilas. Duh," Nox replied.

"Are you sure you want to do that today? Your friend, the AG, said he'd make sure we had whatever we needed to bring Walt in but let's give him a few more days. I'd like to go in with a warrant and my ducks in a row."

"Nice try. I know it came in yesterday, just before dinner."

Nelson smothered a curse. "You heard about that?" He scrubbed the back of his neck as he stalled. He'd taken the call in the hallway while Nox was in the bathroom and had kept his voice down.

"What are you so afraid of? She's a harmless old witch who barely knows what day it is."

"You said the house is full of trash, for starters. And there were lots of dead crows," Nelson replied, making Nox's nose wrinkle.

"What if I promise it's not the *worst* house we've been to?"

Nelson blinked at Nox, hoping he'd realize that wasn't saying much.

"It doesn't smell nearly as bad as the MacCrorys' and only dead animals at Sheila's," he repeated but Nelson shook his head.

"All the more reason to go in with a team of techs in coveralls."

"That'll take too long and Walt's going to hear about it if we put a task force together." Nox gave Nelson's shoulder a playful punch. "We've got this! Besides, he *knows* and we have everything we need now. Let's finish this."

"Okay." Nelson threw his hands up, all out of excuses. "I'll let Merlin and Clancy know that we're leaving," Nelson said as he backed out of the closet.

"If you feel the need," Nox murmured and pulled a T-shirt over his head.

Nelson turned and silently hurried from the room, taking out his phone and sending Clancy a text requesting a meeting at the bottom of the stairs ASAP.

"Boots or sneakers?" Nox called from the closet as Nelson jogged down the hallway.

"What's going on?" Clancy called from the foyer when Nelson reached the banister.

Nelson checked the hall to make sure Nox wasn't coming, then threw Clancy a tight nod. "I just want to sprain or crack a few things. Don't let me break anything important or die," he whispered and Clancy's neck craned in confusion.

"What?"

"I don't have time," Nelson said, giving his head a quick shake. "Don't let me die," he repeated before rushing down the stairs. He waited until he was halfway to turn and roll his left ankle, tipping him toward the rail.

"Stad!"[1] Clancy barked and Nelson's body locked.

He was suspended mid-fall as the hall and foyer blurred around him. His body rocked and swayed from side to side as his arms and legs pulled and jerked like they were attached to strings until the walls and stairs came into focus again.

"Fuck!" Nelson crashed into the painting on his right, slid as he missed two steps, and then bumped his left hip hard on the rail before landing on his ass on the bottom step.

"What happened?" Nox slid into the hall in his socks, crashing into the banister.

"Fuck!" Nelson repeated as various limbs and joints burned and stung.

Nox hurried down the stairs. "Don't move!"

"What happened? I heard a commotion." Merlin had his bag ready as he hopped to see around Clancy.

He had hunkered down next to Nelson and was helping him rearrange his limbs and straighten. "Nox, make sure we've got plenty of ice. There's no telling what he's sprained."

"On it," Nox said, leaping over the banister, then sprinting into the kitchen.

Clancy gave Nelson a stern glare as he helped him up. "I don't know how you knew, but that was a foolish risk to take," he scolded.

Nelson's cheeks puffed out as he nodded. "I know but I was desperate. I've done *everything* I can to keep him upstairs and distracted but we...can't anymore. I *will* break something or die and he was set on going back to Sheila's today," he told them in a hushed whisper, making Merlin chuckle.

"A noble sacrifice for the team," he said as he scooted in closer and put his arm around Nelson's waist to support him.

"Thanks," Nelson said, then gasped when he stepped down on his right foot and felt a sharp, shooting pain in his ankle.

There was a knowing sound from Clancy as he pulled

Nelson's arm around his neck. "It took several attempts to get it just right so you may feel like you rolled down the stairs a dozen times. We might have broken your neck once," he said with a wince. "But I think this should be just enough to buy us a few days."

"Don't you worry!" Merlin beamed up at Nelson. "I'll whip up something to keep you comfortable."

"No. Please don't," Nelson said, shaking his head.

"We have plenty of ice and I threw together a mustard plaster," Nox said as he returned with a bowl and a bundle of ice in a washcloth."

"Good thinking!" Merlin winked at Nelson and there was another humph from Clancy, but he was smiling as they made their way to the study.

"I can't believe *you* of all people fell down the stairs," Nox said, using his foot to push the coffee table away from the sofa so there was more room to maneuver Nelson around it.

"I was looking for something in my notes," Nelson mumbled, earning an eye roll from Nox.

"Now, *that* doesn't surprise me. You and that notepad, Nelson..." He clicked his teeth as Clancy and Merlin helped Nelson lower onto the sofa.

A hand squeezed Nelson's asscheek and he jumped. "Come on, Merlin!"

"Just making sure it's not injured," Merlin said, then gasped when Nox gave him a hard flick on the ear.

"Behave and take this," he said, passing Merlin the bowl and bundle of ice. "I'll get some pillows so we can elevate that foot. Looks like Nelson's getting his way after all. He's not going anywhere for the next few days with the way that ankle's swelling."

He sighed sympathetically as he left them again and Nelson felt pathetic as he carefully reclined, hissing and wincing at the multitude of screaming aches. The adrenaline was wearing off quickly and his body was registering the numerous injuries he had sustained in the stunt.

"Well played, indeed," Clancy murmured and looked impressed as he moved the coffee table around so it was at Nelson's side. "This should keep them busy for a while," he noted as Merlin hunted in his bag and clucked about salves and tonics.

"I hope so," Nelson replied. "They might be busy but I'll be stuck on my ass. What if I need to go to the office?"

"I'll run anything you need to and from the Hoover Building and call anyone who can help," Clancy stated with one of his half-bows.

"Okay…" Nelson didn't know if he'd ever get used to Clancy's deference. "We need to see if anyone's heard from Walt. I want to see if the APB's been released and if his mother has any vehicles in her name he might be using," he said, thinking out loud. Nelson went to get his notebook from inside his coat and swore at the burst of pain in his shoulder.

"Let me help!" Merlin insisted and shooed Clancy away so he could grope Nelson's pecs and abs as he eased the coat off of him. "Here you go, my lad," he said breathlessly as he handed Nelson his notepad.

"You're welcome," Nelson replied, making Clancy laugh from the desk while he scribbled on another notebook.

"Here," Clancy said as he passed it to Nelson. "Write whatever you can think of and I'll run it down for you."

"Playing junior agent, Clance?" Nox said when he returned with a tall stack of pillows. "I put the kettle on for tea."

Clancy shrugged and hugged his chest, regarding Nelson from his perch on the sofa's other arm. "He's done just as much for us and he's yet to let us down," he said and Nox made a pleased sound as he plumped a pair of pillows and guided Nelson back so he was reclining.

"I'm not that tired, real—" he started, but Nox pressed a finger against his lips.

"Let's take this as a sign from nature and gravity that you need more rest. You ran a clerical marathon to clear us and then you spent the last few days using your sexual wiles to distract me, like Circe in a suit and tie."

"Oh?" Merlin turned, alert and eyes twinkling.

"Fine! I'll rest," Nelson blurted so Nox wouldn't go into detail. Merlin looked like he had questions and Nelson wouldn't be able to escape if Nox brought up the cage or their "practice sessions."

"Good," Nox said with a firm nod. "The sooner you accept your punishment and submit to our tender care, the better," he said, then gasped. "My special quilt! That always makes me feel better. And my guitar. I'll sing to you while you recuperate! Be right back!" Nox said as he dashed from the room.

Nelson looked at Clancy, filled with regret. "Can you stop time again, if I can get back to the stairs, and just let me break my neck?"

There was a soft chuckle from Clancy as he stood and patted Nelson on the arm, making him grunt in agony as another wave of aches and stings rippled through him. "I suggest you settle in, Nelson," he advised. "It's going to feel like a very long and ridiculous recovery."

---

1. **Stad!** (Stadd) Stop!

Twenty

Forty-eight hours later, Nelson was almost happy to be driving over the bridge into New Jersey and on the way to Pennsville, his ankle bandaged but feeling much better. After two days of enduring Nox and Merlin's doting, Nelson would have been over the moon if they were headed anywhere but Sheila's house. He had drunk enough tea to fill the Delaware River and his ears would bleed if he ever heard "Wonderwall" again.

But Nelson had considered another tumble down the stairs before they left the townhouse: he was so desperate to avoid taking Nox back to Sheila Forsythe's house. The same instincts that had warned that returning to New Castle with Nox was a bad idea screamed as they drove into Pennsville. He had insisted that it would be better to bring her to the Hoover Building for questioning. His theory was that Walt might come out of hiding if she was kept for a medical and psychiatric evaluation.

"What if he panics and burns down the house and poisons her while she's in our custody? Or what if she decides to sacrifice herself for him and unalives herself?" Nox had argued. "I wouldn't put anything past Walt now and she might not be worth the time and effort it would take to bring her in, she's so unmoored from reality."

"Then, why are you so set on going there now? Why can't we go after we've found Walt?"

Nox whistled and shook his head at the passenger window. "You need to meet Sheila and see what's in that basement. Walt won't give her or that house up easily and he'll flip if he knows we're in there."

"Sounds like another trap," Nelson sighed.

"I know!" Nox rubbed his hands together. "If we can get him to come to us *and* catch him with heaps of evidence that proves it was all his doing..."

Nelson blinked at the windshield, reeling. "Why do I keep walking into them with you?"

"You might be a masochist," Nox whispered out of the side of his mouth. "And it's a lot more fun than checking out utility bills and talking to retired butchers. Not that all of that wasn't *brilliant*," Nox stated and made sure that Nelson knew those weren't minor contributions. "But it's go time! We've learned all we can about Walt and Sheila and it's time to put all that hard work to use and bring it home."

It felt like go time as Nelson parked in front of the small and weathered house on the overgrown corner lot. Nox had warned that it was a mess inside and filled with terrible memories. It certainly seemed haunted and Nelson reached into his coat and unbuttoned his holster when he saw a curtain in one of the upstairs windows swaying.

His pulse was racing as they climbed the steps and entered the closed-in front porch and Nox reached for the doorbell.

"Wait." Nelson grabbed his sleeve. "There's no point telling you not to touch anything, but remember that Walt poisoned three people. Please," he added before letting him press the button.

"Duh! Should I go with Boy Scouts or are we Mormons?" Nox whispered as they waited.

"Don't."

The door cracked and Nelson looked down as a petite woman with wild gray hair scowled up at them. She clutched the halves of her mauve robe together, her dark, beady eyes narrowing as her face twisted.

"I know who you are," she muttered at them and Nox snapped his fingers.

"Nuts! I really thought we could pass as Mormons. He's in a big boy suit and tie," he said, pointing at Nelson.

"Walt told me you'd come but he's not here." She went to close the door but Nox stuck the toe of his boot in the way.

"No worries, dear! We were hoping to get to know you better."

Nelson cleared his throat as he reached into his coat and took out an envelope. "We have a warrant, but I'd prefer to come in and chat without a team of techs taking your house apart and upsetting you," he said calmly.

"You have no right!" she hissed at him and Nox clicked his teeth.

"Sure he does. He's got that warrant and a badge. He can have this place crawling with scientists and investigators in half an hour. Keep up, Sheila." He lowered, planting his hands on his knees so they were eye-to-eye. "Walt is not going to be happy with you if that happens, is he?"

"He'll deal with you," she said to Nox, but she stepped back and opened the door, letting them pass.

Nelson offered her a nod, then gulped loudly as he stepped inside, immediately overwhelmed by the smell. He pressed the back of his hand against his nose to block some of the stench but the heaviness of the air made him anxious and queasy.

"You said it wouldn't smell this bad and I can hear flies," he hissed at Nox.

"You sacrificed something recently, Sheila," Nox said as he craned his neck, searching the dim, debris-cluttered hallway ahead of them. She whispered to herself, a vindictive rush of Latin and

English gibberish as she prowled behind them in her faded robe and dingy white house slippers. They made an annoying scraping sound, but it was almost drowned out by the buzzing of flies when they passed what should have been a dining room. Nelson could make out the carcass of a medium-sized animal on an oak dining table in the dark, cluttered room.

"Where are we headed? The den?" Nox asked Sheila, pointing ahead of them at the end of the hall.

"My smokes are in there," she told him and shuffled past Nox. He held up his hands, widening his eyes at Nelson as he followed her in.

Nelson didn't like the looks of the small back room and decided to post in the doorway so he could keep an eye on the hallway and the stairs. The kitchen was behind him and Nelson ignored the stacks of boxes, dirty plastic microwave dinner trays, and empty styrofoam soup cups littering the counters. Nox was right: it was only half as bad as Julian's or being in the MacCrorys' trailer.

That was a low bar and Nelson snorted inwardly, wondering if he was becoming desensitized and if a fly-swarmed carcass was, in fact, only half as bad as a house full of snakes or a dead elderly woman.

Depends on the woman.

Nelson wouldn't shed a tear over Lonnie MacCrory. And he had a really bad feeling about Sheila Forsythe, as she lowered into a filthy mustard-colored recliner. She pulled an old afghan blanket up to her chin and lit a Virginia Slim. The walls and sloped ceiling of the den were lined with wood paneling and the room's only window was sealed with cardboard and duct tape. A small TV flickered on a stand in the corner, casting the lower half of the room in a gray glow. The volume was turned low and Nelson raised a brow at the televangelist on the screen.

"That's bad for you," Nox scolded her and she mumbled something under her breath before taking a long drag.

"You should worry about yourself," she replied, her scrawny gnarled hand shaking as she raised the thin cigarette to her lips.

"Oh, I do," Nox assured her from his spot by the TV. He had to bend his neck to avoid the ceiling. "Your son has a nasty grudge against me and it's time we settled the matter," he said loudly.

"He's ready for you," she said as she pushed herself back up and shoved her hand into the blanket.

"Fuck!" Nelson reached into his coat, drawing his weapon from the holster as soon as he spotted the pistol and rushed in as Sheila aimed it at Nox.

"Come on, Sheila," Nox complained and swung around when they heard a floorboard creak in the kitchen. Nelson kept his eyes and his weapon trained on Sheila, though, ducking and flinching when Nox yelled. That was all the warning Nelson had before something slammed against the back of his head and he heard a tremendous crack, throwing him forward as everything went black.

Twenty-One

"Hold it right there," Sheila said, aiming her gun at Nox.

He blinked down at Nelson, then at Walt. He was watching Nox with a smarmy grin and a wooden baseball bat rested on his shoulder. "May I?" Nox asked with absolute calmness, holding up his hands as he lowered and keeping his eyes on Walt. "I just have to make sure he's still breathing." Inside, Nox was hanging onto that calm by his fingernails. A conflagration of rage exploded within him at the sight of Nelson on the floor in a rumpled pile of limbs.

"I'm sure nothing important was damaged," Walt chuckled as he leaned the bat against the wall.

Nox's gaze flicked up and was severe as it held Walt's. "I'd start praying now," he said as he pressed the pads of his fingers to Nelson's neck and let out a loud sigh of relief when he felt a pulse throbbing steadily. "He was the only chance you had of surviving this," Nox said as he rose.

"Get back!" Sheila shouted and jabbed at the air with the pistol, but Walt smirked knowingly at Nox.

"He isn't armed and dark magick is beneath him," he told her and clicked his teeth at Nox. "What are you going to do, *professor*?

Dazzle me with one of your silly little tricks or throw some crystals at me?"

"Why did you say professor like that? Like, it isn't totally badass that I get to teach young people about the world and history."

"You sound like a chump and a child," Walt said with a pinched look at Nox. "And the way you carry yourself... What does *anyone* see in you?"

A wide, calculating smile stretched across Nox's face. "Oh, that bothers you, doesn't it?" He searched Walt's eyes and his aura, seeking out the bitterness and resentment. "You tried so hard—killed parts of yourself—to be better than me and it was never enough, was it?"

"Shut up!" Walt spat back at Nox. "There is nothing special about you except your name and your family's money, right Mother?" he asked, earning a sick giggle from Sheila.

"Trash!" she jeered.

"Look at him, Mother!" Walt said, his hand flailing. "He's just a spoiled child. And a punk," he added with a snort at Nox's ensemble.

He frowned down at his jeans, Pink Floyd T-shirt, and vintage leather jacket. "The classics never go out of style and I can't compete with Nelson, suits are his thing. I'd definitely look like a kid on his way to court next to him," Nox mused airily.

"You see what I mean?" Walt said to her as he shook his head at Nox. "*This* is who the great Darach Clancy would pick to be the new king."

"Nobody picked me to be anything," Nox answered wearily.

"No, you were born to it!" Walt countered quickly, petulant loathing etched on his face as he advanced on Nox. "Would it have been so easy to shirk your destiny if you hadn't been spoiled from the moment you were pulled from your pitiful mother's womb?"

"Whoa!" Nox raised a finger in warning at Walt. "You don't want to bring my mom into this. You're in enough trouble."

That earned another cackle from Sheila. "He's just a little

smartass, Walter," she said and he nodded as he squared up to Nox.

"You'd rather swan around campus like some dark prince of the anthropology department and do stupid Netflix documentaries than be a god. What is it you're so afraid of?" he asked in a seething whisper as he studied Nox. "Is it the responsibility and the pressure? Or does it bore you, the idea of having to think of anything but yourself?"

"Well…" Nox rubbed his chin, pretending to ponder the matter while he waited for Nelson to wake up. "Maybe all of the above. I don't consider myself to be a very selfish person, but I think we're all afraid of losing our autonomy…" He winced as he tipped toward Walt conspiratorially. "In this case, it could be literal autonomy. If you believe in mythology and old prophecies," he added with a wink.

There was a flicker and a slight flexing of Walt's brows before he shook it off. "What would be the point of that?" he said dismissively and Nox laughed.

"You really didn't think about that, did you?" he asked with a wide-eyed look at Sheila before swinging back to Walt. "How many seats do you think there are in here?" He tapped his temple. "Can't see *Him* sharing control and us playing rock, paper, scissors when we can't decide what we want for lunch or if we want to end humanity. Can't really enjoy the perks of being a god if your soul's been immolated."

"Don't listen to him," she said with a snort. "He's just making excuses because he doesn't want anyone to have that power."

Walt made a knowing sound and looked down his nose at Nox. "You're so enamored with your virtue that it's made you weak and stupid."

"And you're so enamored with what you think a professor and a sun king should look like that it's made you blind," Nox countered. "You believed your mother's delusions and you assume too much, Walt. That's going to be your downfall," he predicted, making Sheila scowl.

"Don't listen to him. He knows his will is weak and that you would be better than he is. And even if he's right, who would ever forget your name? I would be the mother of *a god*."

Nox's face twisted as he recoiled. "Now, *that* is selfish. And this is why your plan will never work, Walt." He shook his head and winked at Walt. "Watch this!" he whispered and lifted two fingers, causing Sheila's hair to swirl around her as Nox gathered all the air in the room, then hurled her at the wall.

"No!" Walt yelled as she slid to the floor and the gun hit the rug with a hard *thunk*.

"Ah ah!" Nox pointed when Walt tensed to dive for it. "And why would you bring a gun to a Badb fight?" he asked, grinning mischievously and enjoying Walt's wariness as he prowled closer.

"You have no idea of what I'm capable of," Walt said and raised his nose smugly, but he jumped when he backed into the doorjamb.

Nox followed, smiling with delight as he grew warmer and happier. The reckoning was nearly at hand and it would be *glorious*. "Trust me, Walt. I know exactly what you're capable of."

Walt shook his head stubbornly. "No. You don't know me. You don't know what I know."

"Let me tell you what I know," Nox began silkily and saw the goosebumps that spread up Walt's neck and the first flash of fear in his eyes. "You were seventeen when you cast your first curse. You sacrificed a rabbit in the moonlight to Hecate because you wanted to be valedictorian *of your high school*. It didn't work because you childishly slapped together practices and bound them with clumsy dark magick. *And* because it was selfish," Nox added simply, causing Walt to flinch.

"Who told you that?"

"I saw it!" Nox whispered excitedly. "I saw the things you buried and the things you burned *and* what your mother made you do with her on Samhain," he said with a gag and shuddered. "She was sick and she lied to you about her father and your father so you'd be just as sick as she was."

Tears filled Walt's eyes as his gaze swept to his mother's unconscious body. "What are you talking about?"

"She was right about Clancy. He was the same man she was obsessed with when she was at Princeton."

"There are pictures! Pictures of them together," Walt argued, but Nox shook his head.

"At a banquet after he received an award and when she followed him to a gallery. Clancy never slept with your mother. He barely knew she existed."

Walt visibly reeled. "What? What are you saying?"

"She *wanted* Clancy to be your father but he went on a sabbatical the week before you were conceived and laid low until he transferred to Georgetown four years later. Your mom cracked after he left. She got hammered and asked a man to have his way with her in the parking lot of a bowling alley and told herself it was Clancy, that he came back for one night because he couldn't forget *her*," he said with an incredulous look at Sheila.

"Are you saying she wasn't good enough for him?" Walt challenged and Nox shrugged.

"You brought my mom into it first. Sheila was wrong about who her father was, but she was lied to," Nox said, sighing sadly at Walt as he closed the space between them and warmed the room and the lights in the kitchen. "You were both twisted by the lonely, unanswered wish for a father's love and I am so sorry about that. But you should have sought therapy, Walt, not another man's destiny and the lives of seven innocent girls."

"No!" Walt screamed, squeezing his eyes and his fists as tight as he could. "Clancy doesn't matter anymore. You don't know what I've learned. You don't know who I am *now* and what I'm going to do."

"What did I tell you?" Nox sang as he wagged a finger. "You made too many assumptions," he said, feeling himself glow even brighter when Walt shrank away, backing into the cramped kitchen. A soft light radiated from Nox and Walt was crying as he shielded his face.

"What do you mean? I know—" he started shakily. "How are you doing that?" he asked, but Nox cut him off, shushing softly as he guided Walt to the table until he stumbled into one of the chairs.

"Why don't you take a seat," Nox suggested and kicked one of the legs, turning it for Walt. "You're not the only one who can gae intill smoake and blind thy mind to time. I thought you were ill—that you had a cold—but it was the dark magick making you sick."

All the color drained from Walt as he sank onto the chair. "You've been here before," he realized, gulping as he looked at Sheila, then up at Nox. "But Clancy despises dark magick and he said you were afraid to break your soul."

"Of course, I was afraid," Nox replied with an obvious look. "I have *some* common sense and value my soul. I won't sell bits of it to demons like you will, but I'll burn myself for the sake of some angels." He cleared his throat as he canted forward, looming over Walt. "And do you know why I can get away with that without getting sick like you?"

"Why?" There was a pleading rasp in Walt's voice as he stared up at Nox, ensorcelled by the growing brilliance.

"Because only one of us is actually descended from the Badb," Nox explained and gently cradled Walt's chin. "That's why I've never feared you and why your curses kept failing."

"Why would you lie and hide?" Walt asked, his voice wavering as he watched Nox with terrified, adoring eyes. A flash of hot gold was reflected in them as they shimmered and tears rolled down Walt's cheek. "Why would you deny what you are? I only tried to take the throne so I could spread *His* light!"

A giggle fluttered from Nox. It was just the tinder he needed to ignite the ire of the god in him. "You tried to take the throne!" he whispered, suddenly giddy with arousal and joy. There was a muffled groan from Nelson as he stirred, adding to Nox's delight. "You said the magick words!" He raised his arms, giving himself over to the Dagda's fury, his soul ascending to meet *Him*. "Do you want to see the throne and feel *His* power?" Nox asked in a swelling growl that caused the pictures on the wall to rattle.

"Yes!" Walt nodded jerkily as he began to cry in earnest. He clasped his hands together and held them up to Nox. "I worked so hard and I sacrificed everything to prove that I was worthy!"

"You were never worthy!" Nox said with an offended sneer. "You sacrificed things you had no right to take and you polluted our light with your lies."

Walt reached for Nox. "I'm sorry! Forgive me!"

"It's too late." Nox set his hand on Walt's forehead. "It's time for you to see *Him*."

"Yes!"

But Walt's ecstatic cry was swallowed by a howl as his skin was seared and whiffs of smoke curled around Nox's palm. "You thought *you* were strong enough to contain this?" Nox asked, reaching through the curses and dark enchantments guarding Walt and snagging the last withered shred of his soul. Nox yanked that wretched husk wide open and filled Walt's eyes with ethereal beauty. "Behold! Tuatha!" Nox commanded, giving way to the incandescent heat.

"No! Stop!" Walt slapped at Nox's wrist, but it was too late.

He wasn't in charge anymore. "*See me!*" an ancient voice bellowed.

"*No!*"

Walt's screams were drowned out by the sounds of buzzing bees and glorious harp song and Nox was blinded by golden radiance. He heard Walt's distant cries and his keening begging but they had quieted by the time Nox's senses cleared and he was himself again. When Nox tugged on his right ear to work out the last of the faint buzzing, Walt was babbling and weeping up at him.

"I saw *Him! He* gave me all these bees and I can see the sun!" He was holding onto Nox's wrist, shivering as he stared with distant, unfocused eyes. They were no longer dark brown but a dull gray as he blinked at the ceiling. "Look at all these bees!"

Chapter Twenty-One

"I see them," Nox lied as he pried Walt's fingers open and freed his wrist. "Enjoy those bees, buddy," he said with a gentle pat on top of Walt's head.

He took out his phone and went over to try and rouse Nelson. He was still unconscious and groaning weakly as Nox lowered and checked his pulse again. It was getting stronger and Nox made a relieved sound, stroking Nelson's brow as he dialed 911 and waited for the dispatcher to answer.

"911, what is your emergency?" a man's voice asked and Nox smiled as Walt tried to catch one of his invisible friends.

"Hello, my name is Professor Lennox MacIlwraith and my partner, Agent Grady Nelson of the FBI, was attacked by Walter Forsythe. Agent Nelson's injured and unconscious and there's an unconscious woman here as well."

"Units are en route. What about you, sir? Are you injured?"

Nox glanced down at himself. "No, I'm fine. Mr. Forsythe's behavior became extremely erratic while we were questioning him and then he attacked my partner and his mother. But I was able to subdue him and I don't think he's going to hurt anyone ever again."

"What do you mean?" the dispatcher asked warily.

Nox cringed at Walt. "He seems quite lost now and I don't think we'll be seeing any more of Mr. Forsythe."

Twenty-Two

"Can you hear me, Agent Nelson?" a young man's voice beckoned as the darkness receded and Nelson heard voices and the chaos of a crime scene.

Nelson opened his eyes, then grunted when a penlight was aimed at his pupils. The back of his skull throbbed and burned and his ears rang. "Give me a minute," he said, blocking his face and trying to see past the halos of light. "Where's Nox?" He tried to get up but he was swaddled in a blanket and strapped to a stretcher.

"He's right there. I'll send for him if you'll let me check you out," the younger man said in a competent and gently authoritative tone. "I'm Bryn Cadwalleder. You've been unconscious for a while, Agent Nelson."

He had big, seeking green eyes and his dark hair was pulled into a tight bun. He was wearing paramedics' coveralls and they were inside an ambulance. Bryn gestured at the commotion outside and Nelson blinked, numb and befuddled when he could finally make out the bodies of officers and agents. A row streamed out of Sheila Forsythe's house with boxes as another row marched past them on their way inside. Reporters and their crews were assembling on the sidewalks and in the street and Nelson could see Sheila in the back of a police car. She was sobbing and screaming at him.

"What the hell happened?" Nelson asked while freeing the buckle on his chest, earning a wry chuckle from Bryn.

"Not 100% sure about the finer details, but I heard you took a Louisville Slugger to the back of the skull. It looks like you ducked though, so it could have been worse. Babe Ruth is in the other ambulance having some kind of psychotic episode," he told Nelson, widening his eyes suggestively. "Thinks he saw a god and the sun."

Nelson's mouth went dry and his heart lurched, thudding to a halt. "He saw a god and the sun?"

"Something like that. Not my business," Bryn replied briskly. "We tried to check Mom out for injuries because she was unconscious when we first got here, but she's a biter and she hit one of the other medics so she was ejected from the game."

"She was unconscious?"

"They said Babe Ruth attacked her after he knocked you out of the park."

"I see..." Nelson didn't but he kept quiet, deciding it was better to wait until Nox could fill him in. He didn't want to contradict Nox or incriminate him. "You know, I'm feeling much better now. Thank you," he said, throwing off the fleece blanket.

"Sure you are." Bryn pinned Nelson with a hand to his chest, stunning him. The younger man was surprisingly strong for his size and age.

"I'll be fine. I need to go," Nelson insisted, then reared back when Bryn gave him the evil eye.

"You'll wait until I clear you to go and you have a ride. I overheard your sexy sidekick say he didn't drive."

"Alright," Nelson said, keeping his tone easy as he sat back.

He endured the rest of the exam and was cleared to go with a probable concussion and orders to see a doctor if he experienced any mental confusion, difficulty keeping his eyes open, or sudden loss of consciousness. Nelson was also ordered to get plenty of rest and avoid strenuous physical activity for a week, much to his dismay.

"I'll be driving him home and someone will be with him at all times," Clancy told Bryn and accepted Nelson's keys. "I rode up with Merlin," he said before Nelson could object and nodded at the Bentley parked behind another ambulance.

"Looks like he's in *good* hands, then," Bryn said with a smirk and a salute for Clancy as he left them.

"He was...odd," Nelson said, earning a humph of agreement from Clancy.

"Wasn't he?"

Merlin was with Nox and they were discussing something in hushed whispers about hounds when Nelson and Clancy joined them.

"Are you okay?" Nox said, pushing Merlin out of the way and reaching for Nelson.

"Probably a concussion but I'm fine." Nelson tightened his arms around Nox, breathing him in and checking him for any signs of injury.

"I'm fine." Nox leaned back in Nelson's arms and cupped his cheek. "We will do nothing but rest for *a week*," he said with a hard look at Merlin and Clancy. "What did you think of the paramedic?" he whispered and Clancy nodded.

"He could very well be," he said, causing Merlin and Nox to gasp and trade wide-eyed looks.

"What?" Nelson asked them, looking from face to face but Nox waved it off.

"He might be...special. I think he noticed me but I won't make a thing about it if he doesn't want me to." He shrugged, then wrinkled his nose at Nelson. "I have more important things to worry about than spectral hounds and we have to make a stop at the bookshop on the way home. I want to tell Howard and the others that it's over and make sure they know they're safe before they see this on the news and worry." He gestured at the vans and crews and Nelson winced.

"Good thinking. Let's go," Nelson said with a faint nod, careful not to aggravate the pounding ache at the back of his skull.

"We'll meet you there," Merlin said, waving as he left them.

"I was hoping I'd get a chance to drive your car, Nelson," Clancy confided and gave the keys a toss.

"No!" Nelson attempted to snatch them back but stumbled, his shoulder bumping Clancy's.

"Just let it happen," Nox said as his arm slid around Nelson's middle and he was wrapped in calming warmth.

"Fine," Nelson grumbled.

He glared at Clancy's head all the way to Adelphi, begrudgingly accepting Nox's hand as they rode in silence together in the back seat. Nox wasn't ready to go into detail about what had happened after Nelson took a line drive to the skull. He said it was better to wait until later, when Merlin was there, because he wasn't telling that story more than once.

Merlin had called ahead and Heidi was at the store with Howard, Tony, and Aubrey when the four of them arrived.

"What is it? What's happened?" Howard asked, stepping forward bravely as Tony held the girls' hands.

"It's over," Nox said to them, his voice low and wavering with emotion. "Walt and his mother are in custody and they won't be able to harm anyone ever again.

"Thank goodness!" Howard had his handkerchief out and had to cover his mouth to hold back a sob.

"Holy—! Wow!" Aubrey looked dizzy as she fanned her face. She began to shake and cry, throwing herself into Tony's embrace.

"It's okay! We'll get through this together," he promised her as Howard and Heidi hugged and cried.

"Bless you all," Howard told them as he rocked Heidi.

"We'll see," Nox replied with a solemn bow. "We have to get Nelson home so he can rest, but we'll see you all soon."

They all said their goodbyes and Nelson was relieved when Clancy parked his car in front of the townhouse.

This time, Nelson *did not* snatch the keys from Clancy and thanked him calmly when they were handed over.

"It was my pleasure," Clancy replied, as he headed inside with Merlin.

"You handled that very well," Nox said, sliding an arm around Nelson and escorting him inside.

Merlin and Clancy had already poured themselves drinks and had one ready for Nox, after he eased Nelson onto the sofa.

"Out with it!" Merlin wasted no time when he returned with an ice pack in a towel. "What happened after poor Nelson was knocked out?" He hissed sympathetically as he gently pressed the bundle against the back of Nelson's skull. "Just lay back and rest, lad. I've put the kettle on and will have some tea for you shortly."

"Thank you, but *please*, no more tea," Nelson said sincerely before clearing his throat. "Nox?"

He gave his glass a swirl, then winced at them. "I really don't know what to tell you," he said, waving for them to listen when the three of them protested loudly. "I wasn't entirely...there, so I'm a little unclear as to how it happened."

"You weren't there?" Nelson repeated, earning a sheepish wince from Nox.

"Walt used up the last bit of grace I had left to give when he hit you," he told Nelson. "I decided he could take his chances with the god, since he was so keen to meet *Him*, and then I let the Dagda take the wheel."

"Huh." Nelson hoped he was in shock and that Walt hadn't permanently damaged something, because he didn't know how he was supposed to feel or what he was supposed to do about what Nox had done. "Did Walt attack Sheila?"

"She was definitely going to shoot me, Nelson," Nox said, seemingly unbothered as he refilled his drink.

Nelson looked at Merlin and Clancy. "Are you two alright with this?" he asked and Clancy laughed as he joined Nox and held out his drink so it could be topped off.

"Feels like justice to me," he said with a raise of his glass to Nox.

"Agreed," Merlin said as he raised his as well.

"What if Sheila starts talking?" Nelson asked them and Nox's neck swiveled.

"About what? How her son was supposed to be a god and how she discovered that Clancy's an immortal who used to be a different teacher at a different university decades ago?"

Clancy shook his head. "I was able to take a look at the basement and no one will believe that either of them is sane."

"I removed the pictures of you," Nox told him. "There's a chance you could talk your way out of this and keep your job."

"Absolutely not," Clancy said. "I'll be handing in my resignation soon. I have no business in either position anymore. Not with the way Walt was able to manipulate me and the access I gave him."

"Are you sure? There will always be more monsters," Nox said with a lift of his brows but Clancy shook his head.

"You can take over for me when you get back."

Nox grunted, shaking his head and holding up a hand. "I don't want to talk about it. I told you to give us a week to rest and for Nelson to recover."

"Very well," Clancy conceded, bowing his head at Nox before raising his tumbler. "A toast, then. To the end of the Moon Murder Mysteries. Good job, Nox, Nelson."

"Here here!" Merlin cheered but Nox waved them off.

"It was a team effort. We did what we had to do but it should have never needed to be done," he said sadly. "I am relieved that it is over and I am grateful that we were able to put the past behind us and work together again." He finished his drink and handed Merlin his glass. "I'm taking Nelson upstairs now. Lock up behind you when you're through."

He accepted a kiss on the cheek from Merlin, then helped Nelson to his feet. "Are you sure you're alright?" Nelson asked him as they made their way upstairs.

"I'm tired, Nelson," Nox admitted and he looked truly tired. His eyes, his hair, and his smile had lost their shine and he carried himself up the stairs like his legs and his arms were made of lead. "I'm not sleepy tired. I'm...tired in my heart and my soul and all I want to do now is rest and take care of you until I *have to* do the other thing."

"Okay. We'll rest."

"And you'll let me take care of you again?" Nox asked with a cocked brow, humming skeptically.

"I don't have a choice, do I?"

Twenty-Three

The study doors remained closed until Nox opened them a week later. The university, the FBI, Merlin, and Clancy had honored Nox's wishes, staying away and giving them time and space to wallow at home, in blissful peace. Nelson had been a surprisingly good patient and had allowed Nox to dote on him, bringing him tea and most of his meals in bed.

But, they couldn't wallow in bliss forever and Friday morning had arrived, so Nox woke up early and snuck out onto the terrace at sunrise to do yoga, enjoying the brisk spring morning. He paused in the kitchen to put the kettle on and did a Tarot spread while he was waiting for it to boil. The cards confirmed that it was time for Nox to put the case behind him and allow himself and his family to heal. He was centered and prepared when he opened the study doors and faced Merlin's boards.

He used a cup of strong coffee from the French press as a shield, sipping as he peeled off notecards and reports. They went into the wastebasket along with the crime scene and autopsy photos. Nox saved the pictures of the girls—the ones of them beautiful and laughing—in a photo box for later, promising he'd put them in an album with pictures of Heidi, Howard, Tony, and Aubrey for company.

Nox had used moonwater and a sea sponge for purification as he was washing the boards. He started at the top, letting the water drip through the words, blurring them as they trickled down each board until the names and dates were no longer recognizable. But Nox saw their faces and heard the echoes of testimonies as he dragged the sponge in wide strokes, leaving clean slate behind. Nox didn't know what would happen after his birthday, but he could rest easier knowing that Howard and Tony would look after Heidi and Aubrey and vice versa.

He was burning everything in the wastebasket when Nelson lowered onto the terrace steps next to Nox.

"Good morning?" Nelson asked into his mug as he sipped.

Nox squinted up at the sky. "I think it could be."

"How long do we have until Merlin and Clancy show up?"

"They'll give us until midmorning. It would be rude to interrupt us before we've had our coffee."

As predicted, Merlin was the first to arrive at 9:00, letting himself in and hanging up his magenta cape. "I see you've cleared the boards. That's already so much better," he said as he looked around the study. "Just needs some juniper and mugwort smoke."

Clancy arrived a few minutes later with a box of glazed donuts, passing it straight to Nox. "It is a good morning," Nox decided as he took one out and stuffed the entire thing in his mouth, sighing happily as he chewed it. "Gods, that's good. They're still hot!" He held the box out to Nelson but he shook his head.

"Knock yourself out."

"I probably will if you let me eat all of these," Nox murmured as he took it to the sofa.

"Might we discuss our impending trip?" Merlin attempted with a cautious wince, but Nox shrugged as he chewed.

"Sure. Nelson and I talked about it and we're leaving early next Sunday morning. He's in charge of the itinerary and he has a special day planned for me. Try not to be a wet blanket," he said, causing Merlin to splutter in protest.

"I am *never* a wet blanket."

Nox snorted and rolled his eyes. "You are too. You do nothing but complain unless we take your car or a luxury SUV and the only fast food you will *ever* eat is Taco Bell."

"What can I say? I prefer to live más."[1] Merlin held up his hands innocently.

A heavy sigh rolled from Clancy as he glanced at Nelson. "And this is why I stopped going on the birthday camping trips."

"No, it's not," Merlin argued gently, his eyes glittering with tears as they touched Clancy's. "This will be the first we've taken as a family since Lucas..." His voice crumbled and Clancy nodded as he looked away.

Nox sniffed hard and cleared his throat. "You're going with us, Clance?"

He nodded, his smile wide and forced. "Merlin and I talked and we think it would be best," he said, earning a soft hum of agreement from Merlin.

"We think it would be prudent if Nelson and Clancy stayed by your side as much as possible that week," Merlin said with a pointed look at Nelson. "Just in case there are any accidents," he added and Nelson nodded.

"That's probably a good call," he agreed.

Nox caught the exchange, his eyes narrowing as they darted between his three. "Fine. Clancy can come with us too and we'll all travel to Coudersport together," he said with a shrug. "I'm not sharing my tent with you two. You can stay in the cabin and keep each other company."

"I want nothing to do with a tent," Merlin replied haughtily but he winked at Nelson.

Nox didn't care if they had conspired to make him more cooperative. He was looking forward to Nelson's romantic diversions instead of dreading what could be his final days.

Clancy cleared his throat, hugging his chest as he lowered onto the arm of the sofa. "You took a chance, letting the Dagda handle Walt. I put in a call and he is truly gone. They did a scan of his brain and there is significant damage."

"I imagine it's completely fried," Nox said, with almost no remorse. He felt a slight twinge of guilt, then looked at Nelson, recalling how terrifying it was when Walt smashed the back of his head with a bat. "He had it coming," he said simply, earning a hard look from Nelson, but Nox waved it off. "It's a shame that Heidi and Howard won't have the satisfaction of knowing that he got what he truly deserved."

"Walt is in very good health," Clancy noted, grimacing. "Aside from the fried brain, of course."

"And?" Nelson prodded.

"He's got a long life ahead of him. Possibly another thirty-five, forty, fifty years..." Clancy widened his eyes at him. "That's a long time to spend in that particular cage."

Nox made a knowing sound. "And it's filled with bright light and bees," he whispered, making Nelson swear under his breath.

Clancy rolled his eyes. "Poor Walt," he said dryly. "But I am more concerned with how you're feeling after sharing your vessel with a god," he said to Nox. "I assume that's the first time you've done that."

"I don't know..." Nox scratched his head and pretended to consider, then pointed at Nelson. "How do I feel to you?"

He threw Nox an offended scowl. "Don't make this about sex. He's being serious."

"So am I," Nox replied with a shrug. "You know what I'm feeling almost as well as I do and you're going to see right through me if I lie and say it wasn't a big deal. And I'm not the one who made it about sex, *He* did. Along with a millennia of history and mythology."

"Okay," Nelson said, nodding slowly. "He's still scared because he doesn't know how to prepare for what's coming. But he's secretly proud of himself because he's figured out how to block the Dagda and he doesn't need me anymore to get to *Him*."

"Not totally true," Nox countered. "I can channel *Him*

without you and I can go to *Him* at will now. But I wouldn't dare without you."

"Good." Nelson's stare pinned Nox. "He still feels like heaven but he can do way more magick than he lets on."

Nox gasped dramatically, acting shocked. "Snitched on by a cop!" He rose to his feet and went to pace by the French doors where he could see the sun. "The thing about magick is...it's ridiculously easy if you already have it in you. You're manipulating physics and elements and energy is kinetic and water moves by osmosis, right?" He looked around, receiving hesitant nods. "That's all it is!" He laughed and held up his hand, willing the water from his veins and his pores until it spilled over the sides of his palms. Then, Nox pulled the heat from his core, easily finding enough to create a flame, making Merlin cry as he cheered and clapped. "Magick is only hard when you have to learn it. I don't," Nox said, closing his fist and extinguishing the flame with a soft hiss. He wiped his hand on his jeans, then held it up so they could see that it was fine. "I just have to learn how to stop suppressing it."

There was a flat, thoughtful grunt from Clancy. "That's very impressive and encouraging. Can you learn enough by Alban Eilir to save your life? Because the Dagda can hold the heat of the sun."

Nox snorted and rolled his eyes. "The Dagda can hold the heat of the sun," he mimicked in a low, serious grumble. "I don't know. Maybe. A lot can happen between now and the equinox." He swung back to the doors and halted when he saw a crow on the terrace steps. It picked at its feathers before hopping closer to the glass. Nox's head tilted as he watched the crow staring back at him, then smiled when it cawed and took flight. "We leave on St. Patrick's Day and Nelson's in charge."

"Very well. I'll finish purifying the study and then I'll begin gathering everything we'll need for the trip," Merlin declared as Clancy stood.

"I'll be ready to go on Sunday morning. You'll understand if I spend the next week with Ingrid and the girls," he said with one of his customary bows.

"As you should," Nox replied, excusing him. He picked up the box of donuts and gave Nelson a nod. "Let's go. I have a lot to do next week, so Tony can cover for me while I'm gone and...indefinitely. We might as well get a head start on our packing," he said with a lewd wink but Nelson nodded, serious as he followed.

"I already did. My duffle bag's in the car."

"I didn't mean actual packing but good job, Nelson," Nox said with just a smidge of facetiousness.

"Thanks," he replied as they climbed the stairs. "I packed my tightest T-shirts and sluttiest cargo pants," he added dryly and Nox almost dropped his donuts and fell down the steps, he laughed so hard.

---

1. **más** (mahs) Spanish for "more."

Twenty-Four

"Sunday, Sunday, Sunday!" Nox announced with great dramatic flair, bouncing on the bed as the sun's first rays touched the bedroom windows and startling Nelson from a pleasant dream.

He had been driving through the country, coasting through peaceful stretches of prairies and farmland in the Continental with Nox at his side. It was one of his favorites and one Nelson was always happy to return to. He scrubbed his eyes, closing the file on that dream and tucking it in the front of his brain for later.

Reality was *almost* as good as his dreams, though.

Aside from the uncertainty around Nox's birthday, it was hard to find things to worry about and Nelson experienced moments of euphoric relief, knowing Walt and the case was behind them. He'd actually *relaxed* and enjoyed the quiet time at home with Nox and Merlin. After their success in apprehending Walt and closing the Moon Murder Mysteries, the Attorney General made sure that Nelson was granted plenty of time off to rest and recover. And Nelson told himself they *might* be free to build a life together that didn't revolve around seven shattered innocent girls.

"It's Sunday," Nelson confirmed as he grabbed Nox's wrist

and yanked him down and into his arms. "I get to celebrate mo anam cara all week," he said and kissed Nox, praying for the *whole* week and more Sundays with him.

But Nelson had noticed some concerning changes in Nox, as they got closer to his birthday. He started to float on Friday, his steps getting lighter and lighter as he jogged down the steps and skipped down the halls.

When he wasn't running.

Merlin had joked that it was like Nox was six again, the way he raced between the kitchen and the study and Nelson had even caught him chasing a tennis ball in the back terrace.

"It's this or sex," Nox had explained, winging the ball at the wall and sprinting after it before it could go over the fence.

So Nelson loved Nox as if it were the last time and their last day on earth, cherishing every cry and sigh, savoring every sacred drop of saliva, sweat, and cum. They were both lightheaded and shaky as they kissed and giggled in the shower.

Nelson was actually whistling as he dressed in a Henley, cargo pants, and a lightweight field coat, instead of a suit.

But his high was hampered and Nelson's hopes for a perfect road trip were dashed when he and Nox came out and found Clancy and Merlin packing bags into a black Range Rover.

"What's that?" Nelson asked as Nox locked the front door, pointing at the SUV.

Nox was distracted for a moment, his hand pressed against the door as he chanted a prayer. Nelson bit down on his lips, giving Nox a moment to say goodbye. "Thank you," he whispered, then took a deep breath as he turned. Tears clung to his lashes but Nox flashed Nelson a bright smile. "What's up?"

"Um..." Nelson was frozen, too aware of Nox's fear and sadness. He felt Nox's panic cresting, along with his desire to flee and Nelson felt an answering compulsion to *help* Nox escape. "We're going to be alright," he rasped and Nox nodded quickly.

"I know!" He swallowed hard. "And I get to go glamping. I can't wait!

"Right," Nelson said as he turned back to the street, recalling that he had a job to do. He was going to give Nox the best birthday week of their lives if it killed them. Or, destiny did. Whichever came first.

But Nelson's plans for their road trip had already hit a very big snag, before they'd even started.

"What's wrong?" Nox asked him and Nelson nodded at the vehicles and Clancy and Merlin.

"What are they doing? What's that for?" He pointed at the Range Rover, causing Nox to hum curiously.

"That's Clancy's car... We're going on a trip," he said slowly but Nelson still didn't understand.

"We don't need Clancy's car. We're taking mine."

"You want to take the Continental?" Nox's mouth opened and shut as he stared at Nelson. "I thought you knew that Clancy would be driving us. The trip up to the cabin is pretty rough once we get outside of Coudersport. There's no road where we're going," he explained but Nelson's tongue pushed against the inside of his cheek as he stared at the Range Rover. It was a nice enough vehicle but Nelson wasn't leaving his car in Georgetown if there was a chance he wasn't coming back. There was an envelope in the glovebox with instructions and Nelson had even stated in his will that he was to be buried with his car.

"You can ride with Clancy and I'll follow in the Continental," he said, ducking his head at Nox as he headed for the car.

"But the roads are—"

"I'm taking the Continental," Nelson stated and Clancy held up his hands, confused as he watched them from the sidewalk.

"What's going on?" he called.

"Change of plans, team," Nox announced. "We're taking the Continental," he said, earning a faint smile and a nod from Nelson as he opened the driver's door and took off his coat.

"What?" Merlin cried. "Does it have heated seats? My hips can't take that long of a drive without heated seats."

Nox hushed him. "You'll be fine. If you're that worried about your old hips, run inside and get a hot water bottle."

"A hot water—!" Merlin spluttered as he went to retrieve his things from the back of the Range Rover and relocate them to the Continental's trunk.

There was no objection from Clancy. He cut off his engine and obediently moved his bags to the other car. The Continental wouldn't be as comfortable for the long ride and it was perilously unequipped for off-roading, but Nelson didn't care. He could fix his car when they returned or they wouldn't and it wouldn't matter if he broke an axle or ripped off a fender.

"Thank you," Nelson said as he threw an arm around Nox's neck and kissed his hair. He was sentimental about absolutely nothing except his car, and Nox understood that Nelson couldn't leave it behind in Georgetown if there was a chance they wouldn't be back.

Once they were on the road, Merlin clucked and complained about the firmness of the back bench and lack of lumbar support for about fifteen minutes, then simmered down and entertained them with a story. He told them of the Algonquin sun god, Glooskap[1], and his malevolent brother, Malsum[2]—the wolf.

According to the legend, their mother died while giving birth to them and as Glooskap rose from her body he formed the sun and moon, animals, and the human race, while the malicious Malsum made mountains, valleys, rivers, serpents, and every manner of venomous thing to vex the race of men.

But each brother possessed a secret as to what could kill him, and vicious Malsum set out to learn his brother's secret. Glooskap, being the wisest and most cunning of all beings, told Malsum an owl feather could fell him. Of course, Malsum immediately captured an owl and brought Glooskap down only for him to rise the next morning with the sun. Malsum tried again and again to no avail, Glooskap returning every morning like the dawn. Then, Malsum used Quah-beet[3], the Great Beaver to deceive his brother and learned that only a flowering rush could kill Glooskap. Enraged by Malsum's scheming, Glooskap found a fern root and immediately slayed the treacherous Malsum.

"What is most fascinating to me," Nox chimed in, raising a finger. "Aside from the beauty of the allegory, are the striking similarities we find in Glooskap and Malsum with other gods across the different mythological systems. Like the Nordic gods Odin[4] and Loki[5]. In fact, Malsum being a restless lord of mischief returns after he is slain as *Lox*, chief of the wolves."

"Yes!" Merlin clapped in the back seat excitedly as Nelson turned off the highway, taking the exit for the Pennsylvania Turnpike and the diner. "And this is an excellent illustration in answer to Nelson's question about where deities come from and if they are only Celtic. If we accept that the sun is its own autonomous, fixed thing and that heat and fire are independent elements different gods can harness, instead of just one god. Then, it would absolutely make sense for every region of the earth to have their own pantheon of deities that interacted with nature and the world around them in similar ways. In fact, we have a preponderance of evidence in thousands of years of mythology that proves it! The idea that one single deity would control the sun and the universe and the destiny of all things doesn't even make sense when literally everything before it suggests something entirely but similarly different."

Nelson nodded thoughtfully as he steered the car into the diner's parking lot and found a safe spot where the doors wouldn't get dinged. "So how does this new and radically different religion become the prevailing dogma throughout half of the world?"

"Walts," Nox said with a shrug. "As we see with Jesus, it doesn't take a lot to convince the world of your divinity. Turn water into wine, walk on water, be resurrected… Even though we only hear of Jesus returning for just a brief moment and to only a few, so is that a resurrection or an apparition? None of that suggests that Jesus was all that powerful or unique in any significant way from other mythological sons of gods. Look at Apollo[6]:

he could heal and had the power of prophecy *and* he could shapeshift and generate actual sunlight." He chanted Apollo's name and pumped his fists. "And *everyone* loves Thor[7]. But it is in Jesus's cult where his true power lies and the manipulation of that cult by mortal men that makes Jesus different and truly unique. He is extremely adaptable and his father invisible, so it's easy to claim they're on your side."

Merlin nodded from the backseat. "You couldn't get away with that with an earthbound god like Glooskap. Which is why I suspect they prefer an amorphous, invisible one who says whatever serves *their* ends."

"Makes sense," Nelson said as he parked, then turned to the backseat when no one but Nox prepared to exit. "We're here."

Clancy blinked back at him. "It would appear so."

"Whatever," Nox said as he opened his door and got out. "You two can be downers or you can join us for breakfast." He swung his door shut, stuffing his fists in his hoodie as he jogged across the parking lot.

Nelson grinned as he watched Nox. "What do you say? Are you going to be downers or join us for a *family* breakfast?" He got out and was pleased when Merlin and Clancy followed.

Nox had already asked for a table and was chatting up their server when Nelson slid into the booth next to him. Merlin and Clancy had obviously decided to make the best of it for Nox's sake, plastering bright smiles on their faces as they sat across from them.

"This is..." Merlin's eyes were wide as he took in the diner around their booth. "Extraordinary," he whispered.

It was a typical roadside diner, as far as Nelson could tell, with tired, blue-collar patrons and equally tired blue-collar servers. Lots of baseball caps and flannel and lots of cups of coffee and plates of fried eggs. There were several sets of antler and stag neck mounts decorating the walls, but other than that Nelson didn't see anything out of the ordinary.

Clancy stared in horror at the head of a buffalo hanging on

the wall across from them. "Extraordinary," he said woodenly, jumping when their server, an elderly man with a gruff demeanor and a silver high and tight, returned with the coffee pot and began filling their mugs.

"What can I get you gentlemen," he asked as he took out his pad.

"Thanks, Cal!" Nox said, shaking out sugar packets for his coffee. "I'll have the 'Big One' with scrambled eggs with cheese. And could I have that with blueberry pancakes, please?" Nox asked the old man. "With a giant glass of OJ."

"Sure, kid. What about you?" he asked Nelson, who had studied the menu beforehand and was prepared.

Nelson nodded up at the man, his notepad open. "I'll have a Greek omelet with egg whites, add mushrooms, and hold the feta, please. Whole grain toast, no home fries," he recited before flipping it closed and tucking it into his back pocket.

Their server looked at Merlin and Clancy expectantly. "What about you two?"

"Well!" Merlin said, clasping his hands together as he stared at the menu. "There are so many things to choose from," he stalled, glancing at Clancy.

"Indeed, and it all sounds...delightful," Clancy agreed tactfully. "I'll have...what he's having," he decided with a nod at Nox.

"Excellent idea," Merlin said as he closed his menu and held it up to their server. "I'll have what he's having as well." He waited until their server gathered their menus and left them to lean over the table. "What do you think the 'Big One' refers to?" he whispered, making Nelson chuckle.

"Probably your impending heart attack. That plate was loaded with calories and cholesterol before Nox added cheese to the eggs," he warned but Nox cheered, rubbing his hands together.

"Life is short, Nelson. And when in Rome," he added with a wiggle of his brows.

Nelson cleared his throat and shook his head faintly at Nox, silently ordering him to tune the Dagda out and watch what he was talking and thinking about.

"Thanks!" Nox said as he reached across the table and took Nelson's hand.

Nelson squeezed it back, giving Nox a moment to ground himself. "I guess the dysfunctional duo don't eat at diners often either," he said with a nod at Clancy and Merlin, in case Nox had missed anything.

He smiled and sat back as their server returned with their juice. "Merlin has a personal chef and Clancy goes to the kind of restaurants that require references to get into and the chef tells you what you're eating."

"That doesn't sound like something I'd enjoy," Nelson said but Clancy held up a hand casually.

"Some people prefer to experience the work of a master in their element, while others prefer to have their meals shoveled onto their plates."

Nelson shot him a disapproving look. "While we're on the subject of meals, are we going to stop and get groceries? I'm not sure how much we'll be able to fit with all of Merlin's luggage." Nelson asked, but Merlin shrugged.

"I have just about everything we need in my bag. I'm sure we'll gather a few more things along the way."

They discussed meal ideas until their food arrived.

"Is that safe, eating things that have been in Merlin's bag?" Nelson asked, earning a hard snort from Clancy as he poured syrup onto his pancakes.

"On a scale of this place to the worst that could happen while we're up at Coudersport?" he asked, utterly serious as he cut off a bite and ate it.

"Fair point," Nelson conceded.

"Clancy is an excellent cook. Aren't you, Darach?" Merlin said, earning a distracted nod from Clancy.

"I had to learn or we'd starve. Ingrid is hopeless in the kitchen."

"Just out of curiosity," Nelson began hesitantly. "Where does your wife think you're going?"

Clancy took a moment, chewing and sipping from his mug as he stared out the window toward Georgetown. "I told her that we're taking Nox on one of his birthday...spiritual retreats and that there's a chance we won't be back."

They were all quiet for several moments until Nelson cleared his throat. "So she knows you're not...a regular person," he said quietly. "Because she might not be as well. How many more are there like us and Nox?" He looked around the table and Merlin raised a hand and rolled it airily.

"We must assume there are many," he said simply. "But we mind our own spiritual business and keep our own secrets. It's the key to our survival. Every now and then you have a charlatan like Walt who uses our dogma and exposes some of our secrets, putting *centuries* of devotion and discretion at risk."

Clancy shook his head. "I did that when I delegated my duties to Walt and trusted him with our secrets," he said, his cheeks turning red.

"What's done is done," Merlin said dismissively. "We've already determined where the breach was, but Nelson has asked about something much more interesting," he continued, smiling at Clancy. "Ingrid is a lovely name with old Norse roots," he observed, earning a tight nod from Clancy. Merlin made a thoughtful sound as he raised his mug and sipped, eyeing Nelson over the rim. "The Norse have a few rather *powerful* crow deities as well."

Nox hummed loudly as he chewed and nodded. "You've got Huginn and Muninn,[8] Odin's spies and his messengers. And the Valkyrie,"[9] he said, glancing at Clancy. "The Valkyrie are particularly interesting and another great example of how numerous mythologies can share the same symbology and have similar or sister deities. The Valkyrie were similar to the Morrígan in that they were the daughters of royalty and the protectors of kings, they were ruthless companions in battle and would feed on the corpses with their ravens."

"Indeed!" Merlin said. "They are mentioned throughout the *Poetic Edda*,[10] wreaking havoc on the battlefield and guiding the souls of fallen warriors to Valhalla[11] to help them prepare for Ragnarök.[12] Much like our Morrígan and were said to be wed to heroes and other warrior deities," he added pointedly.

"That *is* interesting," Nelson said slowly, eyeing Clancy with renewed curiosity.

Clancy shrugged it off. "It's not our business and it has nothing to do with *this*," he said, beating his knuckle on the table. "She understands that this week is special and while we might not always go together, it's best if we take Nox out of town to celebrate," he said and Nox pulled a face.

"I'm special so I get a whole week to be weird in the woods," he told Nelson.

Merlin clicked his teeth scoldingly. "We can blame that on the capriciousness of the season. The sun and the seed have minds of their own and spring begins wherever you see the first signs of it. It is with Imbolc that we first encounter the most variation with dates," Merlin explained. "This season in particular is rather tricky and why we're mindful during the *week* of the spring equinox. Some people opt to celebrate Imbolc closer to February 5th, when the sun reaches the exact astronomical midpoint of 15 degrees Aquarius, or on the second full moon after the Winter Solstice, thus sliding the entire cycle over by four days."

"That makes sense," Nelson said as he stirred his coffee. "Spring doesn't begin at exactly the same time all over the world."

"No, it does not," Merlin said and tipped his head in Nox's direction. "But I suspect that he can feel it happening as the entire earth comes awake with the equinox, whereas you and I might only experience it for a day."

Nox's nose wrinkled as he looked around for their server. "I think I want to try the scrapple."

"A curious dish, scrapple," Merlin began, picking up Nox's

Chapter Twenty-Four

cue and effectively changing the subject. "An ethnic food of the Pennsylvania Dutch with similarities to several Scandinavian and old British dishes like groaty pudding, haslet, and haggis," he noted but Clancy shuddered and leaned away.

"All made with offal and butchering scraps."

"Yes, it's low or peasant food," Merlin conceded and narrowed his eyes. "Always the snob, Darach, and so quick to dismiss anything you deem as simple and beneath you, when scrapple is almost as ubiquitous as sirloin in the southern Mid-Atlantic states, because it has sustained the poor and working classes since they arrived from the Old World. What have you done?" he countered with a lift of his brows at Clancy and making Nox laugh.

"Name one thing you've contributed to mankind the way scrapple has," he challenged.

Clancy waved it off. "I'll leave that to you and my girls. I know I did good work there."

"True enough," Nox replied, nodding as he sat back. "Your girls are brilliant and brave and you and Ingrid should be proud."

"We are," Clancy said, his voice catching.

They became quiet and Nelson wondered if he was the only one pondering the sacrifice Clancy was making and all he had to lose. He was the only one of the four of them who had a family outside of the diner and he'd made terrible mistakes to protect them and Nox.

It was Nox who made their day, though. He was happy as he stuffed himself with breakfast and orange juice, then skipped through the parking lot to the car like he was a kid again.

"That was fun. I'm really glad you guys are here," he told Clancy and Merlin before diving into the passenger side and giving the horn an impatient honk.

---

1. **Glooskap** (Klue-skopp or Kuh-loo-skopp) a sun god of the **Algonquian** (Al-gon-kew-an) peoples, one of the most populous and widespread North Amer-

ican native language groups. Glooskap was described as kind, benevolent, a warrior against evil, and the possessor of magickal powers.
2. **Malsum** (Mawl-som) a malevolent trickster god and twin brother of Glooskap.
3. **Quah-beet** (NA) translates to "Great Beaver," a river deity.
4. **Odin** (Oh-din) a prominent god in Norse mythology worshiped by the Germanic peoples of Northern Europe. Odin is associated with wisdom, healing, death, knowledge, war, battle, victory, sorcery, poetry, and frenzy, and is depicted as the husband of the goddess Frigg. Odin is also associated with the divine battlefield maidens, the valkyries, and he oversees Valhalla, where he receives half of those who die in battle. Odin fathered many children, including Thor, Baldr, Hoor, Vioarr and Vali.
5. **Loki** (Loh-kee) a god in Norse mythology. Loki is the son of the **jötunn** (Yotun) Fárbauti and the goddess Laufey, he sometimes assists the gods and sometimes behaves maliciously towards them. Loki is a shapeshifter and in separate incidents appears in the form of a salmon, a mare, a fly, and possibly an elderly woman.
6. **Apollo** (Uh-pol-oh) one of the Olympian deities in classical Greek and Roman mythology. Apollo has been recognized as a god of archery, music and dance, truth and prophecy, healing and diseases, the sun and light, poetry, and more. One of the most important and complex of the Greek gods, he is the son of Zeus and Leto, and the twin brother of Artemis, goddess of the hunt. He is considered to be the most beautiful god and is represented as the ideal of the **kouros**-a sculpture of a beardless, athletic youth.
7. **Thor** (Thorr) a prominent god in Germanic paganism. In Norse mythology, he is a hammer-wielding god associated with lightning, thunder, storms, sacred groves and trees, strength, the protection of humankind, hallowing, and fertility.
8. **Huginn and Muninn** (Hoo-gin and Moo-nin) are a pair of ravens that fly all over the world, Midgard, and bring information to the god Odin.
9. **Valkyrie** (Val-kuh-ree) name meaning "chooser of the slain," a host of Norse female deities who guide souls of the dead to Valhalla. Valkyries also appear as lovers of heroes and other mortals, where they are sometimes described as the daughters of royalty, sometimes accompanied by ravens and sometimes connected to swans or horses.
10. **Poetic Edda** (Ed-Duh) the modern name for an untitled collection of Old Norse anonymous narrative poems in alliterative verse. It is distinct from the closely related Prose Edda, although both works are seminal to the study of Old Norse poetry. Several versions of the Poetic Edda exist. Especially notable is the medieval Icelandic Manuscript, Codex Regius, which contains 31 poems.
11. **Valhalla** (Val-hal-luh) "hall of the slain." It is described as a majestic hall located in Asgard and presided over by the god Odin. Half of those who die in combat enter Valhalla, while the other half are chosen by the goddess **Freyja** (Fray-yuh) to reside in **Fólkvangr** (Volk-fan-gir). The masses of those killed in combat, along with various legendary Germanic heroes and kings, live in Valhalla until Ragnarök when they will march out of its many doors to fight in aid of Odin.
12. **Ragnarök** (Rahg-nuh-rok) in Norse mythology, a foretold series of impending events, including a great battle in which numerous great Norse mythological

figures will perish, including the gods Odin, Thor, Týr, Freyr, Heimdall, and Loki. It will entail a catastrophic series of natural disasters, including the burning of the world, and culminate in the submersion of the world underwater. After these events, the world will rise again, cleansed and fertile, the surviving and returning gods will meet, and the world will be repopulated by two human survivors, **Líf and Lífþrasir** (Leef and Leef-thrahss-eer) Life, and the Love of Life.

Twenty-Five

Nox's return to the cabin outside of Coudersport was supposed to be bittersweet. In his head, Nox had imagined a stoic, subdued arrival and to face his fate with his head held high.

Instead, Nox was *stoked* when the Continental crawled around the last bend and rolled into the meadow. His eyes watered at the sight of Merlin's timber frame "cabin" and memories stirred of the few precious birthdays he had shared with his father there. Lucas preferred tents and had said that Merlin's cabin was the opposite of camping with its sleek, modern kitchen with high-end appliances and decadent bathrooms. Clancy certainly didn't mind the luxury and had still gone with them in those days. It felt like that again as Nelson pulled to a stop at the edge of the wide clearing.

But Nox's return was made even more magickal by the sight of a large white cotton canvas bell tent and the team of decorators by the lake. The tent was set up just far enough away to afford them privacy, but a short walk if they wanted to join Clancy and Merlin for a meal or utilize their plumbing.

"I want to check out the tent first!" Nox said, throwing his door open, but Nelson caught his arm, halting him.

"We're early and they're not finished setting up yet. Help Merlin and Clancy unpack and I'll let you know when it's ready," he said, momentarily dashing Nox's hopes.

He reminded himself to behave and that they had days to play and explore. Nelson had probably spent a fortune on the lavish-looking tent and had promised that there would be more surprises.

"You're the best," Nox murmured, planting a loud kiss on Nelson's lips before getting out and bounding up the cabin's front steps. "Let's get to unpacking!" He rubbed his hands together, ready to get the work out of the way so he could thoroughly devote himself to goofing off with Nelson later. "Those can go upstairs," he told Clancy as he carried two of Merlin's suitcases through the front doors. "Since he'll be staying here," Nox added with an imperious tilt of his chin. "Just me and Nelson in the tent," he boasted, earning a chuckle from Clancy.

"We'll still hear you from up here, though, with the way you carry on. I told Nelson to have them set up on the other side of the lake but he didn't listen."

Merlin clicked his teeth from the kitchen. "What's the point of dragging you along if he's going to be on the other side of the lake?" He was arranging jars and cans in the pantry.

Clancy waved him off. "I don't think Nox is at risk of being attacked like the others. But there's no telling when Nelson might need our help to save him again."

"Exactly," Nox said as he detached himself from the conversation and went to check out the snacks in the luxury kitchen's now well-stocked pantry and refrigerators. "Always listen to Nelson. He knows what's best and he will put *me* first, no matter what."

He helped himself to some fresh berries, nuts, and cheese slices, then fell into an armchair by the fire with a bottle of champagne and a book. Nox flipped idly until the front doors opened and Nelson leaned in.

"It's ready!"

"Yes!" Nox brought the bottle, leaving the book.

Nelson took his breath away when he offered Nox an arm and escorted him down the steps. "Happy birthday, a chuisle mo chroí."

"It's not my birthday yet," Nox reminded him weakly but Nelson clicked his teeth.

"You heard Merlin, the equinox isn't just one day. You get a whole week to be weird in the woods and I get a whole week to cherish you."

How could Nox feel bittersweet about that? "You're the best thing that's ever happened to me. The best thing ever."

That made Nelson blush and mumble and his hand was shaking when he took Nox's and told him to close his eyes. He led Nox around and flipped back one of the flaps before announcing that it was safe to look.

"Whoa!" Nox was surprised at how much bigger it was on the inside. He tripped to a halt when he recognized his mother's quilt on the bed amongst the decadent throws and white hotel linens. "Nelson!" His favorite copper and crystal bowls were scattered around the tent and on the round dining table in the center. Dropping to his knees, he had to touch the rug to be sure it was real and truly the big Irish Donegal rug from his study at home. "How did you do this?" Even his robe and his favorite pajama pants were laid out on the bed.

"The hardest part was sneaking the rug and quilt to the decorator. I had to make sure you were *out* last night and keep you busy this morning."

"Oh, Nelson..." Nox was crying as he lowered onto the decadent bed and gave it a test bounce. He could see the lake through the doors and the sun was shining behind Nelson. "I'm home."

"It's good, then?" Nelson asked, scrubbing his beard as he looked around. He'd stopped shaving after he went on leave and Nox *loved it.*

"It's perfect."

Nelson smiled bashfully as he went to an antique armoire and opened it. "We're already unpacked and our toiletries are on this side." He rambled as he pointed out the basin and where all of Nox's things were and explained how the different appliances worked.

"We have our own place to eat if we don't feel like going up to the cabin," he concluded with a wave at the low table and throw pillows at the foot of the bed. "I brought your box of toys. It's in your bedside table," he added in a rush.

"*What?*" Nox turned and lunged across the bed, laughing as he opened the drawer. The hat box was there and the key to the chastity cage was taped to the lid. Nox believed he had left the cage and the box behind in Georgetown and was touched as he peeled the key free. "You should keep it. I know you said you don't want me to wear the cage anymore, but I'll always belong to you and no one will ever be able to touch us in the Nelsonspace."

He held the key out and Nelson laughed but it was watery as he took it. "I don't think these are meant to be this romantic."

"Who says?" Nox held onto Nelson's hand. "It felt pretty romantic every time you unlocked it and took it off."

"It did," Nelson murmured as he lowered to his knees in front of Nox. They kissed and Nox gasped, sounding scandalized as Nelson eased him onto his back.

"In the middle of the afternoon with the tent open?"

"I went over tent protocols with the dysfunctional duo," Nelson said as he unzipped Nox's jeans. "They should announce themselves from the porch and approach slowly so we have time to make ourselves decent or tell them to go away."

"If this tent's a rockin', don't come a knockin'," Nox said, toeing off his Converse and shimmying out of his jeans. "You've thought of everything, Nelson."

But it was clear that Nelson did not want Nox thinking. He teased Nox's semi-hard cock through his boxers until he was hard, sucking on the head through the black cotton. His fingers trailed along the hems and traced the cleft of Nox's ass, making him shiver and moan impatiently. Nelson wouldn't rush, he shushed and slapped Nox's hands away every time he tried to touch himself.

"I'm taking care of you this week. Starting with this."

"Oh?" Nox asked, the single syllable a high squeak as a hot, slick lube-coated finger slid into his ass. It was quickly followed by another and Nox gave himself over to the decadence of the tent and his lover's skillful touch and beguiling lips.

A sweet, spring-scented breeze wafted into the tent and Nox was in heaven as Nelson's beard swept along the insides of his thighs and between his asscheeks. He didn't have to hold back, he was wild and free as he undulated on the bed, panting and begging Nelson's name. He came, a rush of cum and joy that burst from Nox and left him giggling and lightheaded, as Nelson plied him with more fruit and wine, like an Appalachian Dionysus.

"I could get used to this," Nox said and opened wide so Nelson could feed him another large grape.

"That's the point." Nelson had changed into a white robe and had lit all the candles in the lanterns around the tent as the sun began to set. "Should I send for dinner? Clancy's on standby and will be preparing salmon en croûte with glazed carrots and a microgreen salad."

"Soon," Nox said as he curled a finger, beckoning Nelson. "I'm hungry for something else at the moment."

"What's that?" Nelson asked, strolling to the bed.

Nox sat up and tugged the belt around Nelson's waist free and parted the halves of his robe. "You."

Nelson was perfect as Nox licked and nuzzled his cock to life, whispering dirty, encouraging words until they were both frantic.

"Can I ride this?" Nox gripped Nelson's length, stroking and coating it with lube. He was so hard and Nox was losing the ability to play it cool, he was so aroused. They were surrounded by the sounds and smells of spring and crisp, fresh air. Nox could feel the sun as it sank and the moon as it crept over the horizon, calling to the darker aspects of his nature.

Chapter Twenty-Five

"If you wish."

Nelson reclined on the bed and Nox heard the mother goddess in the night as he rose onto his knees and mounted his mate. He'd found one god and discovered magick in these mountains, years ago when he was a child. Tonight, Nox saw a crow reflected in his lover's eyes. He sensed a diffcrent magick stirring in his veins and discovered a new power as he raised Nelson's hand to his throat.

"Are you sure?" Nelson's hand spread around Nox's throat, strong and steady. "You know how hard you—"

"I need you to!"

He could never deny Nox. Nelson's hand tightened, blocking the flow of blood and the rush of pressure in Nox's head was as immediate as the hard pulsing in his core as lights began to flicker. His ears rang and colors bloomed before his eyes, matching the pleasure coiling in the base of his cock. He heard Nelson slowly counting between each crash of his heart and Nox was floating, tethered to the earth by an outstretched arm. Nox closed his eyes and saw stars and a shower of black wings and heard a crow's call.

Nelson let go, his hand sliding from Nox's neck, supporting his shoulder as he went limp, his back bowing as he burst into pleasure and heat. There was a muffled roar from Nelson, his hand tight around Nox's waist as he bucked off the bed.

"Are you okay?" he asked before either of them had a moment to recover. Nelson anxiously patted Nox's cheek and huffed his name as their chests heaved.

"I'm here!" Nox fell forward, kissing away Nelson's fears and laughing. "I'm here. *He* didn't get me."

Nelson cradled Nox's cheek and searched his eyes. "What was that? You felt different."

"In a good way or a bad way?"

"I don't know." Nelson swept the hair away from Nox's eyes, the touch as light as a feather and reminding him of his mother. "It was powerful, though. I could feel everything vibrating and hear the tent rattling around us."

A sly smirk curved Nox's lips. "I think...*that* was the Badb."

Nelson's eyes widened and he opened his mouth to say something, but paused when they heard a loud gurgle from Nox's stomach.

"I'll let them know we're ready for dinner," Nelson said and reached for his phone on the bedside table.

Nox clutched his stomach when it gurgled again. It suddenly felt hollow. "Good. I am *starving.*"

Twenty-Six

They were not exaggerating when they said that Nox was too wild to keep in the city the week of Ostara. He awoke, eyes blazing gold and ready to devour Nelson and the day. And Nox was potent and enchanting, fingering and teasing Nelson until he was slick and ready, then driving him into the mattress. After, neither felt brave enough to attempt the camping shower, so they donned robes and slippers and strolled hand-in-hand up to the cabin.

Merlin pampered them with mimosas and breakfast in a bubble bath, wheeling in a cart bearing another elegant meal by Clancy. Nox and Nelson fed each other asparagus, wrapped in prosciutto and dipped in soft, runny egg yolks, and French toast with warm maple syrup.

But Nox couldn't sit still in the tub for long so they pulled out one of the canoes so he could burn up some of his energy on the lake. He pointed out the various types of trees and talked about the many species of birds and bugs they might find in the woods. Nelson's heart felt like it was glowing, seeing Nox so happy to be surrounded by nature and free to run wild.

"Let's see if we can find all the stones!" Nox said once they pulled the boat back onto shore. He grabbed Nelson's hand and dragged him along as he headed for one of the oblong boulders at the edge of the lake. He bent and picked up a flat rock before he jumped on one of the rectangular stones. "I used to think these were here because of the lake, to admire the view," Nox said, then whipped the little rock at the water, sending it skipping across the surface. "One, two, three, four, five, six...gah!" he counted before hopping down and gesturing for Nelson to follow. "I can get up to ten. We'll see who can get the most skips later," he said as he marched to the trees on the opposite side of the clearing. "I never put it together. I never knew what was so special about this place, except for all of this," he said, pausing and taking in the woods, the meadow, and the lake. "I thought we came back because it was heaven, right here in Pennsylvania. But Dad and Merlin kept coming back to be close to this stone circle. *Our* stone circle," he added, shaking his head. "I was so oblivious when I was a kid."

"Most kids are," Nelson observed, giving Nox a hand up when they reached another large stone that was leaning against the side of an old, sprawling oak.

He scaled up the side of it and grabbed one of the tree's larger branches, pulling himself up and allowing his body to dangle as he rested his chin on his forearms. "I used to be able to make it to that big branch at the top before I got too heavy," Nox said, his eyes scanning the canopy above them before he swung and let himself drop in front of the toppled stone. He dusted his hands and looked around before pointing at another rough-hewn boulder nestled amongst the trees about forty-five feet away. "That's where Dad took me camping when I was eight." He laughed as he swept his unruly black waves away from his face. "But I never noticed before!"

"You two went camping in a lot of places," Nelson reminded him as they made their way to it. The sun was setting and they paused to watch it sink behind the trees beyond the lake.

"We were in the woods," Nox said, when he turned and continued, nodding at a break in the trees next to the large stone. Nox ran and bounded onto it with barely any effort, jumping like he had springs on his feet. "Right over there." He leaped off, waving for Nelson to catch up as he wandered to an open spot at the base of another oak tree. Nox lowered to a knee next to a pile of brush, a soft laugh wafting from him as he held up a hand, warming it on an imaginary fire. "I found it, Dad. I came back," he whispered. He stood, turning and searching around him. "I could feel that the stone over there was old and sacred but I never thought to ask about it."

"You can feel the stones?" Nelson asked, fascinated as Nox became even more radiant and lighter.

"Of course," Nox said as he held out his hand to Nelson.

Nelson reached for it, thrilling at the rush of warmth and peace as Nox kissed his knuckles. He went easily into Nox's arms, sliding into a lazy waltz. They turned slowly, Nox humming as he guided Nelson around and around in a tight circle under the tree.

"Now, close your eyes," Nox whispered. He waited until Nelson obeyed, then carefully twirled him. "Keep them closed," he crooned and extended Nelson's right arm and pointed his finger for him. "Now, see if you can find it."

"I'm not a witc—" Nelson started to object, but Nox stopped him with a kiss.

"Be quiet for a moment and see if you can feel it."

A frustrated breath huffed from Nelson. "Fine." He held out his hand, prepared to disappoint Nox, but almost as soon as he was quiet, Nelson felt something pulling him. It was very faint, but there was a soft, yet insistent shove against his back as his center was pulled, tugged toward something. "I can feel it!" He let his feet carry him, going with the invisible current. He stopped and opened his eyes, gasping as his palm grazed the stone.

Nox was smiling at Nelson, his eyes glowing bright in the darkening woods. "You're right, we camped in *a lot* of places, next to old, magickal stones like these. I think Dad felt safest around them and like he was protecting me. That's why we were here that night, when I caught him using magick to make that spark when he tripped."

"This was where you first learned that *you* were magick," Nelson realized and went back to where Nox had knelt by the tree. He swung around and had to duck and lean to see through the trees, squinting until he spotted a light from the cabin across the meadow. The stones weren't hard to see now that Nox had pointed them out, but his ancestors had been clever and camouflaged them well amongst the trees. Only the three stones by the shore were exposed but like Nox, most people probably assumed they were there for the lake.

"I didn't know why I was drawn to them, but I'd make my way around these old rocks just about once a day when we'd come up to stay at the cabin. I scrambled over them and used them to climb the trees and even talked to them like they were my friends. But I was too young and too oblivious to ever notice that my favorite playground was an ancient stone circle."

Nelson winced as he shook his head. "I don't think your parents or Merlin or Clancy *wanted* you to notice when you were little," he said, making Nox snort.

"No…" He cut his eyes in the direction of the cabin. "I was kept in the dark about a lot of things and I didn't have any reason to question *why* they picked this place."

"I didn't mean to upset you again." Nelson gathered Nox in his arms and turned them away from the cabin. He'd rented the tent to keep Nox distracted, but Nelson was glad they had a buffer between them and Merlin and Clancy. Nox had made a lot of progress and had forgiven them for the most part. But he still had moments when he was bitter and needed space, not that Nelson blamed him.

"I'm fine," Nox said, sighing happily as he wound his arms around Nelson's neck, kissing him. "Everything's pretty perfect, actually."

"Is it?" Nelson lowered his head, growling contentedly as he tightened his arms around Nox.

"You're a genius for renting that tent," Nox said dreamily when Nelson raised his head.

He chuckled as he released Nox to get another look at their old campsite. "I was just thinking that it was a good call."

"Genius," Nox repeated as he followed, his eyes burning brighter and his smirk laced with mischief.

Nelson shook his head. "I don't know what you're thinking, but I don't trust Merlin not to spy on us while we're on a walk."

"This far from the house?" Nox snorted and laughed. "Too many bugs and mud upsets him," he said, stepping onto a fallen trunk and pretending it was a trapeze. He stretched his arms at his sides, wobbling dramatically despite being less than a foot off the ground.

Nelson chuckled as he hunkered down and swept the dirt and leaves away until he found what he was looking for, grinning as he held up a small black chunk of debris.

"Is that…?" Nox asked and Nelson nodded, holding it out to him.

"Natural charcoal from an old campfire," he said as Nox took it from him.

"Wow!" Nox blew on it to clear away the dirt for an inspection. "It's a piece of the fire we burned that night, almost eighteen years ago."

"So are you," Nelson said awkwardly, catching Nox's chin and stealing a kiss. "A fire started burning in you, the night your dad tripped and made that spark. You're magick, Nox, and the Dagda was playing with fire when *He* told you to come here." Nelson wasn't a gifted witch like Nox or as clairvoyant as Merlin, but he could feel it in his bones that this place was special, that it was built for them. Nelson had also come to believe in their bond and their stubborn natures. They had been designed to fit together and Nelson didn't believe that anything—even the Dagda—was strong enough to separate them.

"I think so too," Nox replied, leaning into Nelson. "I've never felt as safe or as strong as I do right now, here with you. I love you," he breathed, his lips luring Nelson.

"I love you too." Nelson's toes curled as they kissed and he spotted something bright out of the corner of his eye. Then, Nelson spotted dozens and dozens of tiny pops of light around them and raised his head. He thought they were fireflies at first, but jumped when a warm spark flashed by his cheek.

"What in the...?" he started and gasped as the night was filled with hundreds of floating sparks.

"It's us, Nelson. *We're* magick."

Twenty-Seven

On Tuesday, the crows arrived. It was the eve of Nox's birthday and he had woken up famished. For breakfast and for Nelson. His euphoric howls filled the glade and Nox felt like a god as he flipped back the tent's front flap to greet the morning.

"Whoa," Nox said as he took in what must have been close to a hundred crows on the lake's shore, all watching the tent. "Nelson, you should come and look at this," he called weakly while Nelson finished brushing his teeth at the basin.

"What is it?" He was patting his face with a hand towel when he joined Nox at the door. "Whoa. Is this Hitchcock bad, or a good thing like a Disney movie?"

"I don't know..." Nox admitted out of the side of his mouth. "I guess we have to wait and see if they eat us or start washing the laundry."

"I believe," Merlin said as he came around the side of the tent, huffing as he leaned on a cane. "That this is what we call a good old-fashioned omen," he explained waving at their visitors.

Clancy was following, looking pleased as he studied the birds. "They haven't attacked, so I think it's safe to assume it's a good omen," he said, earning a wry snort from Nox.

"Attack me? Why would they? I've never disrespected a single crow in my life. Mom taught me that they have long memories and can pass on their grudges," he said as he wagged his finger at them.

Merlin humphed in approval and nodded. "They most certainly do. But I believe they have come because they sense a battle is brewing and they are waiting for your command."

"That's silly," Nox said as he made a shooing gesture. "I have no need for battle crows today," he added and they all stared in shocked wonder as the birds cawed and took flight, circling above their heads before they flew off over the lake.

"Well!" Merlin laughed up at the sky, then smiled at Nox. "I believe we have our answer, Lord of Wild Things," he said as he held onto the cane and offered Nox a dramatic bow.

"Knock it off," Nox said with a dismissive wave. "I'm hungry. Anything happening for breakfast?" he asked Merlin.

"Yes! I was just about to send you a message to let you know that breakfast was ready, when we spotted the birds and came out for a look. Darach found the waffle maker and he's created quite the spread," Merlin informed them, causing Nox's stomach to roar.

"Let's go!" He was far more excited about the waffles, now that their visitors had left.

Breakfast with Merlin and Clancy was delightful again, reminding Nox of the family meals they shared when his parents were still alive. After, Merlin remained on the shore and under a shade with a book, while the three of them went out on the lake to do some fishing. No one was in the mood to clean or cook trout so they were thrown back, but Nox was thoroughly relaxed and enjoying himself until Clancy ruined the mood.

"Have you given any thought to this morning's omen and what you'll do tomorrow?" he asked Nox while casting his line.

"Nope," Nox replied as he reeled his in, preparing to abandon his pole and escape to the other end of the boat or go for a swim if Clancy didn't take the hint.

Chapter Twenty-Seven

"I wish you would," he sighed and raised a brow, his dry condescending tone grating on Nox's nerves.

"Okay..." He nodded slowly, pretending to consider. "Can we get a boombox and play some music while you're teaching me how to cast badass spells and block them? I was hoping for an intense training montage before I have to fight *Him*."

"I'm sure we could find a boombox, but I don't have any spells I can teach you, unfortunately," Clancy said, earning a sarcastic chuckle from Nox.

"I didn't think so, Clance. I know that this is the right place and this is probably the right time, but aside from that, I've got nothing but hopes and wishes to go on. But I'm not going to dwell on it until it makes me sick. Not if this is all I've got left with you and Merlin and Nelson."

"It's not," Nelson stated calmly as he cast his line. "We'll figure it out together," he added, ending the conversation in Nox's mind.

"There you go," he told Clancy with a shrug. "Nelson says it's going to be fine and that we'll figure it out together and I believe him."

"Good," Clancy replied, looking pleased as he offered Nelson a nod and went back to his fishing pole. "As long as Nox isn't facing this on his own. I think that's why we failed all those times before."

"What do you mean?" Nox asked, frowning.

Clancy sighed at the reel in his hands. "We've always protected the heir and made sure the line continued because *our* lives depended upon it. Without the heir, there is no need for us and we would feel our age and begin to decline. We stayed close and kept the vow, protecting the heir but never interfering with the cycle because..." He laughed, shaking his head at the lake. "Because one cycle was supposed to bring about the end of another. That was always the way. And it was always the way for the heir to carry the burden alone. Who decided that?" He looked at Nox, then at Nelson.

"It wasn't me," Nelson said, shrugging a shoulder. "I'd never let Nox carry it alone."

"But that's it!" A tear was rolling down Clancy's face as he reached and gave Nelson's knee an affectionate swat. "You would break the cycle—the cycle be damned—to spare Nox from the burden, while those of us who had sworn to protect him would watch from the sidelines while he fell."

"We have different ideas of what our duties are, I guess," Nelson replied dismissively and Nox kicked him, hard. "What?" Nelson asked and Nox beamed, unabashedly proud of *his* man.

"I really did pick *well*, didn't I, Clancy?"

"You did and I couldn't be more pleased," he replied, earning a flat stare from Nelson.

"What are you two talking about?"

Nox smirked as he sat back and hugged his pole, no longer interested in fishing and content to enjoy the view and the company. "It never occurred to Clancy or Merlin that they could break the cycle or their vow. They've done unspeakable things to help me, but they've always played by the prophecy's rules. It never occurred to them that they could simply...not, and break the cycle. But you..." Nox sighed dreamily at Nelson, ignoring Clancy's hard eye roll. "You don't give a damn about the vow, the cycle, or some god. All you care about is me and you'll do anything—even risk breaking your own neck—to save me," he said with an exaggerated wink at Clancy.

"You knew," Nelson accused, making Nox laugh.

"I heard Clancy yell stop. But most importantly, I *felt* the pause and I felt it, each time my love was broken," he added seriously, giving them each a scolding look. "Nelson went to so much trouble, it behooved me to go along with it."

"I had no idea that he even knew," Clancy said with an irritated grunt. "A little warning would have been nice."

Nelson shook his head. "I couldn't warn you. I had a moment to come up with a plan and I would have chickened out if I'd given myself time to think it through," he admitted in his deep, steady rumble. Nox and Clancy burst into laughter, scaring away the fish, thus ending their fishing expedition.

Nox was still giggling over Nelson's clumsy sacrifice hours later. He had been sent up to the cabin so Nelson could prepare the tent for another surprise. Nox made good use of the time by taking a long, hot shower in Merlin's bathroom. Nox killed a little —a lot—of extra time by shaving *everything* and giving himself a very thorough cleanse.

He was as clean as a whistle and whistling when he strolled back down to the tent, dressed in a soft cream V-neck sweater and jeans. It was getting chilly as the sun set but Nox couldn't imagine a more perfect evening.

He was proven wrong.

Delicate white flower petals were lining his path when Nox came around the front of the tent and the little deck was covered in candles—each one safely glowing in its own jar. Nelson was waiting inside, dressed in a dashing tux, sans tie, with an armful of wildflowers.

"You didn't have to do all of this!" Nox protested as he went to Nelson, taking the flowers and putting them aside on the table, then began to cry when he heard their song. They started to turn as Keith Whitley sang "When You Say Nothing At All." Nelson hummed and sang along softly, his tone and pitch almost identical to Whitley's. "Thank you," Nox whispered as he rested his ear on Nelson's chest and shut his eyes, listening and cherishing the moment as they danced.

On date nights, they would go for long drives and Nelson would occasionally get carried away and sing when the right song came on. He was teasing the first time he squeezed Nox's hand and sang it to him, but they both quickly realized how true it was. After that, Nox added various versions of "When You Say Nothing At All" to all their playlists and got goosebumps whenever Nelson sang along. Nelson said Whitley's version was his favorite, but Nox's was whatever version Nelson was singing.

"We should eat before our food gets cold," Nelson said once

the song was over and Kacey Musgraves began to sing "Love Is A Wild Thing."

"Is this our 'Cuddling In The Country' playlist?" Nox asked as he went to the low table at the foot of the bed and lowered onto one of the large throw pillows.

Nelson looked concerned as his gaze flicked to the speaker, then back to Nox. "Was I not supposed to use it? We're in the country and I thought cuddling would be ideal," he explained, making Nox groan. Nelson was so adorably innocent and chivalrous.

"It's perfect," Nox insisted, setting Nelson's mind at ease.

He grinned as he worked a cork out of a champagne bottle and nodded at the covered dish in the middle of the table. "You can look," he said and winked at Nox just as the cork popped.

"I am extremely curious," Nox confessed as he lifted the silver cover and cheered at the mound of steaming Kung Pao Chicken resting on a bed of fluffy jasmine rice. "My favorite!"

"I know," Nelson murmured as he filled their glasses, then sat across from Nox. He reached for Nox's plate, filling it first and handing it back to him. "I have ice cream and warm brownies for dessert."

"Heaven," Nox declared and raised his glass for a toast. His gaze was grateful and filled with promise as it held Nelson's and they tapped their glasses. "Thank you for this perfect night and for creating this...heavenly hideout. I was dreading this week and tomorrow but I'm not anymore. I have never felt safer or stronger than I do right now, here with you, and I am *so thankful*. Thank you for bringing a little bit of home with us and for loving *me*— your Nox—and for helping me stay connected to him."

Nelson waved it off, looking away as he blushed. "I didn't know what else to get you and I was afraid Merlin and Clancy would drive us up a wall," he mumbled.

"A very distinct possibility," Nox said as he sipped. "Although, they have been remarkably well-behaved and extremely functional as a duo since..."

"They have, but let's keep the conversation light," Nelson suggested while he filled their plates.

"Amen," Nox agreed heartily and picked up his chopsticks. He scooped a mouthful of food into his mouth, feeling truly content as he watched Nelson eat. His gaze drifted around their luxury accommodations before settling on Nelson again and Nox let out a dreamy sigh.

"What?" Nelson asked, his brow cocked warily.

"I was just thinking about how much like heaven this is and how far we've come since Minnie's Motor Court.

Nelson choked on a laugh and shook his head. "Don't remind me! That place was *so bad*. I still have moments when I wake up and I'm scared I'm there again."

"Oh, no!" Nox cried as he reached for his champagne. "That's terrible, Nelson."

He waved it off with his chopsticks. "It doesn't last long and you're always there to make me forget."

He'd surprised Nox again. "Wow. That's lovely. Thank you." His eyes strayed to the candles on the deck, the swaying flames drawing his attention. Nox heard a crow's call, summoning him as the dancing fires stretched and blurred. He nodded and allowed himself to get drowsier, wading in as the hypnotic, lulling flicker pulled him from the tent and into the heart of the flame.

In it, Nox saw three fiery crows, rising warrior goddesses with burning tresses and great blazing feathers. The most fearsome of the three spread her wings and Nox saw *Himself* and Nelson, wrapped in fire and writhing in ecstasy. Then, Nox saw himself, rising like the sun with three mighty crows, ablaze as they took to the sky.

"Nox!" Nelson's panicked cries were accompanied by sharp slaps to Nox's cheeks. "Nox, wake up! Look at me!"

"I'm okay!" Nox laughed and reached for Nelson, ecstatic and crying. "I'm okay!"

"You didn't look okay," Nelson said as he pressed his hands against Nox's cheeks and brushed the hair away from his face.

"You were so pale and your eyes rolled back and you were babbling about fire and crows. It wasn't like your other trances, when you're with *Him*," he explained.

Nox nodded, taking Nelson's hands in his. "I was scrying," he stated calmly but Nelson frowned.

"I don't know what that means."

"I saw into the fire and had a vision."

"Like a fortune teller with a crystal ball?" Nelson asked and Nox hummed.

"Just like that but without the dubious implications," he scolded. "I wasn't trying but I was given that vision, it came to me."

"Okay..." Nelson searched Nox's eyes, concerned. "And what was the vision?"

"Fiery crows!" Nox said with a high, watery laugh. "They were *mine* and I was rising like the sun, Nelson."

"That's good. Right?" he asked slowly as he rubbed his brow.

"It's great!" Nox said, getting up and pulling Nelson with him, around and onto the bed. "I think we should do it now."

Nelson's brows pinched as he frowned. "It? Like...intercourse?"

"Yes! But the whole shebang."

"The whole... No." Nelson shook his head and attempted to back off the bed but Nox went with him, shushing soothingly. "I don't want the whole shebang."

"It's going to be fine!" Nox promised, certain he'd read the omen correctly. He couldn't really see any other way to interpret it. "We were being held in a great flaming crow's embrace, against her breast, and we rose with the sun, Nelson. If that doesn't scream that our purpose is divine and blessed, I don't know what it means," he said excitedly, working on buttons while pinning Nelson down.

"We should ask Merlin and Clancy."

"No," Nox said and shook his head. "They're sleeping peacefully and they were happy today. If the worst should happen and I blow this, at least their last day was a good one. Let's go now while I'm feeling like I'm on top of the world and I have the goddesses' blessing," he urged.

"Do we have to tonight? Won't they be on our side tomorrow?" Nelson argued but Nox shook his head.

"What if *He's* expecting it to happen tomorrow too? What if *He's* resting, enjoying a night of peace before we have to face each other?"

Nelson raised a brow at Nox. "The element of surprise?"

"Exactly! I have spiritual and tactical reasons for wanting to do this!"

"I get that..." Nelson stalled, his eyes straying to the tent's doors. "I think you should talk to Merlin about your vision. Isn't that his thing, omens?"

He was scared. Nox could feel it in his aura and see it in his eyes. He took Nelson's hand, placing it over the eye on the center of his chest.

"I wouldn't risk losing *us* if I didn't feel strong enough, but I'm ready! Trust me, Nelson."

There wasn't a moment of hesitation. "Okay. I guess we're doing this now."

Twenty-Eight

"Okay. I guess we're doing this now."

Seven magickal words.

Nox *knew* with every particle of his being that they were going to make it. There had never been a truer or better heart than Nelson's and there was no way Nox was letting him down. Not when Nelson had proven time and time again how far he was willing to go for Nox.

"I have never been more in love with you and I have never felt more loved than I do right now. That's why I know I'm strong enough. *You* are where my greatest power comes from."

"I'm scared as hell but I know we can do this," Nelson said, lifting his hips and shoving his trousers down. They scrambled out of the rest of their clothes and faced each other on the bed, standing on their knees. Nelson took Nox's hands in his, kissing the knuckles. "What do we do now? What's the plan?" he asked, his gaze solemn as it touched Nox's.

"The plan?" Nox shook his head. "I still don't have one so we're going to have to do what we do best and play it by ear."

"Great..." Nelson looked around the bed, leaning toward his bedside table and searching the floor.

Nox gave his arm a swat. "What are you doing?"

Chapter Twenty-Eight

"Looking for my antacids."

"You don't need them and we don't have time." Nox grabbed his face and kissed him hard, putting his whole heart into it.

There was a soft groan as Nelson angled his head and gathered Nox in his arms. That was all it took for Nox to find the sneeze-like tickle in his soul and hear harps and bees. Nelson's embrace tightened and his fingers twisted in Nox's hair, keeping them locked together as they both ascended and were wrapped in rapturous light.

Nox held on, sucking on Nelson's tongue and thinking only of him until he felt soft, cool grass under his feet. Birds chirped and sang as a breeze ruffled the leaves in the trees and a harp plucked softly. He opened his eyes as Nelson opened his and they blinked at each other, confirming that they were both still alive and together.

Once Nox was sure, he looked around them and was pleased to find that they were in the stone circle. It was a sunny, mild afternoon and the cabin and tent were gone and all the stones were upright, creating a wide ring around the meadow.

"You made it," a familiar man's voice—Lucas's voice—said tenderly. He was the impossible, lost, older version Nox *should* have had, that the Dagda had deprived him of, with streaks of gray in his hair and his beard and wrinkles at the corners of his eyes.

Nelson gasped as he covered himself and averted his eyes. "This is my worst nightmare."

"No." Nox pointed at the lie in front of him, his ire swelling into hatred. "Do not come to me as my father. I *know* that is false," he said with a disgusted sneer.

"Alright," *He* said, in Lucas's gently reassuring tone before giving his head a quick shake. His hair bounced with the movement, the ash blond turning shiny jet black and *His* flannel and khakis vanished, replaced by a simple black silk robe. It was open and flowed as *He* glided toward Nox, his tattooed, naked body a perfectly identical replica of Nox's. "Is this better?" *He* asked sweetly, throwing the robe off and turning for them.

Nox's head tilted as he inspected his ass, nodding. "The extra squats and adding the locust pose to my yoga routine's paying off," he noted and raised his brows at Nelson. "I do that for you," he added but Nelson shook his head.

"Not the time," he scolded.

"Never a bad time for a great ass," Nox murmured to himself, then pulled his gaze to *His* face. "But I can work with this," he said, keeping his thoughts to himself, in that deep place the Dagda couldn't feel or hear. *He* had played the wrong card again because Nox would have been helpless if he had to face another Nelson. "I bet it's better for you, too," Nox said as he circled *Himself*, pretending to study his own tattoos and admire his own form.

"Mmm..." The Dagda purred as *His* hands glided down *His* neck and over *His* chest. *He* appeared to be enthralled as *He* traced a nipple, shivering in delight at the sensation before *His* hands splayed over *His* abs and swept lower. One curved around *His* semi-hard cock as the other caressed an asscheek. "So much better and now you can see how beautiful we'll be together."

"But will we stay beautiful or will we grow fearsome and ugly?" Nox challenged and *His* hands stilled in their sexual exploration and *He* frowned, confused.

"What do you mean?"

Nox clicked his teeth as he approached *Himself*, raising a hand to cradle *His* cheek. There was a jolt of euphoric radiance and Nox was momentarily addled. He shook it off and caressed *His* cheek "The world out there...it's beautiful!" he whispered and watched carefully as *He* reveled in Nox's touch, nuzzling his hand and purring in delight. Nox hummed seductively, his thumb brushing the Dagda's lips with false fascination. "But there is so much darkness. You only had a glimpse of it with that fake Badb and I fear for the world when you see what's become of it."

"Then I will fix it," *He* said simply.

"That would be wrong!" Nox countered, laughing as if the Dagda should know better. "It is all part of the cycle and we must trust that it will—that mankind—will fix its own mistakes."

"Will they?" The Dagda replied, sounding dubious. "Or will they repeat the same mistakes until all the good is gone and the entire world is lost to darkness?"

Nox hesitated because he had feared that himself in his lower moments. "Empires rise and fall. That is the way it has always been. Sometimes, they crash and burn when they reach those inflection points, but something bigger and better is always reborn."

"Always?" The Dagda laughed, mimicking Nox's patronizing tone. "Have they outgrown their greed and obsession with power or are they still making wars and stealing from each other?"

"Oh." Nox's head pulled back as he feigned surprise. "You were planning to share your power and control of the world, then?" He widened his eyes, daring the Dagda to deny that *He, Himself* craved power and complete control.

He stared back at Nox as if *He* had never been doubted or *His* intentions questioned before. "I would know all and my reasoning would not be flawed. It could not be because one can only be just and merciful when they have all the power and control."

"How can you believe that and would you be interested in some oceanfront property in Arizona?" Nox asked *Him*, laughing and shaking his head.

Nelson coughed softly and gave Nox *the look*. "Not the time for sarcasm."

Nox held up his hands, smiling at the Dagda. "My hamartia[1]. And will it be my downfall?" he admitted and wondered out loud. "Perhaps I'm going about this the wrong way, attempting to convince a god of *His* fallibility..."

"I have all the time in the world," the Dagda said with an airy wave, inviting Nox to give it a shot and proving *He* had a sense of humor. He raised the other hand, licking *His* knuckles while eyeing Nox with ravenous, covetous hunger. "Tell me why we shouldn't purge the world of all that evil and all that pain?"

"Because you would be purging all that is good as well!" Nox said, clasping his hands together as if to beg *Him* to be merciful. "I know you have seen it in Howard and Aubrey and Tony. And every student who steps into my classroom, brave and ready to grow their minds." He gasped, clutching his chest reverently and allowing the Dagda to feel his love for them. "I would fight to defend the last scrap of that goodness in the face of any evil because I have seen the power one kind act or one good person has and how they can change the world."

"Perhaps..." The Dagda narrowed *His* eyes, circling Nox, more interested in assessing and admiring his naked backside. "You are romantic and sentimental, but I find that arresting. Your compassion and sense of duty beguile me, I must admit."

"Maybe you should keep me," Nox suggested, finding the chink in the Dagda's armor he'd been waiting for. That—*he*—was the Dagda's greatest weakness and what *He* wanted most after all.

"Keep you?" *He* asked, sounding intrigued.

Nox shrugged as he sauntered closer. "Why not? Who says you have to raze what's in here to make room for you?" He bit his lip, offering the Dagda a teasing, mischievous grin. Nox slid a hand over the Dagda's shoulder and sucked in a gasp as he felt another pulse of radiant, joyful arousal. They were both quaking as he pulled the Dagda closer, their frantic breaths creating a hot breeze that shook the ground and fluttered the leaves in the trees around them. "What if you could have me and keep me by your side?" he crooned silkily, noting the golden sparks of lust in the Dagda's eyes as *He* watched Nox and considered the proposition.

"Have you?" *He* asked with obvious fascination.

Nox made a sultry sound, nodding and nipping at *His* lips. "We both know that's what you truly want, isn't it?" he huffed, then sucked on the Dagda's lower lip, creating a swell of lush heat that rolled through them and throughout the clearing.

"Oh." Nelson covered his mouth, looking stunned. "I... I guess this is better than fighting..."

Nox groaned in agreement. They were both achingly hard as Nox's tongue swirled around the Dagda's. *His* kiss was seeking

Chapter Twenty-Eight

and possessive as *He* molded Nox's body to *His*. Nox pulled his lips free, flashing Nelson a cocky wink as the Dagda lapped at his jaw and up his neck, already drunk with desire. "I'm romantic and compassionate on the streets, but I'm a sexy, slutty demon in the sheets. Why would you give up that?"

"I do not deny that I have long desired you," the Dagda said, whispering the words along Nox's clavicle. "Could it work?" *He* mused and dragged his tongue over Nox's shoulder, growling as *His* need grew fierce. "The two of us...together, side by side..."

"Why not?" Nox pouted, writhing against the Dagda and ratcheting up their hunger until they were both trembling. "Why should you deny yourself that which you yearn for and deserve the most? Why should you sacrifice do chara?"[2] he asked sweetly as he slid to his knees.

Nox's hands spread and gripped as they glided up *His* thighs, around to *His* ass, and up *His* abs, scratching and creating goose-bumps as they roamed the Dagda's body.

"Mo stór!"[3] *His* fingers sifted through Nox's hair lovingly. *He* was enthralled as Nox pressed his lips and nose into *His* sac, moaning and licking with lewd abandon.

"Um..." Nelson's neck craned as he moved in for a closer look. "We're going to classify this as masturbating," he said, licking his lips and pushing out a loud breath. "I...think I'm into this."

Nox made a wicked, knowing sound as his tongue washed up the Dagda's shaft, swirling around the head to collect a drop of honey-sweet pre-cum. "Hmmm..." he chuckled drunkenly, swooning up at The Dagda. "I've always wanted to do this but I've never been flexible enough," he said, then opened wide so he could take *Him* deep into his throat. Nox sucked hard, moaning like a siren as his head slowly bounced up and down, tugging at the Dagda's cock and whipping the three of them into a hot frenzy.

"Oh...that is so good," the Dagda said huskily, *His* voice ragged with need. "I've always wanted *this*," *He* said as *He* pulled Nox to his feet and captured his lips for a searing, stunning kiss.

He was flying too high, too fast and meant to slow them down and steal back control by ensorcelling Nox with *His* hands and *His* lips.

"Show me!" Nox pleaded, as he tipped back his head so the Dagda could ravish him.

He was lifted as the Dagda's teeth scraped his neck and *His* tongue left a scorching trail along his neck, shoulder, and chest. Nox whimpered as his nipple was bit and sucked hard, sending bright bolts to his sac and throbbing hard-on. He gave into the carnal lust, urging the Dagda on with wicked chants.

"Take me! Show me how beautiful we can be together!"

"Yes!" The Dagda cried, wrapping Nox in *His* arms and laying him in a bed of soft, loving earth and sweet-smelling flowers. "So beautiful!" *He* promised, parting Nox's thighs and tracing the cleft of his ass reverently. A shiver of blissful delight rushed up Nox's spine as the Dagda's finger strummed his hole, before one, then two slowly nudged into the tight, flinching ring. "Oh, mo stór..." *He* whispered as *He* fingered Nox, each tender slide of *His* fingers sending waves of searing pleasure up his spine and down his limbs.

And Nox was so wet! Pre-cum dribbled from his cock but he was shocked at how slick and ready he was to be mounted.

"Now," he demanded, twisting his fingers in the hair on the back of the Dagda's head, demanding *His* lips and *His* body.

"Now," the Dagda agreed, *His* intoxicated laugh carrying through the meadow as *He* dove into Nox's mouth and slid hard and deep into his ass with one swift, slick thrust.

"*Yes!*" Nox howled as he curled a leg around the Dagda's hip, locking them together. "That's it! More!" he begged.

His head lolled in the dewy grass, wreathed in heady-scented primrose and daffodils as bees buzzed around them. They were incandescent with heavenly pleasure as driving, consuming heat filled Nox's core.

Nox let out an ecstatic cry, filling the glade with glorious harp song, as his nerves thrummed with incandescent joy and he felt his

Chapter Twenty-Eight

soul igniting. He heard his mother's laughter and his father singing, a faint Irish lullaby calling him home. But Nox was *burning*, his vision growing brighter and brighter as the sky and the meadow began to fade.

"Stop!" Nelson yelled. "Nox, come back!"

"Can't. Iss so good," Nox slurred as he wound his arms and legs around the Dagda. He laughed and shook his head, remembering how safe and loved he felt in his Nelsonspace. "Iss good… but I've had better," he managed to mumble, seeking, seeking, seeking until he saw Nelson leaning against the door in his classroom. He was all that was loyal and noble and the Dagda could never arouse Nox more than that taunting curl at the corner of Nelson's lips when their eyes met. He heard a crow's call and reached for that loyal, noble light, remembering the soul-deep satisfaction and ultimate peace he experienced when Nelson spilled himself deep in Nox's core. "Wait!" he wrenched himself away from the rapture, twisting his fingers in the Dagda's hair to whisper in his ear. "It's so good but it could be better. D'you wanna see the stars? D'you wanna see the heavens?" he dared *Him*, curling a finger behind the Dagda's back, summoning Nelson.

The Dagda raised *His* head, delirious with lust and caught in Nox's spell. "Tell me how," *He* demanded as *His* hips continued to pump, swift and brutal, desperate in *His* desire to take them higher, to take them into the sun.

Nox had *Him* right where he wanted *Him*. "Are you strong enough, Grian?[4] Can you handle my Uaithne?" he taunted, earning a defiant laugh from the Dagda.

"I have before," *He* said and glanced over *His* shoulder at Nelson. "Give it to me, Uaithne," *He* commanded without slowing *His* pace.

"As you wish," Nelson said, throwing a hard, dubious look at Nox as he got into position behind the Dagda.

Trust me. Trust in us.

Nox reached deep into his Nelsonspace, where he burned the

hottest and the brightest, just as Dagda's glorious light spilled into his core and threatened to outshine him.

"Yes!" *He* shouted, *His* thrusts halting when Nelson grabbed *His* shoulders and took over. Nelson's pelvis smacked firmly against the Dagda's ass, setting a slower, grinding, prowling pace.

Nox could breathe again and his senses began to clear but the Dagda was insensate, babbling in English and Gaelic as Nelson drove harder and faster.

"That's it!" Nox reveled in his love and faith in Nelson, incandescence bursting from him as the Dagda's screams grew louder and more animalistic, possessed by the primal, relentlessness of Nelson's spirit. *He* howled as light spilled from *His* eyes and *His* mouth, heavenly harps and impassioned cries filling the night as Nelson filled *Him* with steady, rolling thrusts. "You're almost there," Nox whispered in the Dagda's ear as their pleasure reached a golden, molten crescendo.

"No! Wait!" The Dagda sensed *His* essence igniting but it was too late. *His* eyes rolled and *His* jaw stretched into an ecstatic, melodic sob as a scalding tide flooded Nox's passage and propelled him into bright, blinding euphoria.

"Du thabairt dorais du glé, for mu muid céin am messe."

Nox heard Nelson's low, steady chant and felt his good, honest strength driving slick and steady in his core. Nelson's arms closed around him and it was Nelson's lips and tongue tangling with Nox's.

"Du thabairt dorais du glé, for mu muid céin am messe," he repeated, his hands in Nox's hair and locked around his ass, possessive and strong.

"Don't stop," Nox whispered, wrapping an arm and a leg tight around *his* man, *his* wolf, *his* mighty Uaithne. "Take me home, Nelson."

"You're already home," Nelson said and captured Nox's lips. They were both crying, their hands interlocked and palms glowing, as Nelson came, pulling Nox with him into pure, safe peace. "Du thabairt dorais du glé, for mu muid céin am messe."

Chapter Twenty-Eight

Nox smiled at the smell of their tent and the familiar scent of his lover's body. He could already tell before he opened his eyes that he was in a bed with fine cashmere and cotton linens. The air was chilly as it touched his skin, causing Nox to shiver and giggle.

"You did it," he whispered into the corner of Nelson's neck, blinking back tears.

"We did it but it was mostly you," Nelson said as he rose on an elbow, cupping Nox's cheek. "Is it you? Are you my Nox?" His voice broke as he searched Nox's eyes.

"It's me, unfortunately," Nox teased, laughing as Nelson's lips crushed his.

"Thank God," Nelson said when he raised his head and took a deep, relieved breath.

"Not God, actually," Nox started, raising his finger, then paused. His lips pursed and his left eye squeezed shut as he did the math. "Thank...me, I guess," he said, shrugging.

Nelson's frown deepened until his lips twitched and a laugh exploded from them. "I love you so much but shut up," he said as he rested his forehead on Nox's, whispering his name and a sacred *I love you.*

"I love you too," Nox whispered back, then bit back a snorting giggle.

"What?" It was a wary rumble.

"You know, that puts you at 2-0." Nox's smile was beatific as he rubbed the tip of his nose against Nelson's.

"2-0?" Nelson parroted.

Nox sighed contentedly and pecked at his lips. "Your holy dick. It's undefeated."

"Ah." Nelson sounded disappointed. "Could we leave that part out when we tell—"

"Knock knock," Clancy called from several paces away from the tent. "Are you both alive and decent?"

"Yes!" Nox laughed.

"*No,*" Nelson said, rolling them and bounding from the bed.

"Just a moment." He snatched their robes off the floor and tossed one at Nox.

"I don't mind!" Merlin declared breathlessly, throwing back the flap at the front of the tent just as Nelson was tying his belt.

Nox took his time, stretching and rolling his head around to get the kinks out of his neck before donning his. He nodded as Clancy peeked inside. "Now, we're decent."

"And you're..." Clancy rolled a hand at Nox. "You?"

Merlin hurried to Nox, reaching for his cheek. "Are you well, my child?"

"I'm *fine*, Merlin," Nox said sincerely, smiling at Nelson. "We did it. *He's* gone!"

"We heard it and we saw all the light!" Merlin was shaking as he hopped and waved excitedly at Nox and Nelson.

Clancy nodded, chuckling in disbelief. "We came running to see if we could help when we saw the light coming from the tent. But we weren't sure what to do when we got here. The tent was on fire but we could hear..." He coughed suggestively, throwing them a wide-eyed, suggestive look, earning a loud hum from Merlin.

"Sounded wilder than any orgy I've ever been to, let me tell you," he said and pulled at the collar of his psychedelic paisley pajamas and fanned himself. "Wasn't sure if I should start smudging or recording for my OnlyFans."

"No." Nelson shook his head and pointed at the door. "It's done and I'm done for the night. Go back to your cabin and we'll explain everything later after we've had some sleep."

"As long as you're both well," Clancy said, bowing and backing through the door.

"We're both fine," Nelson replied and shooed Merlin so he'd follow Clancy out.

"Very well," Merlin sighed and bowed as he left. "Just tell me if that was indeed a wolf we heard."

"Nelson," Nox whispered and pointed at him.

"Fascinating! And well done!" Merlin said, offering Nelson a soft clap of his little hands.

Nelson grabbed one of the bolster pillows and threw it at Merlin. "Not another word until tomorrow"

Merlin waved, then shouted in protest when Clancy yanked him out of the tent, making Nelson and Nox laugh.

"Bedtime," Nelson said with a toss of his chin at the bed.

Nox didn't feel remotely tired. If anything he felt alert and refreshed and like he could swim across the lake. But he could see that Nelson was barely hanging on, his eyes were so heavy and he was leaning against the bed for support.

"Let's go to bed." It was his turn to guard Nelson and Nox would make sure nothing disturbed him while he slept.

---

1. **Hamartia** (Huh-mar-dee-ah) a fatal flaw in a character of a tragedy that leads to their downfall.
2. **Do chara** (Duh ca-Ha-rah) Your beloved.
3. **Mo stór** (Muh stohr) My most beloved, my treasure.
4. **Ghrian** (Gyree-un) Sun

Twenty-Nine

Nelson was alone when he opened his eyes and stretched, reaching for Nox, only to find the other side of the bed empty. He heard the sounds of birds chirping and distant splashes while he pulled on pajama pants and a robe and washed up at the basin.

He found Nox sitting on one of the long stones by the lake, bundled in his mother's quilt. His hair was wet and he was smiling, blue-eyed again, and relaxed as he watched the rising sun reflecting on the water.

"Good morning?" Nelson asked as he sat next to him, earning a soft chuckle from Nox.

"It's a good morning," he confirmed, settling against Nelson's side.

Nelson put an arm around him and they were quiet for several moments. "Did you go for a swim?" he asked, trying to estimate how cold the water was this early in the spring.

"I needed some exercise. I was getting too restless and I didn't want to disturb you."

"Restless," Nelson said with a knowing hum, then gasped when he remembered what day it was. "Nox!" He popped up and spun toward the tent and the cabin. "It's your birthday!"

Chapter Twenty-Nine

Nox was laughing as he stood and pulled Nelson into his arms. "It's my birthday." He kissed Nelson and tapped their foreheads against each other. "And I can't think of anything else I need right now."

"Me neither," Nelson whispered.

Nox and the world were safe from the Dagda and Nelson would get to see *his* MacIlwraith live a long and happy life. There would be other cases, but they had solved the one that would haunt them the worst and Nelson knew that Howard, Heidi, Aubrey, and Tony would take care of each other and heal together.

And he and Nox would have all the time in the world together. Possibly, an infinite amount of time, Nelson realized as he recalled what Merlin and Clancy had said about their proximity to the heir keeping them "young." It was also likely that the FBI would give them autonomy to investigate whatever they wanted, as long as they didn't mess up *too much* or embarrass the bureau, so they were truly the masters of their own destinies.

Finally.

For Nelson, it had been easy to cram himself into his father's and the FBI's mold of the perfect son and agent. He had thought that was a sufficient destiny and *could have* been content, but Nox had always chafed at the invisible grip fate had on his path and his future. Nox had been so stubborn and had fought so hard, he'd defeated a god and altered the collective destiny of the human race.

But fate had chosen the *right* MacIlwraith in Nox. He understood that love was the strongest magick and that power, no matter how supreme it might make you over all others, could not make you better or stronger. In the wrong hands, it could make a man incredibly weak and foolish and it could devastate the innocent when wielded irresponsibly. True and real power came with accepting that it shouldn't be used and Nox would always tread lightly. He was a *good* god and Nelson was grateful to the depths of his soul, knowing that kind of power was in

Nox's hands now instead of the Dagda's. Or, the former Dagda's.

He raised his head and squinted at Nox. "So... Are you *Him* now?" he asked, causing Nox's cheeks to puff out as he considered.

"I think I might be..." He held up his hands. "But we might have also experienced the creation of a new god and had a first-hand glimpse at why some of the historical record around proto-Christian deities is so spotty. It might have been moments like this that were lost in translation or erased by the victoring dogma."

"Knock knock," Clancy called as he and Merlin approached.

Nox turned to greet them and both Clancy and Merlin bent into deep, sweeping bows and remained with their heads down as Nox went to them.

"Eochaid Ollathair,"[1] Merlin said in a watery whisper.

"Saol fada chugat, mo rí,"[2] Clancy said solemnly.

"Stop it!" Nox ordered, flailing a hand dismissively. "I'm still me and I wouldn't be here without your help. Thank you," he said as he pulled Merlin into an embrace.

"My sweet boy!" Merlin cried into Nox's chest, his sobs shaking his little frame. "My sweet, sweet boy! I've been so afraid of losing you!"

"I'm not going anywhere," Nox told him, wiping the tears from Merlin's cheeks and kissing his head. Clancy was crying as well when he and Nox hugged, clapping each other on the back and swaying for a moment as they laughed and congratulated each other.

Clancy's hand trembled as he brushed the hair from Nox's eyes and regarded him. "I knew you and your mother were too special, too magickal, to be wasted like all the others."

"It was Mom's spirit and her goddess who gave me the power to transform and balance dark magick."

"You are the equinox, half light and half night," Clancy confirmed as he went to bow again, but Nox stopped him.

"Just Nox," he corrected with an affectionate pat to Clancy's chest. "And what will you be? You're free now and I hope I'll never have use for a general. Will you stay with us?" he asked, his eyes soft as they held Clancy's.

"I will, but I called Ingrid and told her I'd like to travel more now that I can retire. I was thinking of getting a boat so we could see the world the way we've always dreamed."

"That sounds awesome, Clance! You and your girl, out on the sea," Nox said and there was a telling shimmer in Clancy's eyes as he nodded.

"It's my idea of heaven."

"But you'll be back?" Merlin clarified, tugging on Clancy's sleeve.

He chuckled as he put an arm around Merlin. "We'll be back. The girls are still in school so we'll make sure we're here for their breaks and we'll miss you all too much."

"Oh, good!" Merlin stated brightly. "I have always adored Ingrid and your girls. It's been such a shame, not getting to see them as much since..." He waved it off, not wanting to bring up their sorest subject.

"I've asked Ingrid to bring the girls up," Clancy told them. "I figured that since we all took the week off and we're all still here... We might as well make it a real family getaway."

Merlin hopped and clapped as he spun to Nox and Nelson. "How wonderful! Isn't it wonderful?"

Nox was beaming as he nodded at Merlin and then at Clancy. "It is," he agreed. His eyes met Nelson's and they were glowing with *good*, loving light and gratitude. There was a rush of warm joy as their hands slid together. "I have Nelson and a family again and we're all going to live happily ever after."

The End

1. **Eochaid Ollathair** (YOKH-adh oll-UH-hurh): The Dagda, the allfather. He is known as the good or great god and the lord of the heavens.
2. **Saol fada chugat, mo rí.** (Sail faddah coogit, muh ree) Long life to you, my king.

Epilogue

Six months later...

It was just about a month short of a year since they had met, but the long-overdue event had arrived and Nox was thrilled as he waited for their guests. Bixby was finally bringing his husband to dinner and Merlin was in the kitchen preparing his specialty, Kung Pao Chicken.

Dinner smelled lovely, causing Nox's stomach to growl as he sipped his whiskey and watched the windows from the foyer.

"They'll be here soon," Nelson said as he passed Nox on the way to the study with a fresh bucket of ice. "Bixby asked if it was okay if they brought Arawn's brother. They're twins, I guess. Bixby said he's a big fan of yours so I said it would be fine."

Nox shrugged as he took a sip. "Merlin always cooks too much and the more the merrier."

"That's what Merlin said," Nelson murmured from the study. He was holding a drink when he rejoined Nox, looking so handsome in a gray, chunky Irish Aran sweater, jeans, and a light beard.

He only wore suits when he was working and Nox liked the way Nelson carried himself now, in casualwear. His back and shoulders weren't as rigid and he smiled so much more.

"Love you," Nox said, stretching his neck for a kiss.

There was a low, lazy growl as their lips brushed. "You too."

The bell rang, startling them. "We'll continue this later!" Nox said as he turned Nelson and shoved him at the door.

Nelson gave the front of his sweater a tug and patted his hair before pulling the door open. "Hello and welco— Oh, it's you," he said, with a shocked look over his shoulder at Nox.

"Don't just stand there. Let them in!" Nox said as he went to move Nelson and froze when he recognized the two men flanking Bixby. Well, Nox recognized one of them as the paramedic who had taken care of Nelson after Walt had knocked him out.

"Hey!" the younger man on the right said as he took Nelson's hand and shook it. "It's the Lousiville Slugger," he winked at Nelson, then offered Nox his hand. "And his sexy sidekick, the mystery-solving demigod."

"Welcome to our home," Nox said slowly, raising an expectant brow at Bixby as Nelson ushered him and his husband inside and closed the door.

Bixby offered Nelson an apologetic wince and clapped him on the back before reaching for Nox's hand. "This isn't how I planned on telling you two, but we have a bit of a...situation and I figured that since we helped you..."

That was all Nox needed to know. "Of course," he said with a sweep of his arm at the opened study doors. "Pour yourselves something to drink and tell us your story."

A Letter from K. Sterling

Dear Reader,

Thank you so much for your time and for reading *Nelson & MacIlwraith III*. I hope you had fun unraveling this mystery with Nelson and Nox and are excited to read their next adventure! Before you go, I'd appreciate it if you'd consider leaving a review. Your review would really help me and help other readers find their way to us. And I promise, I read and appreciate every single one of them. Even the negative reviews. I want your honest feedback so I know how to steal your heart.

Please help me out by leaving a review!

Once again, thank you from the very bottom of my heart. I love you for sharing your time with us and hope we'll see you again soon.

Love and happy reading,
K.

About the Author

K. Sterling writes like a demon and is mother to Alex, Zoe, Stella, and numerous gay superheroes. She's also a history nerd, a *Lord of the Rings* fan, and a former counterintelligence agent. She has self-published dozens of M/M romance novels including the popular *Boys of Lake Cliff* series and *Beautiful Animal*. K. Sterling is known for fast-paced romantic thrillers and touching gay romcoms. There might be goosebumps and some gore but there's always true love and lots of laughter.

Made in the USA
Monee, IL
24 March 2024